MW01680280

THE 2023 WRITER'S BLOCK ANTHOLOGY

Edited by

CALLIE ROWLAND

Hydra Publications

ISBN: 978-1-958414-23-1

Hydra Publications

Goshen, Kentucky 40026

www.hydrapublications.com

FOREWORD

The 2023 Writer's Block Anthology is a compilation of the winners of the Writer's Block Short Story contest sponsored by Louisville Literary Arts and Hydra Publications. All genres were submitted, with Sarah Thomas winning with her short story, Liftoff. Read her story and the other nineteen finalists as part of this anthology.

LIFT OFF

SARAH THOMAS

WINNER OF THE WRITERS BLOCK SHORT STORY CONTEST 2023

I always knew that I would die from falling—falling down the stairs, falling off a precipice, falling in love with the wrong man.

Since I was small, stretching to reach the dark banister that ran the length of the stairs in my parents' house, I had to concentrate on each step, as my head was inhabited by visions and sensations of that first misstep, the panic feel of air under my toes, the impact of hardwood on soft skin and muscle, the crack of bone, the whisper of my mother's long skirt as she rose from the piano bench, the melody replaced by the dissonance of the crash. I'd imagine all of this, nearly launching myself into catastrophe, as I concentrated on my feet and made my way, gently, to the landing.

I didn't realize that this feeling had a name until my husband and I moved to Switzerland: *l'appel du vide.* The call of the void.

"*C'est tres commun*," my friend explained, taking a drag of her cigarette, though it was more associated with skyscrapers and mountaintops than staircases. "*Ce n'est pas suicidiare*," she assured me, but it is the desire for freedom, and the uncertainty that comes with it.

"*C'est comme ça*," I said, as I did when I didn't know what to say, but that time, I meant it.

That conversation was a lifetime ago, but it still feels recent—the first time I felt at home in Switzerland, the first time I had a friend of my own, and even though she is dead now, I still feel like this here, especially walking by the lake. I used to have such pride in the haunting beauty of my old hometown, that the longest bridge in the U.S. spanned Lake Pontchartrain, but next to its Swiss counterpart, it appears flat, brown and featureless, its belly sliced by a bridge to nowhere. Along with my friend, Lake Geneva was the first Swiss thing I loved. When I started calling it Lac Leman—its local name—it felt like a cheater's intimacy, and when I started joking that New Orleans, "Wasn't so bad, because the French used to own it," I knew I had completed the betrayal.

~

The man that calls me Honey is showing me the places in the garden where daffodils have begun to break through the frozen earth. He is clasping my hand tightly and his glove is scraping the skin on my wrist as we walk from patch to patch, and he narrates the outlook for this piece of ground that is ours, that he will put in onions instead of beans this year, and that our neighbor says we're going to get too much rain. I nod and look down at my hand clasped in his gloved one, and wonder why the gardener is holding my hand, and then he says, "What's wrong, Honey?" And I know he is not the gardener.

I remember my mother saying that tea is supposed to steep for four and a half minutes, and now when I make tea, I guess when four and a half minutes is and then check the wall clock in our kitchen. It's been five minutes, but I was close, and this is a small triumph, because some days time becomes flexible and diffuse: four and a half minutes might be two, or twenty, the tea gone suddenly cold when I seemed to have just dropped the bag into the water. These small tests of my mind feel reflexive because I see the edges blurring, things falling just out of the frame, and quizzes reel them back into order, momentarily.

"Mom, are you okay?" A woman who I know is my daughter asks, who seems to have hurtled through time as well, because now she has variegated silver and dull brown running through her wheat-colored hair that was uniform. I look at the small child at her side, round and seamless, with unclouded blue eyes looking out to an uncomplicated world, and I think my daughter's hair is what has happened to us. Time propels us from this perfect, smooth lump of humanity into something warped and streaked, our love colored by resentment, our trust corrupted by experience, even the drama of sadness dulled by knowing it will end.

"Yes, sweetie," I say, and pull the waterlogged tea bags from the mugs, toss them into the bin. Four and a half minutes, nearly to the second. I smile at her, and the child giggles.

The man that calls me Honey is standing by the door.

"Where did you last put them?" he asks in a voice that seems pushed through the spaces between his teeth.

"I don't know," I say, and for a moment I have forgotten what I am looking for, but I see that he has on a jacket and boots, and I only have on a jacket, so I know my boots are missing—the soft brown leather ones, the ones I wear nearly every day, and we are trying to go somewhere, and now he is angry at me. I hurry over to the shoe closet, and he says, "You just looked there, Honey," in the pushed-through voice, so I run up the stairs, away from his eyes, and there is relief in just being unseen.

I get down on my knees and look under the bench in the kitchen, and my heart rate is rising—*Why do I have to wear these boots?*—but I cannot ask him this, not at this point in the hunt, so I throw open the back door, and there they are, sitting outside, a bit muddy. I feel such relief I begin to laugh a little.

"You aren't very good at not losing things, are you?" he asks, behind me now.

I don't know how to answer this: the tangle of double negatives, the question that he seems to know the answer to. My mind flashes to a student paper and my own hand crossing out words to shape the question into something more comprehensible, a thing more clearly parsed: *You are~~n't~~ very good at ~~not~~ losing things.~~, are you?~~*

"I don't know," I answer.

He shakes his head, defeated, as though this answer confirms something grave, though it is entirely noncommittal.

I am in a field full of boys in school clothes speaking French, and I am young again. They are cutting through the grass with their bare legs, fixing small wooden rockets onto pipes and slabs of split wood and bricks. Their faces are contorted into the shapes of the faces of the men they will one day be —wrinkles linking their brows, concentration behind their eyes. They are equipped with matches and glass bottles full of water.

"*Depeche, toi! Elle se casse!*"

"*Écoutez, nous avons encore dix minutes avant le décollage!*" I shout over the sound of the wind in the grass, and their voices, and the train, making its way across the countryside below us, on its way to Geneva, full of people having coffee and important conversations. But it doesn't matter to us, with the wind on our necks and the pulse of anticipation at our wrists. How balsa wood and baking soda and matches can propel a heart to the sky.

It's ten minutes to lift off, I've told them: *le décollage.* I had to look up the word for lift off during the unit on rockets, and I remember it made me laugh that it was so close to *décolletage,* and so whenever I said it, I thought of a woman's breasts peeking out from a low-cut top. When I told my husband this, he growled in my ear, "*Your décolletage makes my rocket décollage.*"

"Was I an astronaut?" I ask him. Sometimes, when his mood is light, and I feel brave, I ask him these questions without being afraid. I am looking at a row of books on the wall in our landing. There are books about the moon missions, and astrophysics, how to make your own rocket and a memoir of John Glenn.

He puts down his book and walks over and puts his arms around me from behind, and says, "No, but you taught an astronaut."

I can tell that my judgment was right, and this was a good day to ask such a thing. "I did?"

"Yes," he nods. "You were a science teacher. A damn fine one."

He winks at me, and there is something ignited—like a cut wire being reattached to its source.

He reaches up and pulls out a book; *Beyond Earth* is written on the spine.

"One of your old students is an astronaut now," he says,

and opens it. On the front page, it is written, *For Madame Roberts, thanks for believing in me.*

He runs my hand over it, like it's written in braille, and it is nice to feel the smooth page, and to see my name written, *Madame Roberts,* like I am a person to be respected, and I feel grateful for this JM, who has granted me a sort of sophistication that has lasted even until now, tucked into a forgotten book.

I smile at my husband, and I see something settle over his face. Hope, maybe.

~

My daughter is walking with me along the lakeside, her hair back in a bun, her face pulled tight and girlish. The air is warming, and the walled gardens that flank the water have telltale tendrils of spring escaping between cracks and over gates. A vine has wound around a bike left against a wall all winter.

~

She asks me to recite a poem. This has become a ritual that I like and don't like: the performative nature of it, the role reversal, but part of me feels in on a secret ruse, that I am humoring her desire to quiz me. I recite "A Red, Red Rose" by Robert Burns, and when I say, "Red, red," I reach into the pram and rub my nose against my grandson's tiny nose, smooth as a river pebble, and he giggles. It feels good to have the power to do this, to remember the words and to make a thing, even a small one like this, happy.

Until the seas gang dry my dear and the rocks melt o'er the sun,
And I will love thee still my dear til the sands of life have run.

My daughter holds my hand for the rest of the walk. We go back to the house; we sit in the kitchen with the window open to the garden, where the stalks are heavy with green tomatoes. They stay for tea. My daughter offers to make it for me, but I say, "No." Even if I lose my way, my life is populated by people asking me guiding questions to urge me to the next motion. I know that I have forgotten something, because the tone is not of curiosity, but of extreme gentleness, the vocal equivalent of averting one's eyes.

"Mom, did you turn the stove off?"

Now I turn the stove off, because there is a yellow sticky note in my husband's handwriting that says *Have you turned me off?* and one on the front door that says *Lock me and take a key!* This at first—how long ago, I'm not sure—felt like spying, and it irritated me and made me feel juvenile, because I believe that I am a very smart person, or I used to be, and that memory of intelligence is still firmly rooted in my brain. But now, it feels more like a little conversation with these objects in the house, giving them life and personality, as though after asking *Is there water in me?* the coffee pot might get up, pour itself a cup, and light a cigarette.

While I am tidying the kitchen, I hear my daughter speaking to my husband in a whisper. "*She is still amazing*," she is saying, but it is in a way that does not sound like a compliment, but a reduction. It is the way we might tell a dog what a good boy he is, what a very good boy, when all he has done is sit down on the carpet.

~

We are sitting on the floor of my parents' living room in the Garden District, and I am leaning against the piano bench, which is digging a trench into my back. My little sister is lying on the floor in front of the television, and my folks are on the couch. I can hear my mom's nerves; her coffee cup softly rattles as she nestles it back into the saucer. She wears long skirts, even in the heat, her legs crossed at the ankle, her feet bare. My dad is smoking and peppering us with bits of biographical information about each of the men on the ship. He was a Gulf Coast oil and gas man, married to things that burn.

"Aldrin graduated from MIT, just like your uncle," he says.

"They say Cal Tech is even better than MIT now," says the man who will become my husband, eager to say something dissenting, his eyes darting from the screen to my father.

"California," my father says evenly, shaking his head, and

blows his smoke toward the TV, making the rocket appear all the more potent, about to blast into outer space.

We have been watching for over two hours, but finally the announcer says we are at *T minus 1 minute 35 seconds,* and we all straighten up to see history. I get the sudden feeling that something terrible is going to happen—the rocket will burst into flames, killing all of the men inside that my father has been describing for the last two hours. And suddenly, I am not in my own living room anymore; I am in the living rooms of the wives and children of these men and praying that the rocket goes straight up into outer space like it's supposed to. And then for a moment, I wonder if any of these wives or children secretly want for the rocket to explode or never to return, a black wish to only gravely regret if it comes true.

Thirty seconds and counting. The astronauts report in crackling voices: "It feels good."

T minus 25 seconds.

Then, my sister begins counting alongside the announcer. By 10, we are all chanting in a sort of trance, bound together by this electricity and smoke and fear. "*5, 4, 3, 2, 1... Ignition, lift off!*"

We launch up, cheering and hugging for these strangers in Florida that are off to the moon, and it all feels like we have accomplished something together, just by witnessing it on TV.

The man who will be my husband looks like a boy, like the boys in the field will look in twenty years, his eyes lacquered with the thrill of possibility. He hugs me, squeezes me so tightly that for a moment I am afraid my ribs might snap, and when he lets me go, he says, "We are going to explore the world."

"I think I want to explore space," I say.

He laughs, and doubt dilutes his shining eyes. "Space?"

"I want to be an astronaut," I say.

"Girls can't be astronauts," my little sister says.

"But they can make them," he says into my hair, and squeezes my behind at an angle that my parents can't see.

But my mother sees, and she obscures her knowing smile.

~

My daughter and I are walking through the forest behind the house, the sticks snapping under our boots. She is pregnant, musing about the unborn baby and whether he will be a musician. She is a gifted pianist, and she asks if I remember her first recital.

"Of course," I say, seeing again her small frame at the hulking piano, a braid down her back.

"What did I play?" she asks.

"Cannon in D."

"It was Für Elise."

"Yes, Für Elise, how could I forget?"

She stops walking. "Mom, you're forgetting a lot. Haven't you noticed?"

"That was nearly thirty years ago my love," I say (but of course, I have noticed).

"But Für Elise was special," she says. "You said you'd give me a hundred francs if I could play it without mistakes."

"You never did, though," I say, feeling mean, though it's simply true.

"No, I never did." Her hand trembles as she slides it into her pocket.

"I'm sorry. Let's go home." I reach out and touch her shoulder.

"Okay," she says and steps off the path. She gestures for me to walk ahead. We'd stopped for a few minutes; there were no signposts. I take a breath and walk down the hill. I don't hear her footsteps behind me. When I turn around, she is pointing in the other direction.

~

I am on my knees in the garden, looking between the tomato plants. I do not know what I am looking for, but I know it is important. I see that I have on my wedding ring, some relief. The dirt below my face is deep brown, nearly black, and I think it is a blessing that as my tears fall into the soil, they disappear.

A fist appears in front of my face. It's attached to the sunburnt arm of the man who calls me Honey. He makes a show of opening it, like a magician, and inside is a pearl. I feel my earlobes, and the left one is empty, naked. "Thank you," I say, and I move to take it from his hand.

"No, let me," he says.

I stand, wiping the tears with my fingers, and they leave streaks of dirt on my face.

He fixes the earring in my ear and with great patience, wipes the dirt from my face. "You aren't very good at not losing things, are you?" he asks.

I look down at my hands, rimmed in black earth, and as he waits for me to answer, his wrinkles fade away and his eyebrows grow thick and dark. He was handsome.

"I haven't lost my wedding ring, or you, or my mind," I say.

And he looks at me with astonishment. He says, "Well, at least two of those three are true, Honey." He says this kindly, but there is poison in it. I cannot locate the poison, because I cannot remember the last thing that I said, and I am sure that today I cannot ask him.

The hand in my hand is small and soft, the feeling of palming a buttered biscuit under my mother's table to slip it to my dog. The air is cold, the sky clear and punched through with holes of light, the stars harsh in their precision, and I am naming them and guiding his blonde head up to take in the expanse of the sky.

"*C'est Orion,*" I tell him, pointing out the three stars on his belt. Orion is the easiest for me to find, the belt unmistakeable. I remember learning that the stars of Orion's belt were over a thousand lightyears away from each other, and this made me wonder if they knew that they were part of the same thing, like a woman seeing her future husband across the chasm of a dance floor.

The boy's ears are cold, and I wonder fleetingly if I

should have gone down to get his cap, but his mother and her father were down there in the cellar, drinking cognac and whispering conspiratorially, when the boy looks up at me and said, "*Je veux partir à l'aventure.*"

"Me too," I say. He nods, hungry for the unknown blackness outside the kitchen door. I felt our kinship.

"*C'est Ursa Major et Ursa Minor, la mère ourse et son petit ourson,*" I tell him, growling like a mother bear. He growls back, his teeth glinting white in the moonlight.

The clearing is white with snow, the crunch under our feet loud in the silence of the forest. The clearing is crowned by three angular Toblerones, remnants of the war. I hoist the boy on the slope of one, his lightness surprising. I never knew a human could be tossed at will. I tell him to be careful and to look up. He sits like an ornament on a concrete pedestal.

"Wow," he says, with only a hint of his Genevoise accent lilting the word. *Wow-a.* He is still mine, his Americanness, his sweet Southern awe just generations removed.

"And that is the North Star, *mon cherie,* and it can guide you home, no matter how lost you are."

The warmth of his head in my hand, his murmur of awe, the crisp silence and cloud of our breath, the perforated heavens. And then we are blinded, a flash in our faces. I wonder if this is death, come down in a shock of brilliance to take us.

"Oh my God, what the fuck, Mom?"

It is my daughter.

She wrenches the boy off the Toblerone and pulls him close to her chest—to hug him to safety, but he is afraid now and crying.

"You could have been killed."

"By what? The stars?"

"By wolves."

"There haven't been wolves here for years."

"You could have frozen to death."

"Not in ten minutes."

"We've been looking for you for over an hour."

"We were fine."

"You. Are. Not. Fine," she shouts. And she begins to cry.

The man who calls me Honey puts an arm around her to comfort her, as she clutches the boy, the three of them wrapped around each other like a nesting doll, and I look to them across the white distance and feel nothing of kinship, like a foreign body in my own alien orbit.

I am forty now, and pregnant, though he does not know it yet. We are walking along the pale fingers of a cliff, a volcanic speck on the Aegean Sea, and I am imagining what the sea would look like filled with a thousand ships, their white sails a precursor of blood, how Helen must have felt breathing it all in, the sweat and fury propelling these men through the water, knowing they were coming for her.

My friend who died of cancer gave me the book I brought. She underlined bits, and as I read, I feel that she is still alive, her pen in my hand as I trace the lines. One is, *You must love in such a way that the person you love feels free.* This makes me wonder if she has underlined them as instructions for my life, or if she underlined them alone, with no agenda. She never married, and I feel the weight of her judgment for my trifling domestic choices. For a moment, I am angry at my dead friend, even though my husband has taken me here to escape the grief of her loss.

A young couple walks to the cliff edge with a child on his shoulders and a baby on her breast. I have the maternal instinct to lurch for them, tell them they are too close—*Don't jump!*—but I bite down on my anxiety and try to let this feeling dissipate into the brine of the wind, to let things take their course.

"I guess it's too late for us," my husband says.

Part of me wants to rescue him from this defeat. I want to tell him that, *Just maybe, it's not too late, for it is early still.* But there is a kernel of fury his comment stokes, as though I am an empty vessel rather than a thing entirely of my own. I want to explain that I am not Helen; I am not even the men muscling through the water; I am the sails carried on the wind. I am the wind.

"Speak for yourself," I say, with too much salt in my words. I tell myself that when he goes back to Switzerland, I will stay here and live on this cliff.

Later that night, I walk into the bathroom, and he is

sitting on the toilet crying like a child. I wrap my body around his, and despite what I tell myself, I know that in this life I will never leave him.

There is a thump on the kitchen window, the crack of bones, a spot of blood and feather on the glass pane. The man that calls me Honey hurries from the other side of the garden, bends among the onions and scoops the small thing into his hands. For a moment, I am jealous of the bird—I see the lines of tender worry etched on his face, and I yearn to see him hold me like this when I am limp and bloodied.

He looks up, and I realize I am watching him without movement. I open the door.

"Honey, can you get me a shoebox? Put a hand towel in it, please."

I glimpse the bird, who has a beautiful yellow head and black eyes that are still open.

"Now," he says.

I go upstairs to the closet and then begin to lose the instructions—*Why am I up here? He has asked me to get something.* I think we must be going somewhere, so I grab my boots and walk back downstairs. I look outside and see him holding the bird. I remember the shoebox. But he sees me bewildered, boots on the floor. I know that I am caught.

Our daughter has returned for the first time in many weeks, with a wariness that appears to be something that I have earned. She has not brought my grandson, and I am sure she sees the pall fall over my face at the empty space around her legs, but she only shrugs.

I make the tea while they sit at the table, calculating the steeping seconds in my head as my husband tells her of a bird that he is trying to nurse back to life after it careened into our window. He says he should not have left it there alone, that when he returned it was gone, blood across the floor, a trail of feathers, and he's sure that a cat got it, dragged it away to finish it. The guilt pulls his face into the mask of an old man, his eyebrows drawn severely. I wonder how long he has looked like this, or if it is just today. I pull the bags out and glance at the clock. *4 minutes 40 seconds.*

Nearly perfect.

My daughter tells him of his kindness, says our grandson takes after him, that he wants a rabbit of his own to take care of, smiling thinly at me and blowing the steam from her tea. I think that I should take this grandson into the forest while he is still pink and malleable, where he can see the hares running and the ibex with their outlandish horns and even the wolves, and I will teach him that a rabbit is not a toy to keep, no matter what his mother tells him. I think my daughter sees this working inside my head, as though my thoughts are scattered in her mug amidst the tea leaves, and she tells me to join them. She asks me to recite a poem, "Brown Penny" by Yeats, and I do, but when I arrive at the penultimate verse a blankness washes over my mind, like light whiting out the page.

. . .

For he would be thinking of love,
Until the stars had run away, I pause.
Until the stars had run away. I close my eyes.
... *And the rocks melt oer the sun.*

My daughter says, "*And the shadows have eaten the moon,* Mom, that's the line."

But I am certain I know this other line about rocks melting, and it is not wrong.

"No, it's the rocks melting," I say.

"No Mom, you've forgotten it," she says, her face crumpling now, and my husband begins to rub her back. I think it's a good time to leave them.

I go upstairs to find the book the poem is in, to see who is right, and as I ascend the stairs, I hear my daughter's quick words, "Not long now," and, "Forgetting everything," and her father is murmuring something softly.

I stand at the bookcase and am overwhelmed by all the spines. The variety in color, font and subject. The poetry, the history and the cosmos, the photo albums and children's books, the expanse before me, an anthology of our life, contained in this shelf that he built when we were young, to hold these artifacts.

What am I looking for? I don't mind that I've forgotten. I pull out a book that details how a rocket ship works, explaining Newton's third law of motion—*When two bodies interact, they apply forces to one another that are equal in magni-*

tude and opposite in direction—the exhaust shooting skyward into the heavens. I am reminded of the thrill of propulsion. *Le décollage!* The blast into the ether. I leave the book on the floor to go back downstairs, to the hushed, familiar voices, and then there is a chirp, a flutter at the skylight. I look up as I step down. There is the gold crown, the black eyes. I am sure it's him, fluttering above the glass: he has escaped the jaws of the cat and cheated death.

This feeling buoys me as I step again, a bit further out, the disappointment of the hardwood catching me, and then a bit further, wiggling my toes in the air. And I gather my breath and nerve, feeling the freedom of nothing beneath my bare feet.

3, 2, 1... Lift off.

AGENCY

CS ACKERSON

This entry to their home had always seemed bigger than it felt right now—stuck here trying to avoid her own reflection. Patsy could see herself in the mirror that hung in the foyer to their home. She tried to focus on the back of her guests instead of her own face and her clothing choices. The wrinkles were unmanageable and she had stopped trying long ago. She reasoned it was expected at sixty-nine years old. The skirt she wore was so pilled that it looked fuzzy in the reflection. Why hadn't she ever noticed that before? She was disappointed that she hadn't done more with her hair that morning. She knew there would be visitors but she had washed the gray bob herself and it was always flat when she did that. Sometimes the whiteness startled her and she longed for the auburn hair she had had thirty years ago. She could almost hear Alan suggesting she make a hair appointment. "Go on. Treat yourself," he would say, but that wasn't what he meant.

She noticed the bald spot on the back of Sam's head and the stain on the back of his wife's jacket. She flitted her eyes back and forth from herself to the backs of these people. "I don't know what to say, Patsy. We're all in shock," Sam Smithfield said, holding her hands in his as he stood at the front door with his wife, Megan, in her blue dress with matching jacket and eyes full of pity. Patsy just nodded and watched the tears well in his eyes. Hers were dry. She could not muster any and her reflection confirmed this. She felt bad for these men who rarely cried. She felt obligated to comfort them and would have liked to offer her own tears but they wouldn't come. She had been surprised at this lack of moisture as the visitors had begun to stream in over Alan's last few days. She considered herself weepy, the type to tear up at the news of a death. It didn't matter if she actually knew the person or not. Just the thought of that loss for loved ones would bring tears to her eyes. She longed for that now. Instead, she focused on the back of their clothes. They were already dressed for a funeral, but her husband wasn't even dead yet.

Over the past few months, she had had front row seats for this rapid decline, but Alan had worked hard to hide it from everyone else until a week ago. "Thanks for coming," she said to the Smithfields as they walked to their car. She could tell Sam was crying, sobbing actually. She was embarrassed for him as he barely said goodbye, snot and tears dribbling. By his reaction she guessed he had not been at the office early enough these past few months to see Alan walk in with his portable oxygen tank.

Alan had started the firm forty years ago when they were

both twenty-nine. Patsy, already at home with three kids and another on the way, waiting at home most nights to serve him dinner at 9pm. Sam had joined him a few years later, and she had always thought he was much younger than Alan. But maybe divorcing and marrying younger women kept him looking younger. She knew Megan was his third wife.

Over the last few months, when a client came into the office Alan would go to the conference room and stash the tank beneath his seat. Patsy guessed that the other attorneys didn't notice this, but his assistant and the receptionist knew. They always made sure he was ready before they brought the client in.

Once Alan was bedridden, the office sent out a memo to his clients. This was before Sam Smithfield and his wife came to visit. Seeing on paper that someone is dying isn't convincing enough for everyone. That was when Alan shifted from not wanting anyone to know to welcoming everyone to see him in the rented hospital bed. A few clients even asked to come to the house to visit. Patsy was surprised that Alan agreed to this. His acceptance was when her tears dried up. It seemed one of them needed to be in denial at all times. The few clients who came to visit looked sad, but she also sensed they were mad. She knew none of them would say so, but their lack of tears gave it away. It really wasn't fair that he hadn't warned them so they could find another attorney. Who knew what kind of business dealings they had going on. She knew some of the clients had been with him since he started. Some were the kids and grandkids of the original clients. She just followed them as they climbed the stairs to the bedroom. They had paid the company extra to haul the bed upstairs. It was so odd letting these people in this part of the house—the part reserved for private things.

She listened as he greeted them like he would have at the office. She knew he was reaching out from the adjustable bed to shake hands with the men. She was close enough to appear if he called for her, but she stood out of sight so they might feel some sense of privacy. Really, she could hardly hear over the constant tick of the oxygen machine. It was pushing fifteen liters now. She imagined the client wanted to ask who would handle their affairs, but they were too proper for that. She imagined calls were being made to Sam and the other attorneys in the firm. Demands made for services Alan had promised them. She made sure to appear after a few minutes to prompt their goodbyes and lead them back downstairs.

She would be lying if she hadn't thought of him dying, but she had never thought it would be like this. She had imagined getting a phone call that the cleaning staff had found him slumped over his desk. Or a police officer showing up saying he had been in an accident. Stress induced heart attack they would find out later. Well, maybe not the stress part but she knew that would've been the cause. The doctors had warned him to reduce his stress after a mild heart attack years earlier. She remembered the odd cough he couldn't shake. The time he dropped a plate because of the pain in his arm. He wouldn't go to the emergency room, but at 9pm he had called a client who was a doctor. He was an orthopedic doctor, but a doctor just the same. Of course, the doctor cleared his morning schedule and Alan showed up at 8am. He had that kind of power over his clients. It was an understood reciprocity, because he always took their calls at home. Patsy insisted that she drive him there, so she spilled the beans about the plate and the cough. He had tried to make light of it, but she had begged, "Alan, I thought you were going to die coughing two days ago. There's something wrong. Please tell him the truth." This doctor was the son of a long-deceased client, and he quickly sent him across the street to the hospital after getting the details.

Dying with warning wasn't what she expected. She thought the work would kill him. But this was a lung thing. She couldn't remember the name of it. Something with *-osis* at the end of it. All she knew was that his lungs would eventually harden up and stop working. And it would be soon. A month ago, she found him sitting halfway up the steps breathing fast and shallow with his lips tinged with purple. She panic-fired questions at him. "Alan. What is it? Did you fall? Are you okay? Do you feel sick?" She didn't wait for the answers, and after catching her own breath she called 911. He sat in that spot until the paramedics arrived. They had lived in the same house for thirty years, but she had never known him to sit in this spot before. The two young men came in with their duffle bags full of help. One was tall and the other had red hair. They immediately took his blood pressure and slipped a device onto his finger. The tall one spoke directly to Alan. "My name is Bobby. Can you tell me your name, sir?" The redhead spoke before Alan could answer. "He's at 73%." Patsy tried to read the tall one's face to see what this meant, but they both moved so fast, one putting an oxygen mask on him and the other rifling through the bag. By now, Alan's shoulders had rounded in submission, and they helped him down the steps one at a time toward the gurney.

Patsy followed them out with one hand on his as she hurried to match their pace. "I'll be right behind you," she said to him.

His breath was returning, and he was in charge again. He pulled the oxygen mask up to speak. "No dear. Call Dennis and have him bring you over. I'll be fine with these young whippersnappers. Isn't that right, Robby?"

"It's Bobby, sir," she heard the young man say.

"Are you old enough to drive this thing, Robby?" He said as the doors to the rig closed. She imagined the young man rolling his eyes at Alan's repeated mistakes. She could never decide if he did it on purpose or not.

Dennis was their oldest. He was probably still working himself, so she doubted he would be home to answer his phone. She called Michelle instead. She lived farther away, but she was always home. "Everything is fine. Your dad was out of breath so I called an ambulance. Can you call the others and let them know I'll be at Methodist Hospital? But wait a little while because I know they are in the middle of dinner and bedtime. I'll call you once I get there, then you can call them," Patsy said calmly.

"Mom, I'm going to call them now. They will want to know," Michelle said over the noise of the TV in the background.

"I shouldn't have called you yet. He was fine once they got him the oxygen. Please don't worry them," Patsy pleaded.

"Oh, Mom. I wish I could come down."

"I will be fine. Tell Dennis to come. Everything is going to be fine."

She figured Dennis would likely show up later once he got home and checked his answering machine. A bachelor accountant at forty-eight, he still had an answering machine and no cell phone. He said he didn't want to be any more available to his boss than he already was. It just meant that he worked late into the evening. At forty-six, Michelle was stuck home with her two tweens since her husband was always traveling. Besides, she was nearly an hour away and it was already after 7pm. The next two, Thomas and Laura, were busy with their young families. There had been a five year gap after Michelle when Alan was working at a big law firm trying to work his way to partner. But once Alan decided to go out on his own, he was home a little earlier for a while. He didn't feel the need to stay late to impress the partners at the firm and was biding his time to save up a bit more money. He knew things would be tough once he started on his own. He explained to Patsy there would be a lag before the money started coming in again. So, for a couple years, Alan came home at six and had dinner with her and the kids almost every night. It was like a second honeymoon for a while. The next three kids—Thomas, Laura, and Becky—came in quick succession all barely a year apart. Now, Thomas and Laura both had kids under five and she hated to bother them at this time of the evening. Becky lived in Chicago, staying there after graduating from law school. She was the only one who had followed in Alan's footsteps going into law. Still single at thirty-nine, Becky was likely still working at this hour too.

By the time Patsy found him in the hospital, the doctor was half out the door. "Mr. Parker, they will set you up with oxygen at home before you leave. Start with two liters and if that doesn't give you enough, we can increase it. They will give you a portable tank also. You need to use it all the time now." She thought the doctor seemed even younger than the paramedics as he nodded at her on his way out.

"That's a big ring on your finger," Alan said to the nurse who was adjusting the cannula tubes around his ears.

"Yes, I'm taken big guy." She winked at Patsy. "Can I get you dinner? I know it's late but I can call and see if I can get something brought up."

"Can I see a menu?" Alan said, making the nurse smile.

"Oh yes, four course meal coming up." She winked at Patsy a second time. "Let me see what I can do."

As she left, Alan lifted his hand and said, "Waiter, waiter, can you take our order?" Alan let out a little laugh, but Patsy did not smile.

They had stopped going out to eat because he could barely get in the restaurant without huffing and puffing so much that he couldn't eat once they sat down. She was okay with that because going out to eat together had never been her favorite thing. Years earlier, they had gone out to a restaurant. She was watching a family at a table next to them. They put the toddler in a high chair at the end of their booth. Patsy looked past Alan's shoulder and watched them settle into their seats. Alan kept talking about work, and his words were consumed by the restaurant's bad acoustics.

"Patsy. What are you looking at?" he asked, turning to look behind him. Patsy smiled and waved at the little boy now looking back at her. The mother opened a package of saltines and put it in front of the boy.

"He reminds me of Thomas as a baby. Don't you think?" Patsy said, smiling with her eyes focused on the boy.

"Sometimes I wonder if you're even in there," Alan said, unrolling the utensils from the napkin. "The lights are on but nobody's home." He laughed at his comment.

Patsy's face fell, and she shifted in her seat so that Alan blocked the boy's face. Blocked her face from the boy. She straightened up her body and looked at Alan directly, "Okay finish telling me about your lawful stuff." She unrolled her utensils and smoothed the napkin over her lap.

"Legal stuff," he huffed. "Sometimes I wonder how you even know to put that napkin on your lap and not on your head, Patsy."

She stopped moving her hands and glared at him. He smirked back at her but quickly put his hand up to summon the waiter when she didn't break eye contact with him. She took the napkin and put it on her head. She moved back in view of the boy. He stared at her for a long moment then smiled. The boy reached for his father's napkin and put it on his own head. They laughed together. She didn't look at Alan again, but she felt him shrink a little.

"For god's sake. Take that off your head," Alan demanded.

She ignored Alan and giggled with the boy until the waiter brought their food. Then she took the napkin and returned it to her lap and they ate the meal in silence. As they left, she waved goodbye to the boy and smiled at his parents. She led the way to the car and neither said a word the whole way home.

After that day, she put the napkin on her head whenever she wanted to shut him up. And it worked. At first, he would get mad and demand she take it off, but eventually he gave up and stopped talking. She would take it off if he was quiet long enough. Sometimes they were able to have a conversation after that. Other times neither one talked for the rest of the meal.

~

After watching Sam and Megan drive off, Patsy returned to find Alan dozing off. He jumped at the click of her shoes on the wood floors. "You can rest for a while. Becky's plane lands in about an hour. Dennis is picking her up and then coming here." Alan nodded then closed his eyes again. Patsy had expected a fight from him, so she straightened his blanket to use her energy. Then she tiptoed out of the room in hopes she wouldn't wake him again.

She thought back to that day in the hospital and wished she had followed that doctor and asked questions. She had heard him say he should wear the oxygen all the time but she knew he hadn't. Had the doctor given any other instructions that would have helped his lungs last a bit longer? Could he have avoided being stuck at home waiting to die if she had been there in time? And now here she was managing the procession of visitors with a box of morphine injections ready for the hospice nurse. She should be crying about this, but no tears would come.

Patsy waited in the kitchen for her children to show up. Two days earlier, Alan had called them all one by one and told them to come for a meeting. She listened as he repeated it for each one. "I need you here on Thursday at 6pm," he said, and before they could respond he finished with, "Everyone." He called Becky first to make sure she could get there from Chicago. Only Michelle asked how he was doing after the request. "Everything is fine. I just need to talk to everyone," he said. She apparently didn't push for more.

Michelle arrived first, then Thomas and Laura came in together. Patsy told each one as they came in that he was resting so they would wait until everyone arrived before going up. Laura searched the cabinet for a bottle of wine. "Anyone else want a drink?" she asked.

"No I have to dri—" Michelle started but choked up. Patsy wondered for a second if she was crying because her drive was so far or if she was the only one in the room who seemed to be aware of why they were there. Either way, Patsy wished she could cry.

"Hit me," Thomas said, holding a glass toward Laura.

Becky and Dennis finally showed up, and the commotion when they came in made Patsy feel overwhelmed. Becky made her rounds hugging everyone. Laura poured Becky a glass of wine while Dennis filled a short glass with bourbon and a few ice cubes. Michelle was full-on sobbing by now. And while Becky hugged Patsy they heard Alan yelling, "Hey, you having a party without me?" It took them a moment to process what he had said, but then the cacophony returned with their laughter. The kids all stood there, but Patsy practically ran to the steps.

"Sorry, hon. Here we come," she said, rushing upstairs.

By the time they all reached the landing, Patsy was busy moving chairs into Alan's room. The hospital bed was a twin so it left lots of room for chairs, but there had never been more than two other people visiting him. Everyone except Michelle had a glass in hand, so they stood helplessly watching but not knowing where to put down their drinks. This was another thing that never happened upstairs. Food or drink was never allowed up here before this makeshift infirmary. Michelle dropped her oversized purse on the floor and took a chair from their mother. Dennis took it from Michelle with one hand and nodded at her to grab another one. Her face was still wet, but now her eyes were serious. "Don't worry. I got it," she said sarcastically. Laura and Thomas looked at each other and shrugged. Becky was already in the room and hugging her dad. Dennis took the second chair from Michelle but kept his drink steady.

"So glad you could join me," Alan said sternly.

"We were waiting for you to wake up," Patsy said as she pushed a pillow behind his back.

"Let's be clear. You were not waiting. It sounded like a block party down there."

"Aw, Dad, come—" Thomas started but stopped when Alan's hand came up to silence him. Alan held it there as he looked at each of them, waiting for silence.

Michelle broke the silence by patting the chair next to her and said, "Here Mom, sit here." Her voice was muffled from her stopped-up nose. Everyone seemed to breathe after that, and they all took a sip of their drinks. Patsy grabbed some tissues from the box next to Alan and handed one to Michelle. She held out the wad to the others, but no one else took any. Once she sat down, she fiddled with the tissues on her lap to keep busy until someone spoke.

"I guess you know why you are here," Alan began. He stopped and cleared his throat and that made everyone look up at him. It was unclear if his voice cracked with emotion or if it was the lung thing causing the catch in his throat. They were positioned around the end of the bed in a half moon shape. They could see each other out of the corner of their eyes, but it only confirmed that they were all called to attention by this. Michelle sniffled and Patsy stared at Alan while her fingers fiddled with the tissues.

"There are some things you need to know. First, the doctor says it's hard to tell how long this will take."

"Oh my god, Dad!" Laura yelped and bent to put her glass on the floor. Michelle sobbed loudly. Dennis folded his arms in front of him, still holding the nearly empty glass. His face was stoic. Thomas shifted in his chair then crossed his legs. He had trouble looking anyone in the eye. Patsy took one tissue and started smoothing it out on her lap.

"Let him finish please," Becky said before taking the last swallow of her wine and placing her glass on the floor also.

"It could be days or weeks or it could be longer. For now, I'm stuck in this bed and in this room. I need you all to plan to be here more to help your mother."

They all started to speak at once, but they stopped when Alan's hand shot up again. Most nodded their understanding instead.

He continued, "I have engaged an attorney at another

firm to handle things for you. He will be in touch in due time."

"Why not use someone from your firm?" Michelle asked through her tears.

Before Alan could answer her, Thomas muttered, "Because you don't shit where you eat."

"For god's sake, T. What is wrong with you?" Laura snapped.

"What in the world does that *even* mean?" Patsy asked, searching the eyes of each of her children.

"Watch your language," Alan said, looking at Thomas. They all quieted down once they noticed Alan's hand up again.

"Go on with your lawful stuff, dear," Patsy said.

"Legal stuff," Becky whispered.

"What?" Patsy whipped her head around to look at her. "What did you say?"

Everyone froze. They weren't used to a reaction like this from their mother. She searched each one of her children's eyes for something. There was no more softness in them. Angles had shown up around their eyes and mouth, and it felt like broken glass was flying around the room. Like an explosion had happened and she couldn't hear anything anymore but the shards were still flying. She wanted to duck. She didn't want to get hurt.

When she realized Alan had his hand up again, her shoulders fell. The only sound was Michelle's sniffles. She took one more look at each of her children. Michelle was looking down and dabbing a tissue at her nose. Becky picked at her fingernails. Thomas and Laura both leaned down to pick up their empty wine glasses at the same time. Dennis was the only one looking at her. His chin was tucked and she could feel his sadness. His face was blank though. Like he had forgotten how to speak. She turned to Alan, who was moving his mouth, and before he could let out a sound she took the tissue and placed it on her head.

Alan let out a guffaw, which made the others look up to see his shoulder shake with laughter. The others started to giggle when they finally looked at their mother. Even Michelle seemed to laugh, but really it was hard to tell if she was laughing or still crying. Dennis had a smile but he made no sound. Patsy was overcome with the joy in the room. She was laughing with them when she realized her face was wet with tears. Suddenly Alan's laughter turned to a cough which silenced the room. Everyone looked up to see Alan holding his hand up while continuing to cough uncontrollably.

"Oh Alan, put your hand down," she snapped. "I think that's enough for one day." She stood and retrieved his water from beside the bed. She held the straw up to his mouth and he leaned over to drink. She looked at each of her children's faces. The angles had softened and she could almost feel them all exhale. She smiled at them and set the water down. "Who wants to help me get some dinner for your father?" She didn't wait for an answer, but as she walked to the door the tissue floated from her head onto the bed near Alan's hand. He moved his hand over it and left it there.

AND SHE FADED INTO ME

WHITNEY VALE

August turned cool for one day, the day my mother died. The previous day's humidity swallowed by sudden showers made the Kentucky soil soft, pliant as a bruised Magnolia blossom. I stood in the hospital stairwell with the heavy metal door cracked open a couple of inches. I held my cigarette away from the opening and the smoke cooperated by floating up instead of out. Mom's room was just down the hall. I needed a break, and just didn't want to risk missing anything by taking the elevator down five levels to the discreet smoking area set up outside. I dropped the butt and nudged it to the small pile I had been making over the course of the last twenty-four hours. When I looked up, I saw my sister walking hurriedly toward our mother's room.

"Hey!" I hissed. "In here!"

Laura, pulling her suitcase behind her, grabbed the metal

door and wrangled her bag, purse and frazzled self into the stuffy stairwell.

"Where have you been? We expected you hours ago."

"Good to see you too. I took the earliest flight from L.A. I could get. We got diverted to Dallas mid-flight—I don't know why—and sat in the airport for another hour with my mobile—and no way to reach you. Have you ever considered the movement called 'Get on Board with Technology'?"

After a joint laugh, I stammered an apology.

"Look, it's been grueling. Mom's fluid is building up again —and she doesn't want any further intervention. We're just waiting for you."

"What are you talking about?"

"You know what I'm talking about. Instead of taking off the fluid, the doctor will give her a sedative, and she'll fall asleep—"

"Like a pet?"

"Oh, come on! I told you this on the fucking phone. The doctor explained to her if she had to be intubated again, it would be for the rest of her life. She would be on tubes and machines—she wouldn't be able to speak to us, or eat— "

"A few of her favorite things."

"Right."

"She's been waiting for you, Laura. Before she takes the sedative."

"Give me one of those."

"I thought you quit."

"I did."

"Oh. Right. Here." I shook out a cigarette, and several fell to the floor. That's when I realized my hands had been shaking.

"You okay?"

"Coffee and cigs are not stabilizing meals."

Laura had pulled one puff when Nurse Tim pulled open the door.

"She the sis?"

"Yes," we both said at once.

"Be careful of the smoke, and maybe take a few breaks outside. If you're caught that's it for you—and the rest of us addicts."

We followed his pale blue form down to Mom's room. Hush spread like a white cloud when we pushed open the door. Mom's face, moist from illness and her natural sheen, was drawn. Her hospital gown had slipped off one shoulder, and she looked like a wizened child in a bed much too large. Blazing brown eyes, slightly protuberant, remained her strongest feature as her skin thinned and her body shrank.

"Laura!" Mom's voice was thick. Fluid.

"Mom! I'm so sorry, I got here as fast as I could."

"That's all right, Sweetheart. You're here now."

I leaned back against a wall and watched Mom look at Laura. Maybe it was the lack of sleep and food, but memories filled me up, and I thought I might drown in them, small hurts, not so subtle comparisons, and the rest of the usual suspects in sibling rivalry. I mean, I don't recall Mom ever calling me "Sweetheart". Can that have been true? Maybe when I was an infant, a toddler. But at that moment, hoping a slippery white wall would hold me up, I thought, *Was I ever your sweetheart?*

"Mom, I know what you want to do. I don't want you to."

And just like that, Laura asserted control over the scene. And it felt like she also wiped out the three years I had been caring for Mom. White knighting from L.A.

Red oozed up from the floor into my body, threatening to blow out an artery. I had walked into Mom's hospital room on a previous emergency visit as two doctors stood over her, mopping up blood as it drained from her neck. She once told me they were all evil. And they looked it that day, white-robed vampires with syringes.

"Laura, we talked all this out with Mom already, I told you."

"It's for the best, Hon."

"Who's best, Mom?" Laura darted a look at me. The cold wall grew arms and held me back.

~

The door swung open and Dad walked in with his odd duck footed gait. It wasn't a waddle exactly, but the splay of his feet always made him seem awkward. Except when he was dancing with Mom. I remember him telling me when I arrived back in Kentucky after twenty years away, "Your mother and me, when we were first married, we had a fairy-tale love." I had never known my father to say anything remotely fantastical. The marriage I remembered was more *Who's Afraid of Virginia Woolf,* though I suppose that was a Grimm enough comparison. I always suspected she felt a little sorry for him.

She turned her gaze from Laura to Dad. A ghost of a

smile touched her lips before lifting off again. She pursed them, deep smoker's lines indenting her pale skin.

"Look, here is Laura, come at last." Her voice was getting hoarser. "And you have come at last too."

"I had to feed the dogs. I told you."

"Oh, yes. Chloe and Zip..." She laughed her half-laugh as she looked off toward the window, slightly ajar. The smell of dampness and the swollen creek snaked in.

"Dad, I think Mom is being precipitous."

Jesus. She actually said "precipitous". Mom had been dying for almost three years, how could it have been *precipitous*? What the fuck is precipitous about congenital heart failure or failed kidneys.

But I knew. I knew that it couldn't feel any way but rushed. Death is always a surprise. Death is always in such a damn hurry to make off with our hearts.

Mom patted Laura's hand. I hated to see the resemblance between them. It made me feel more left out. And yet, I loved to see the resemblance between them, because it meant I wouldn't feel so alone. After.

"I'm very tired, Sweetheart. I'm ready. I can't do this anymore."

"But, Mom, please..." Laura held back her tears but they tangled up her words. Dad looked like he was going to collapse. I had my wall.

"No. I've had a long time to think about this." She buzzed the nurse's station. "I really am so happy to see you. I am so proud of you. And isn't it wonderful your sister came back here to live?"

Laura bowed her head over Mom's hand. Dad sat on the

bed. I slowly moved from the wall to the foot of the bed. The door opened, and the doctor walked in.

"Don't you have anything to say to me?!" Mom directed this to Dad, who began to cry.

"I love you," he said. "I love you."

"I love you, Ma," I whispered, my voice left someplace on the floor.

Mom looked toward the window once more. And the doctor came forward with his syringe.

Mom turned her head to the doctor who had been with her for some twenty years. They didn't like each other. But she smiled at him. And he, before bowing his head for a moment, smiled back.

He administered the sedative. And it was fast. She fell asleep, faster than she could close her eyes all the way. Under her thin lashes, a glimmering teardrop remained, refusing to fall. "It could be hours," he murmured before leaving us to our shock.

"I'll be back in a minute," I said, pushing away from the bed and the softly breathing form. I ran to my stairwell and yanked open the door. Bile backwashed my throat. I was hungry and lightheaded. And I wanted to smoke. Laura came in just as I lit up, grabbing the pack from my hands. And we stood there, nearly motherless, and smoked in silence for maybe a whole blessed minute.

"It was your idea." Thrust from Laura.

"It was not my idea." A half-hearted parry from me.

"You didn't let me speak to her on the phone!"

"Oh, for fuck's sake. Don't you get it? She didn't want to talk to you! She had made her decision—"

"Well—"

"Is a deep hole in the ground."

"What?"

"Oh, something a teacher used to say. Never begin a sentence with 'well'. It's just a deep hole in the ground."

"Excuse the hell out of me."

And we didn't speak for a few minutes, just filled up our lungs and the gray space with smoke.

"Look," I said, "she knew you couldn't talk her out of it, and she also didn't have the energy for an argument. She was done. She told me months ago she was done, just afraid to let go. Wasn't sure she'd be going to heaven."

"Heaven, really?"

"We can't all be comforted by atheism." I lit another cigarette. "We can't all be comforted by distance either."

"Oh, that's right, blame me for your choices. No one made you come back here."

"I know that. I know that. And mostly I'm glad I came, I just am mixed up between the right thing, wrong thing, love her, hate this. I can't find myself anymore. I feel like the drudge sister in a cliché. And you, only visiting a few times—"

"I have a job!"

"And I didn't, which made it easier. But Mom would have preferred it was you. She wouldn't have turned down six meals in a row from you. And you would have just ordered something in—"

"I can't believe this. Mom is dying and you're doing the Smothers Brothers."

"Oh, Laura, I can't remember Mom ever hugging me." At which point I started to cry.

Laura stood there, dumbfounded. It's funny how specific relationships are to the person experiencing them. She was the favored one. I knew she loved me. But I wasn't special.

"She must have."

"There is not one photograph that bears witness to that... phenomenon." With that, I dropped the cigarette and walked back to Mom's room.

She hadn't moved.

I pulled up an uncomfortable chair and sat next to her. Dad sat on the other side, face red, unshaven. He ate bran cereal every morning; I noticed some dried milk on his blazer. Laura came in and made friends with my wall. I looked at Mom, the giantess of my childhood. I remembered her juggling oranges just out of reach of my outstretched hands. She laughed, relented and handed me one. I remembered catching her singing some old torch song while she stirred some bean soup on a white enameled stove. Tears streamed down her face.

I stared at her slightly visible eyes, watched the slow movement of her chest as it made feathery pushes against the sheet. I felt an overwhelming urge to get in bed with her. I lifted my hips, side to side, and tucked my hands under them. Something I did when I was little, holding my energy in place, holding my stomach, my breath. But I wanted to crawl into bed with her. Then I thought, *Oh, that's something you've seen in movies. You're just wanting to make a pretty picture.* I folded my hands into fists. I didn't care what was true. The truest truth was to lie next to Mom. And so I pushed off the chair and got next to Mom, I stayed on top of the sheet. Her body still gave off her musky odor. I breathed it in deep.

I am not sure how to explain what happened next—I was so tired. I closed my eyes, and I sort of went into a trance. I mean I opened my eyes just a slit and there was the room, Laura and Dad. I closed my eyes again, and gently put one arm across Mom's wren body. And then I saw it, this great winged creature, all white, androgynous—smooth features. A burst of light blinded me, and when I could see, Mom was nineteen, dressed for dancing, polka dotted dress and spectator shoes. I didn't recognize the empty room. A tall open window with billowing drapes also wafted in the scent of the sea. The creature, the angel, flew into the room and swept her up in his arms as if she weighed but a feather. She laughed. And he flew away with her. Boundaries had faded between us. I don't know if I was seeing what she saw as her body closed down or if she saw what I saw as I lay there grieving.

I rolled away from her and stood up. An hour had passed. Dad was gone. So was Laura. I walked to the makeshift smoker's lounge. Laura was sitting on one of the stairs. She didn't raise her head when I walked in. I passed her a smoke.

"I'm glad you're here," I offered.

"Yeah, me too. I'm sorry it's been so much up to you. I figure Dad has been pretty hopeless."

"Better, actually, than I thought he would be. He's helped

a lot for someone who spent most of his life in absentia land."

The door violently swung inward and Nurse Tim, without entering, said, "It's time."

All three of us ran the hard steps to Mom's room. Tim said she could still hear us, to talk to her. A ragged breath struggled out of Mom's throat. The death rattle had commenced.

"Mom, I love you," Laura spoke first and held Mom's hand.

I stood on the side of her bed and stared for a brief moment.

"Mom," I faltered, "I love you. You're going to dance now whenever you want. Mom it's all okay."

She died then. There was the smallest movement in her body as her last breath expelled. Tissue-soft energy pushed through me. With a shock, I realized Mom's spirit had passed through my body on the way to the open window.

Dad walked in, covered his face and sobbed.

Nurse Tim said we could take all the time we wanted. We couldn't really. For a few hours, time had stopped, and then begun its relentless march once again.

~

Back in the stairwell we started to make plans for the funeral. Laura asked to choose the music, and I said I would do the Bible verses for the program.

"Isn't there one about love never fails?"

"Yes," I said, "Yes."

THE CAUSEWAY

CYNTHIA CAIN

An old gravel road ran parallel with the paved one that took her to the Island. Beyond the gravel road, scrubby pine trees and small pin oaks, stunted by frequent fires that laid bare the sandy soils of South Jersey's Pine Barrens, stretched for miles. On their childhood drives to the beach, Lydia's dad had talked about how he and his brother Don used that gravel road, all there was then, to drive from their home in Philadelphia in the thirties and forties. Weekends, they'd fish the shoreline and camp on the beach. Lydia had seen the sepia photographs of them, shirtless and tanned, bachelor sportsmen holding up huge bluefish and sea bass, the leather holsters they propped their surf rods in slung from their waists. Never in her life had she seen her father look that happy.

Lydia loved this feeling, driving alone, the soft rolling sound of her tires skimming the flat macadam road. Around halfway to the island, she'd remember to open her car windows and inhale: the scent of the pines evoked childhood day trips with her father and siblings. They'd walk the sandy trails and he'd point out wild blueberries and crush teaberry leaves, urging them to chew and see how they tasted like gum. It was not uncommon to come across the ruins of a mill or the foundation of a house, the remnants of little hamlets that had once flourished when bog ore was used for iron. Those villages, less than ghost towns now, were abused by time like so much that once mattered.

Today, before she left home, her father stood at the kitchen counter while she gathered her keys and sweater and work shoes.

"I don't like the idea of you driving along that dark road coming home so late. That's an old car your boyfriend sold you. What if you break down?"

He had to put in the bit about Alex selling her the car. Her dad didn't like Alex, never had, and sometimes Lydia wondered whether that made her like him more. Selling her the car for five hundred dollars when he'd paid four hundred was typical Alex. He'd had it almost a year, but he had put new tires on it. Lydia thought he'd be a good salesman; her dad thought he was cocky and disrespectful. When he came over, he parked his car in the top of their circular driveway, no matter how many times her dad asked him to pull it over to the edge of the lower circle in case someone had to go through.

"No one ever comes over here but me," he'd say.

At least today her father hadn't commented on her summer plans. The reason she drove to the beach weekends now, in May, was so that she'd have this job early, ahead of the college students, and could spend summer at the house Alex's dad owned a few miles up the beach. She had worked at home the year before, at Howard Johnson's on the Turnpike, and no way was Lydia going to stay in Mt. Holly again while Alex was a lifeguard on the island.

She'd been lucky to get the job. And she was determined to show the year-round waitresses that she could hold her own in the dining room. Wida's Hotel and Restaurant was known for its unfussy atmosphere and simple good food. The menu, printed on plain card stock, didn't change from year to year, nor did the décor. The massive dining room with creaky wood floors had the same buttery seafood smell, and the square linen cloths were always clean and starched. As a girl, she'd come here with relatives, savoring the freshly ground fat hamburgers and hand cut fries.

A core of seasoned waitresses worked the restaurant year-round, supplemented by college girls in the summer, when the island's population increased tenfold and sunburned families formed hungry lines out the doors of the best places to eat. Lydia thought that next year, she and Alex would finish classes at the state college early and could maybe find their own place to stay, away from his father's heavy drinking.

~

It was late May, just a few weeks until graduation. Lydia, who had all but left high school behind already, drove straight east, exiting the scrubby pines and traversing marshy flatlands, over which a six-mile causeway connected the island with the mainland. Marsh grass gave way to open bay, a vivid barometer of beach conditions, gray and choppy when weather was foreboding, glassy and flecked with shimmers when the sea beyond the island was calm. The causeway dipped and touched down on two or three tiny islands dotted with weathered bait shacks and dilapidated piers, then spilled cars out at the feet of a modern motel perched at the Island's doorway. Lydia took the broad boulevard south toward Wida's. It was just a few miles to the big hotel, one of the island's oldest, built long before she was born. Then, tourists either camped like her dad had done, or stayed in hotels. Private homes came later.

But they had come with a toll. The dunes that she remembered climbing and hiding in as a child had been flattened by construction, and most of the once empty lots from bay to ocean were filled with houses, stores, or parking lots. The beaches had to be held in place by massive stone jetties that kept the island from washing away. It was, her dad had told her often, really only a big sandbar, as all barrier islands were, meant to shift and finally disappear with time.

Lydia parked the old Impala in the lot and got out, sucking in the good salty air. It was early, too early to clock in, but already mist was rolling in from the ocean. It would be a foggy night. She looked up at the building, with its signature mint green exterior and the tall letters at the top that spelled WIDA'S, illuminating the boulevard at night, the long rows of windows for the three floors of modest hotel rooms. There was time to walk to the beach.

She passed the boxy hotel and the shuttered houses squatting in their tiny lots all waiting for the summer invasion. Only locals and weekenders would eat at the restaurant tonight, but in a few weeks, the huge dining room would turn over three or four times. At the end of the street, she leaned over to untie her white Oxfords and held them as she climbed over what was left of the dune. At the top, where the ocean came into view, was a forest green bench. Here Lydia sat, shivering a little, partly from the ocean air still cooled by winter's currents, partly from the always startling sight of waves crashing, ferocious and insistent. The sea here was never entirely placid, but the intensity of the Atlantic varied with the tides and the seasons. Today a few surfers in full wetsuits tested the shore break, getting brief rides in the choppy surf.

Her family had rented a summer house until a few years earlier, when she was fourteen and her brother almost seventeen. He'd been a surfer, rising before the sun to coat his cumbersome board with surf wax and carry it out to the closest beach with a good break. He got a job that summer and rode his bike to the Deli a few miles down the Boulevard until one day in August when a car plowed into him from behind, sending him over the handlebars and mashing his face into the pavement. For the rest of the summer, her parents spent every day over on the mainland sitting with him in the hospital. They didn't rent a beach house again.

Lydia did not hear the man coming, and she jumped when he sat on the bench. He was maybe sixty-five, seventy, and wore a ratty blue sweater and a cap. He had the permanently tanned look of a beach dweller, the watery eyes of one who had stared at the waves for decades. But then, maybe she was just making him out to be an old sea captain here when closer to home she'd think he was a farmer or a Piney.

He spoke:

So we'll go no more a roving so late into the night, though the heart be still as loving, and the moon be still as bright...

"That's Byron, young lady. You know Byron?"

"Not really. I mean, I heard of Byron, sure." She planned to major in Education but still had a lot to learn.

"Ha! I should have guessed. Ignorance—the way of all flesh. And how about these birds?"

"Birds?" Lydia started thinking about how she might conveniently get up and leave. For the moment her instinct to be polite won out.

"These gulls, swooping above us." The old man waved his arm. "Do you think they're here for nothing?"

She'd never really thought of the omnipresent gulls as birds. "I guess they're here to pick up clams."

"You *guess*."

She nodded.

"These birds are here to tell *you*," he pointed at her and

she leaned away from him so that his finger wouldn't strike her face, "what to do next."

Lydia just looked at him. Pity contended with aversion, but she stayed.

~

The beach was empty now. A surfer in the shore break fell from his board, and it skittered crazily toward the sand. In three weeks the beach would be full of umbrellas and squealing toddlers with sand in every crevice.

"They're scavengers. Dirty birds, noisy, too. Still, beautiful, so graceful the way they swoop. Do you know how many kinds of birds there are in the world? Thousands! Tropical beauties along the Amazon, hawks in Southern swamps, great big condors out west, swooping through canyons that will stun you, they're so beautiful. You'll want to see all of that. Life's short. Don't miss it!"

She had stood up while he spoke, and, picking up her shoes, started backing up. "Oh-kay."

"Aw, go on. Pay me no mind." He bent forward and fumbled in his sweater, pulled out a pipe.

"Bye," Lydia whispered, waved limply, and walked swiftly down the dunes, stopping at the pavement to brush the sand from between her toes and put on her shoes.

~

The hostess, Mae, stood at the cash register, poised for business even though the place was empty. She stopped

Lydia a few feet inside the door, ready to inspect her as soon as she entered the spacious dining room, still slightly musty after the winter's confinement. Empty tables covered with clean white cloths stood waiting for their customers, the wood floors swept spotless. The regular waitresses sat at a round table near the kitchen, eating and laughing. She'd have to sit with them if she wanted to eat, even though she felt like an interloper, just one of the summer girls who came and left, swooping in like the gulls, opportunists. *They* were the real employees, and every one of them made it clear.

"That top is a little too tight." Mae's eyes skimmed over Lydia. "I don't like my girls looking sexier than me."

Lydia signaled that she understood. Mae was at least fifty, fat and gaudily dressed with a wide pouf of hair and garish lips.

"Better get your dinner and check to see what side work you have tonight."

Lydia put her brown polyester vest on over the bright gold ribbed top that Mae didn't like, tied the brown apron she carried over her matching slacks, and walked past the waitresses, who ignored her, through the swinging door into the kitchen. Glaring fluorescent lights overhead bathed the large kitchen, its glowing stainless grills and stoves already firing up to the clack of knives as prep cooks set up behind the pickup line. The head cook tonight was one of the mostly absentee owners' sons, a boy around her brother's age named Joey. The Wida family was a huge extended Greek clan, powerful and well-respected on the Island, and Lydia knew that Joey was a surfer and went to college, nothing more. He had never talked with her, just at her.

"I'll have scallops," Lydia called when he glanced her way. They were permitted anything on the menu except lobster.

"Broiled or fried?"

"Um, broiled, thanks."

"Want anything else?"

"A baked potato?"

"Not ready yet." Of course.

"Okay, just some coleslaw."

"Get it yourself, over there." How stupid could she be?

Lydia ate, silent, strange among the women who kept talking without acknowledging her.

"Nothing good will come of that. She needs to stay in school," Eleanor, the matriarch, commented.

"In school? Pregnant?"

"Get her to a doctor. It's legal now."

"Not for us. Catholic."

"Well."

They were discussing the life and fate of one of their grown children, the potential non-existence of a grandchild, as they sliced through veal cutlets splattered with tomato sauce. Lydia looked at her plate and ate quickly.

"Let's get to work, ladies." Eleanor's vest brushed her arm as she pushed past Lydia. "Kids. Selfish and inconsiderate." Somehow she felt the remark was aimed as much at her as at the pregnant teenager who wanted to quit school.

Lydia finished, cleared her dishes, and re-set the table they'd all used for dinner. She took her place at the assigned station, five of the least desirable tables toward the wall without windows, just as the first customers were being seated. Once the dinner rush began, she was in its flow, taking orders, bringing out monkey dishes of fresh coleslaw she'd once seen the old Greek grandmother mixing by hand, serving fresh rolls and drinks, placing the dupes she tore from behind the checks on the chrome rack in the kitchen, and, when her number lit up on the board in the dining room, loading the big oval tray with six or seven plates filled with shrimp or lobster tails or crab cakes. She remembered to say, "Coming through," when she pushed open the swinging door to the kitchen, "Behind you," when she came up to the rear of a senior waitress about to turn around with a loaded tray, and to carry the full tray of mixed drinks from the bar without looking at it—the best way to keep the liquids from spilling. Hours passed.

The parties of diners shifted from noisy families to middle-aged couples who lingered over their cocktails before ordering. Lydia cleaned and condensed the ketchup bottles and waited for her last party, a boozy tanned couple in bright polyester, to finish. She glanced around at the nearly empty dining room and headed for the back, an unused banquet room where she could sit in one chair and put her feet on another. Her legs throbbed and trembled a little at rest. In bed tonight, she'd feel the pleasant ache of having worked with her body, and the satisfaction of making good money, cash. She pulled the wad of bills from her vest pocket and straightened them, turning the faces in the same direction, placing the fives and then the ones together.

She thought about the summer ahead, working here while Alex lifeguarded. With luck she could get mostly days so they could be together at night. Then college, and what? Marriage? Kids? It felt like a foregone conclusion. But just a few years ago, every possible scenario for her life had still been out there. Summers had been dreamlike, endless, the beach a place where young bodies displayed themselves by day and made tentative contact by night, urged on by the rumbling surf, its waves a cover and an approval.

She remembered a boy she had adored. He'd only been at the shore for two weeks. After the first few days, they had been together constantly, lying face down on the beach by day, whispering their stories and plans while sand sifted between their fingers, meeting at night for as long as Lydia was allowed out. A football player from a high school in Philadelphia who'd come to rent a vacation home with his single mother and younger siblings, Carl had been different from the boys at home whom she'd kiss when they played spin-the-bottle or five-minute honeymoon, but without passion or context. They'd talked, held hands, imagined themselves a couple, and he had promised he'd come back to see her again every summer.

The day her brother was hit, her father and stepmother had stayed at the hospital until late at night. Carl had come over, and after the baby, her half-sister, was safely asleep, they had laid together on her bed, whispering, kissing for hours, their sun-warmed bodies touching at every possible point. Fear and elation filled her even now, remembering how precious and tender those kisses and touches had felt, how guilty she had been the next morning when her father described the injuries her brother had sustained, how the doctor had said that if he hadn't been so fit from surfing, he may not have survived, how his face would be permanently scarred, how he looked, swollen and bruised, his nose smashed flat, his forehead covered with hundreds of stitches. She hadn't even thought about him when she'd been with Carl.

"There you are. Your customers are looking for you." It was Mae, her disapproval piercing Lydia like a parent's scolding.

"Sorry." Lydia jumped up, pulling the checkbook from her pocket as she walked briskly to the table.

"You'll be sorry if you find your name off the schedule," she heard Mae mumble.

All of the other waitresses had left by the time Lydia cleared the table, checked over the side work, and reported to the register where Mae scanned each guest check before dismissing her. "You're on for five o'clock next Saturday and Sunday," was her curt goodbye.

~

Lydia punched the clock in the kitchen and headed toward the door. Joey was alone, cleaning the stovetop and wiping the counters. He was humming a Doors tune: "Green-Eyed Lady". Lydia walked out the service door and took her keys from her purse. The white Impala was one of ten or twelve in the lot. The others were probably guests in the still mostly empty hotel. When she got in and turned the key, the engine sputtered and stopped. She tried again. A grinding sound, then nothing. Again she turned the key, pumping the gas. Mae bustled past and got into her car, pulled away. Lydia sat still for a minute. Who could help?

She thought about the little old man at the bench and his crazy talk. Talk about birds, and all the places she'd never see. Or ought to see. About her dad. He'd probably tell her she'd have to quit if he had to come get her. It was ten thirty and Sunday night. Alex was working late at the newspaper. She couldn't reach him there. Why wouldn't it start? She tried again. Nothing. What the hell was she going to do? She got out of the car and slammed the door. The restaurant lights were out, but the kitchen was still bright. Lydia walked back in. The screen door to the kitchen slammed behind her.

Joey, bending over to slide a huge pot under the counter, straightened up and looked at her without recognition at first. It was as if he'd never seen her. And, most likely, he hadn't actually seen her without the chrome counter and heat lamps that kept them separated. His face had an easy grin that it never wore when he was snatching dupes from the rack and slamming plates of food onto the pickup shelf.

"Hey, can you help me with my car? It won't start."

"Sure. I can try. I'm not real good with cars though. What's wrong?"

He had removed the starched white chef's hat and jacket and wore a tattered, faded T-shirt. His brown hair was curly and long and he had very tan arms and hands. And curly eyelashes.

"Hey. What's your name again?"

His voice had shifted to that softer tone guys use when they notice that a girl is attractive.

"Um. Lydia. I don't know. It just won't start. I tried a lot of times. Usually I can get it going, but it's just refusing to go."

"Well, maybe it's flooded. Wait awhile and try again."

He was still looking at her though, and his gaze traveled down, caressing the round curves of her breasts beneath the top Mae had scolded her for wearing, past her slender waist, and back to her eyes.

"Hey, *Lydia,* why don't you come next door and sit awhile and then we can go fool with it? I need to get these clothes off. Greasy."

He turned off the lights in the kitchen and the glow from the hotel lobby kept them from total darkness. He lived, she assumed, in the large house next door to the hotel with his family.

"Oh. I don't want to bother your parents. Maybe I can just use the phone and call somebody. Maybe there's a service station."

"Not off-season there's not. You'll be stuck here until morning unless we can get it started. Come on. I'm thirsty, aren't you? We'll get something to drink and then I'll check it out. My parents aren't even there. They're in Greece until July."

Everything in the big kitchen was still. A soft buzz from the refrigerators and faint and low, the rush of surf, were the only sounds. Lydia bit her thumbnail and considered this boy, who was considering her back. Now she got it. If she went next door, lots of things could happen. Of all the things she felt, fear was not one. Here was a boy, here she was, and she could decide. If she went, she'd have some explaining to do. If she went, it would change a lot of things. If she didn't go, she might regret it someday. She thought about Alex, about calling her dad, about coming in to work next week. If she stayed, would Joey still bark at her, "I can't read this," from behind the steel barrier?

"I think I'll go out and try one more time. Um, if it doesn't start, I'll be right over."

Joey took a step toward her and touched her face near her eye. "You have a little bit of ketchup or something there." He let his hand slide down her cheek and across her shoulder. "Come on, come over. Okay?"

For a few seconds Lydia stood completely still, and then she turned and walked out the door and across the parking lot to her car. If it started, she'd go home. If it didn't start, she'd go over. Would she? She shouldn't. She would. Her keys shaking with her hand, she got into the driver's seat, pushed the pedal all the way to the floor like Alex had once showed her when his car was flooded, and cranked the ignition. With a rush, it started. Lydia breathed. Without a glance at the hotel façade, she pulled out of the parking lot and headed toward the causeway. By the time she reached the pines, her heartbeat had slowed to a steady jog. She had the feeling she'd escaped something, but she knew she had not escaped anything at all.

~

To her left, the old gravel road lay silent. As she drove, her eyes burning from the night's work and tears, she saw that there were indeed two roads. One, the one she was on, was smooth and accessible. It led to Alex, college, and a job. She'd teach until she had her own kids. A modest wedding, cursory family visits on both sides, summers at the beach, where she'd supervise her own gritty offspring and sit in low webbed chairs, her skin more sunbaked every year. It led to many things she knew well: weekend dances and beer at the fire hall, little league games and aerobics as she grew older and wider. Alex would work at the paper and probably own it someday. He'd go fishing and drink with his friends while she raised their kids and read books she couldn't talk to him about and saved recipes, met with her girlfriends, the wives of his friends, for coffee. Their home would be old, sturdy and cozy. They'd be content.

The other road was there, but it was shrouded and uncertain. It could have gone anywhere: Tanzania or Rome, past the great cathedrals of Europe, Buddhist temples in Thailand, to cable cars in San Francisco, the lush green meadows of Ireland, towering pine passes in Colorado. It led to places she knew only from books and dreams, and along the way were people whose names she didn't know but whose faces, like Joey's, passed through life with a reckless ambition to try out new people, new flavors, new ways. It led to soft sand beaches and sun-bleached ruins somewhere in Greece, to yoga studios and herbal teas, to tiny African villages with the Peace Corps, to white water rafts along the Colombia River with easy friends.

And Lydia drove, staying on the road she knew, toward home.

CLOWNS IN THE KUDZU

CHRIS HELVEY

Less than a year ago there were seventeen of us and we were the most feared outfit in Hoffmann County. Our name was on every radio and television show within two hundred miles and *The Hoffmann Gazette* ran a REWARD FOR INFORMATION LEADING TO THE ARREST AND CONVICTION OF ad every week. For sure we were the real deal.

I mean we were bad. We were the wild bunch that set fire to the African Evangelical Church, where they preached rebellion even though the Civil War is ancient history, punctured the tires on eighteen school buses that were being used to promote that abominable busing, and gave Henry Lawton the beating of his life—which he deserved for being a prick banker who turned down three CLOWNS in one week for a loan.

Yes, sir, this time last year we were riding high and on our way to bursting onto the national scene, but...

Yeah, you knew that was coming—there's always a but when any person or group tries to do something constructive. And we are a constructive group. Sure, we perform certain acts of violence and destruction, but those are only the stepping stones required for ultimate success. Guess you might be wondering what that success is, so I'd better tell you. And while I'm at it, I'll tell you about the CLOWNS.

Let's start with our name—CLOWNS. Now it's important for you to know that CLOWNS stands for Citizens Legally Organized Wholly for National Sanity & Security (we combine those last two letters because "CLOWNSS" looks goofy as hell and we demand to be taken seriously as an organization).

What we do is to try to keep our town and county on the Sanity Road. I mean there is so much goofy shit going on in this world—just plain stupid stuff like global warming, or dangerous like the Muslims trying to take over America, and don't forget about the rich bastards who have millions in the bank but can't be bothered with paying a living wage or giving a man a loan when hard times come a'knockin'. That and all the LGBTQ, UandME and the Chimpanzee foolishness and why college basketball coaches get paid so damn much money and what about all the fricking Welfare Queens and deadbeat dodo dads. Not to mention why it's okay for drug companies to make billions creating opioid crises but Mister or Miss Average All-American Citizen can't legally smoke medical marijuana.

Then there's the black issue. Now, it's not that we have anything against blacks in general. After all, we've known them all our life and some of them are downright good people (better than a helluva lot of whites) and most are all right, as long as they lay off the booze and dope. Which, come to think of it, applies to white folks, too.

In fact, my best fishing buddy is Joma Winston whose skin is so black it looks purple in the right light. Joma and his cousins, Juan and Cletus, are really guys you can depend on. We get along fine. However, there are some agitators, who generally come from the north or one of the coasts, and stir up fires that the CLOWNS have to put out.

You see what we're really about is the protection of American values for all and, to steal a phrase from Le Orange Donald, to Make America Great Again. And we were on the road to salvation, like we were the most feared group south of the Ohio River, only some people didn't understand our true mission and started putting land mines on the path we were traveling.

Bobby Vanover was the first casualty. He was trying to teach Lloyd Bascom a lesson. Lloyd's the prick who loaned Joe McDermott a couple grand to cover a mortgage payment on his farm but made Joe sign a paper that said the place was Lloyd's if Joe didn't pay him back within six months. Told Joe not to worry, that the paper was simply a formality.

Formality my ass. When Joe's soybeans got the blight and he couldn't make his next mortgage payment, let alone pay Lloyd back, good old Lloyd, who'd been his friend for thirty years, lowered the boom. A slick attorney, a sympathetic judge, and thirty days later the McDermott clan, including four kids, had to hit the road.

Last we heard the family had split up and Susan had taken the three youngest kiddos and gone back to her mother's place in South Carolina. Word was Joe had taken up drinking and had spent several nights in the jail over at Campton.

So Bobby, who really was a good buddy to Joe McDermott, put on his clown suit and makeup one night, drove down Highway 155 about a mile past the farm, pulled off where the old Phillips house burned a couple of years ago and parked behind the garage, which was only slightly leaning to port. Then he cut across county under the light of a full moon, with an Army surplus flashlight to help out in the shadowy places.

Now all Bobby aimed to do was burn down an old tool shed that didn't have anything in it except a few bales of barbed-wire, a broken handle ax, a rusty saw, a few pickle jars of nails, bolts, and screws, plus an old Lawn Boy mower that hadn't run since before Rudy G slipped a cog or two.

So nothing of real value would have been lost. All Bobby had in mind was a warning to Lloyd not to slicker anybody else out of their rightful property, but what he got was a belly full of twelve gauge shot on account of this trip wire Lloyd had stretched between a couple of fence posts about fifteen feet from the tool shed. Worst thing was, Bobby was fixing to become a daddy in about two months.

After that disaster things just went south for us CLOWNS —sort of like one of those chain-reaction wrecks you see once in a while on the interstate. First, the sheriff caught Bob Hicks breaking into Douglas Hardware, then Phil Parsons took up with a Holiness woman—one of the unforgiving Jenkins sisters, and a month later the Upton boys got hold of a real bad batch of crack. By the time their uncle found them they'd been dead three days and Tom Upton sure wasn't about to raise them up like Jesus did Lazarus. Then Ollie Miller got the cancer and Richard Broughton got caught kiting checks and, well I'm sure you get the picture.

In less than twelve months we've gone from twenty-four and growing to seven, and some of them are scared shitless. That's why tonight is so important. The CLOWNS have got to make a statement, and I mean a major statement, like a manifesto, and do it right. Which is why I'm hunkered down here in the damn biggest patch of kudzu I've ever seen, keeping an eye on the front of the Clawson place.

I'm not alone. At least not yet. There are four of us still active. Now, the Creekmore boys would be here for sure if they hadn't both got busted for dealing last month. And Tom Gilson will rejoin us as soon as he gets back from his National Guard deployment.

But for tonight, as we teach a lesson to the whole asshole Clawson family, especially that bitch Aimee, there are just four of us. We're all dressed in our clown suits and wearing fake noses, fake hair, and more makeup than Tammy Faye wore on her best day.

Yes, indeed, we aim to make a statement tonight. No way in hell does she get off easy, not after the way she treated my wife when she was so sick with the cancer. Oh, yes, for damn sure, Ms. Aimee Clawson is going to pay.

Good news is I don't have to do it alone. Young Luther is watching up on the hill behind the barn. That gets him out of the main action but gives us an extra set of eyes. Plus, it allows him to be a part of the CLOWN posse—O.J.T. you might call it.

Then there are Chad Sizemore and Tom Dale. They're down in the swale on the other side of the barn, getting ready to start the fire as soon as we get George Clawson on the road.

I glance at my watch. 6:57. Only three more minutes and Damien Burch sets fire to what's left of the Jensen house. Actually, it never was much more than a shed masquerading as a shack and nobody's lived in it since Cooper Jensen took off for Cincinnati close on ten years ago. Roof's caved in on the west side and nothing but mud daubers, house finches, and opossums live there now. So burning it won't be a loss at all. In fact, you might say we're eliminating an eyesore.

Damien will start the fire and then cut out back and slip off through the woods to where he's hid his Jeep, then head for Shooter's to set up his alibi. Now Damien's not officially a clown, but he's not against us, especially when I've slipped him twenty dollars of good drinking money.

Either George or Ethel Winters is almost sure to see the flames right away. Their place is only down the road a tenth of a mile from the Jensen place and their house sits in the curve there, so they'll have a clear view out their front room window. Plus, they're almost always home in the evening and for certain they are two of the nosiest people who ever lived.

If they happen to be in the back, which I doubt cause they watch every damn stupid game show they can get on the TV in their front room, for dang sure one of their dogs—they've got four or five mongrels—will smell the smoke or see the flames and start howling like crazy.

Once one of the Winters calls in, the fire dispatcher will hit the button that alerts all the members of Hoffmann

County Volunteer Fire Post 3. And I'll bet you any amount of cash money you name that Boyd Clawson will tear ass out of here within thirty-seconds after he gets the call. Boyd's always been a little weird where fires are concerned. Fact is some folks think he's not above setting one himself.

Anywho, once he blasts out the action is going to begin. At least the CLOWNS are going to make a statement. Ms. Aimee-the-Bitch Clawson might not agree with our intent or our actions, but too damn bad.

Just thinking about what we're fixing to do to her sets my limbs to trembling and I wriggle deeper into the kudzu. I bet this blasted kudzu has never seen anything like me before, all dressed up in my clown suit, sweating like a racehorse with some makeup starting to run. I reposition my clown nose. Damn, but I wish the CLOWNS could grow as quickly as kudzu—we'd soon have America back on the Glory Road.

Dusk is coming on and the breeze has died down and I can hear a whippoorwill starting up across the road. From down south of town comes the faint whistle of the RCX freight rounding the bend near Harperville.

I open my eyes for a final reconnoitering. Lights are coming on in the Clawson place and I can smell onions starting to fry. I feel my mind smooth and my eyes go blurry and suddenly I'm seven years old and hiding in a clump of sumac on the hill behind Granny Washburn's house. My arms and legs quit trembling and a soft, warm peace flows over me like an undeserved blessing.

Wham!

The slamming of the screen door snaps me back into the evening and I turn my head in time to see Boyd Clawson jogging for his pickup. Thirty years ago, Boyd earned All-District honors as a wide receiver. Now he's so bad out of shape that he can barely jog to his truck. Father Time whips everybody's ass.

Boyd jerks the driver's door open and slides in behind the wheel. I hear the engine fire and then Boyd's left arm snakes out and plants the magnetic flashing light to the roof of his truck. Five-seconds later he's raising dust, heading hard for the highway. Once the front wheels hit the asphalt I'm scrambling up, starting to work my way down the slope.

I smell the smoke before I can see either Chad or Tom. I give a whoop like a barn owl to let them know it's me coming around the side of the hill. They whoop back and I scramble over a sagging barbed wire fence and trot down an old cow path.

Chad waves and I know everything is going according to plan. I slow down to catch my breath. Tom is just pulling the branding iron from the fire. He holds it up and I can see the glowing CLOWN mask emblem Ben Risenhour made for us in the Hoffmann County High School shop class earlier this summer after the graduation exercises were over and the place closed down for a vacation.

The branding iron looks exactly like those you see in old cowboy movies, except instead of the *B—B* or the *Rr* we got this forged steel face of a grinning clown on the business end.

"It ready?"

"White hot," Tom says and twists the branding iron around and we do the handoff just like relay racers pass the baton.

"You ready?" I ask Chad, and he grins and shakes the handcuffs at me.

"Let's roll," I say, and start trotting down the bank as fast as I can safely go. It's only thirty yards to where the old truck road is and we're there before I'm quite ready.

The barn looms dark against the red glow on the western horizon and I take a quick look to make sure my posse is with me. I see their ornery faces and feel my lips curl into a smile. After what Aimee Clawson did to my wife before she died, she deserves whatever she gets and one of the constitutional articles of the CLOWNS Code is to mete out justice and avenge the poor, the weak, and the sick. Poor Carla was all three.

We cut across a swatch of open ground, staying in the shadows when we can and running hard when we can't. This is the danger moment for us. If Aimee Clawson looks out the kitchen window and spots us, she'll just hole up and dial 911, which wouldn't be good for the CLOWNS.

I keep one eye on the window and don't even see a shadow, so things should be all right. We get up tight against the barn wall and ease our way around to the front. Chad has the cassette recorder and he slips around the corner and into the barn.

Seconds later this loud, awful squalling comes wailing out of the gathering darkness and I know he's got the speaker cranked to the max. Sounds like half a dozen cats are in heat or fighting, really a bit of both. And if it's one thing Aimee Clawson purely can't stand, it's cats.

She told my wife so to her face when Carla was bad sick with the cancer and then proceeded to kick Tubby so hard she broke a bunch of his ribs and messed up his insides bad enough so that he never was right again—and all because Tubby had scratched her leg a little. I mean that's what cats do, right? Scratching is purely natural for a cat.

Now that's been almost two years ago and Carla's been dead for over eleven months, but a real CLOWN never forgets a wrong, nor fails to make it right. And I do mean never, as Aimee Clawson is about to find out.

When it happened, Carla had just finished a round of chemo—think it was her last—and some of her friends, believe me she had a lot because she was a real nice person, threw her a party.

Now it wasn't exactly a sendoff. Of course, everybody knew how Carla's story was going to end, only nobody had the guts to speak the hard words, not even me.

Carol, Lori, Marcie, and Ann and two or three more of her girlfriends from like forever got together and planned this party for Carla, with cake and punch and little gag gifts. Then they invited about all the women in the county who knew her and some, like Aimee Clawson, who'd maybe met her once or twice.

Yeah, I know they meant well. Really they only wanted to try and cheer Carla up. Only they shouldn't have invited so many, especially not Aimee Clawson.

Right off she showed herself by asking for some expensive whiskey that she knew nobody had and then talking about her new Porsche when nobody else at the party drove anything but a Ford or Chevy or Toyota.

Next, she walked around our house like it was her rental property, fingering all of Carla's pictures and keepsakes, even her collection of doll furniture from when Carla was a little girl. Plus, all the time she was wandering around touching things, she was making snide remarks about how dusty this picture was and how that table needed polishing.

But the worst was when she started talking about what a good friend she was of Carla's and how she needed to start cooking meals for me and having me come over to her place for Sunday dinner sometime—like I ever would. I mean she was eyeing me like I was a big slab of prime rib and with my wife there in the same room, struggling to hold on to life. That shit pissed me off big time.

I got all this from Marcie Banks and Ann Groves who were like Carla's best friends and they both are honest as the day is long. Why Marcie works at Farmer's Union Bank and Ann teaches Sunday School for First Methodist, so I know they can be trusted to speak truth.

Sure, I knew Boyd Clawson. We'd gone to school together and played ball on the same team. Back then he'd been all right, only sorta stuck on himself. These days he was okay I guess, only a bit of a jerk at times, but it wasn't him the CLOWNS were going to teach a lesson.

I snap out of remembering and take a quick look around. Tom has got the trip wire strung between two stalls and he and Chad have hid themselves real good. A tiny brown sparrow flies into the barn and heads for the rafters and I watch him beating his wings. Right then the screen door slams and I tighten up like somebody's twisting my guts in a vise.

Plenty of security lights at the Clawson place and I catch a good look. It's her all right — hair twisted up just so and that long, thin face, and that funny skipping kind of stride. I ease back behind a bale of hay and wait.

She's inside the barn now—I can hear the shuffle of her footfalls on the loose straw. From the yard a night bird calls out and then I catch a whiff of her perfume. For just a second I think about how much we are going to hurt her. Now I was raised to know that in one light it's wrong to hurt another person. But after what she did to Carla, well, with apologies to William Jefferson, I just don't really feel her pain.

She's stopped moving and I figure she's looking around trying to figure out what happened to the damn cats. I'm afraid she's going to turn around and head back toward the house, which would really change the equation. I'm worried I've let Carla down, not to mention leading the CLOWNS to another setback. We surely don't need another of those right now.

But right then old Chad comes through like a champ. He fires up the recorder for just a second—one little cat hiss—and it sounds so real that if I didn't know better I'd lose twenty bucks betting it was an actual cat.

She comes on—that second of sound was simply more than she could resist—and Chad hits play again and a loud meow spurts out and then she really starts moving fast.

I hold my breath, but not for long, because Aimee Clawson lets out this wild scream and then I hear her body hitting the barn floor, but I don't pause to savor that sound because we're already moving.

Tom is the closest CLOWN, and he throws an old sheet over her head and gets his knee smackdown on the middle of her back and, before anybody can say Bo Diddly, Chad and I are there, too.

Chad goes to work with the handcuffs, which is a mess because she's struggling like a coon in a gunny sack, and Tom has to help him because I'm busy tugging her slacks and panties down.

She's screaming, of course. Only with that sheet over her head and her face mashed into the dirt the sound is muffled. Tell the truth I wouldn't mind hearing her scream a time or two, but it's better, safer this way.

By the time I've got her slacks and panties down Tom and Chad have her handcuffed and hogtied and I pick up the branding iron.

She begging now and starting to cry, but what I'm really hearing is Carla crying after what happened to Tubby, knowing he was an innocent creature and that she was dying and that Aimee Clawson was a first class bitch and there wasn't one damn thing she could do about it.

I'd like to savor this moment, but time is rolling right on. Time and rivers, they just roll on and I know we'd better do the deed and get out while the getting is good. Young Luther is a nice kid, but he's green corn and he'd never think of a way to stop Boyd if he comes back early for some freaky reason.

I take one satisfied look at the glowing clown's head, take

a deep breath, and press the business end of the branding iron against Aimee Clawson's ass.

She screams so loud it feels like my eardrums are breaking apart, but I pull out my Case and cut the ropes tying her legs together and Chad and Tom get the cuffs and sheet off and we hightail it out the barn door with her screams following us like a bad dream.

It's almost hard dark now, for which I'm grateful. I run hard across the open ground and then start jogging down the old fire lane the CCC cut back in the 30s. There's a pond here somewhere, only I can't seem to find it. Just when I'm about to go to Plan B, whatever the hell that is, I catch a glimpse of moonlight glittering on water and I stop and fling the branding iron.

The splash strikes me as a punctuation mark to the evening and I take one final look back at the barn and the house and for a moment almost feel a touch sorry for Aimee Clawson.

Almost. But then a memory of Carla comes drifting sweet on the night wind and I smile because I've fulfilled my promise to her and to the CLOWNS. I look straight up at the moon and shout, "CLOWNS Forever!" Then I wipe a single teardrop out of the corner of my left eye and start jogging after Tom and Chad.

We've surely conducted a successful vengeance tonight for someone who never had a chance to do it herself. But there are dozens more wrongs that still need to be righted and, since our lousy stinking partisan-ass government can't even stop a telemarketer, I reckon it's up to the CLOWNS to stand up for the common folks.

CLOWNS in the cities.
CLOWNS in the country.
CLOWNS in the kudzu.
CLOWNS forever.

I crest the rise then and pound on down to the truck. The smell of smoke is strong and I can hear the sirens wailing. I figure up in heaven Carla is smiling and that Tubby is smiling, too, wherever good cats go.

CROSSING THE BRIDGE

CARROLL GROSSMAN

I bounce up the two tall steps onto the Greyhound bus. It smells stale: dirty clothes, body odors, food scraps and cigarette smoke all trapped together, not much air moving. The crowded bus stops too often, but nothing dampens my enthusiasm for going home to get ready for a trip to our nation's capital. For the first time, I'll be spending the summer with my mom and my Uncle Tad in Arlington, Virginia. I don't mind that the woman sitting next to me comments on every sight out the windows and that every bump in the road reminds her of an accident that has happened in that place: "See that old oak tree over yonder? Molus Creech got drunk and run his car right into it. Like to have killed him." I only need to nod every now and then. She's in charge of the conversation.

A few hours later, the bus stops in the same wide place by the side of U.S. Highway 119 where my mother had stood waiting a few years ago with her suitcases stacked on the ground beside her until Rex stopped and put her bags in the trunk of his car and they hurried away. I run across the road and on over to the big old house. All is quiet. I take the two steps in one onto the front porch, knock and turn the knob on the front door. Daddy's lying on the couch, a quilt pulled up to his chin and his feet sticking up under the quilt like tandem tents. I sit my suitcase by the door and walk over to stand beside the sofa. I touch his cheeks, a little bristly, and his forehead, which is damp.

"Hi, Daddy," I say. He opens his eyes and smiles.

"I'm so glad to see you. When did you get here? Was I sleeping?"

We talk. He wants to know what I've been learning and who my friends are and do I have a boyfriend? I tell him about my friends, and I tell him how I struggled to do well in chemistry. I fail to mention that I haven't received many As on my report card due to "going wild" according to a teacher or two. Throughout the school year I danced morning, noon or night and got grounded; I ran, jumped in the air and threw my legs around the waist of the boy I was dating and got grounded; I sneaked into the dorm after lights out and got grounded. I might tell Mom just to hear her holler, but not Daddy. He would be too disappointed.

I ask him about being sick.

"I've been having this pneumonia for two or three weeks."

"Have you seen Dr. Foley?"

"Oh, yes, he came to see me and gave me a shot and some pills I've been taking. I'm startin' to get my strength back, little by little. I've had to get someone to come in and cook every now and then."

"Oh, Daddy, will you be okay for me to go with mother for most of the summer?"

"Honey, you don't want to miss going to Washington, D.C. You never know whether you might have another chance like that again. You go. Are you hungry?"

I look in the kitchen: the refrigerator, the cabinets, not a lot of food. I find a jar of cooked pinto beans that I warm up for us and make some fresh cornbread to go with the beans. Daddy walks to the kitchen by holding onto the wall and the backs of chairs. He trembles a little with the effort of eating but eats a full bowl of beans and a big piece of cornbread with butter. He says my cornbread is almost as good as my mom's. I make sure he takes his medicine and drinks a full glass of water, too.

After he gets back to the couch, I carry water from the spring a quarter mile up the holler and fill the bucket as well as a jar for the refrigerator. No one has been taking care of that chore. I tell Daddy I need to get ready and catch the bus to Mam-ma's to talk with Mother and Uncle Tad to be sure what time we'll be leaving tomorrow to go to Arlington—Arlington, Virginia. It is two words to me, as it seems far away, like the history it represents, desirable and unbelievably exciting. Arlington, Virginia.

"Do you need a quarter for the bus?"

"Thanks, Daddy, I've got it. See you after while."

I descend from the bus near the gray swinging bridge that crosses the Cumberland River between Baxter and Loyall and ends just a few hundred feet from Mam-ma's front gate. I rub my hand along the rough hedge and smell paw-paws growing in the yard and see the grass cut short just the way Mam-ma likes it. I think for a minute about the times Mam-ma has allowed me to use her old push mower to accomplish that job. I can almost hear the sound of the always sharp blades rifling through the grass as I walk up to the front porch. I love my mam-ma. I walk across the porch past the 'porch rockers' and push open the front door.

"Mommy, Mom," I start to yell, then realize that Mom, Mam-ma, Aunt Jenny, Aunt

Rhonda, and Uncle Tad are all sitting right there in the living room. Mom stands, and I wrap my arms around her. She hugs me back a little bit. They're all sitting there close to the walls with their arms crossed over their chest or stomach, whichever is bigger. No one is smiling except Uncle Tad. They don't waste a lot of time telling me how good it is to see me and no time at all inquiring about school. Uncle Tad asks, "When did you get in?"

Before I can answer, Aunt Jenny chimes in, "Have you met the woman who's been living with Carr?"

"Daddy's sick. No one's 'living' with him."

"Yeah, I heard he was sick, but that woman was there before he got sick." Aunt Jenny's lips curl.

I told them there was only Daddy at home when I got there, that I found him on the couch resting, that I helped him cook something to eat, that we ate and then I caught the VTC bus to Loyall.

"I'm so excited..." I say.

"You always would take up for your daddy, no matter what."

I can tell no one in that room is in a good humor. I ask myself, *What are they so mad about?*

Just then Mother, in the middle of lighting a cigarette, throws the match onto the coffee table and walks out the front door and slams the screen behind her. I hear her feet hitting the porch and steps, nearly running.

"Where...?" I start to ask.

"To the bridge, of course," says Mam-ma.

"See what you and your daddy's gone and done?"

"You better go git her." They're all commenting at once.

Confused, I race after Mother, who is now on the bridge, and it's swinging fast and wide. I stumble on a loose board and nearly lose my balance.

"Mom, Mommy, Mom—Wait!" She stops. "What in the world is the matter with everybody?"

"They're mad and I'm mad because your dad has that woman living with him."

A little voice inside me wants to ask how she can be bothered when she left so long ago. Instead, I say, "Mom, if he does, she's not there, and besides he really cannot take care of himself right now. What's he supposed to do?"

"Well, I can't have you fussin' and arguing all summer."

"Mom, I'm not making a fuss. I don't want to fuss or argue. I asked Daddy if I could still go home with you for the summer even though he's sick. He said yes, I should, that I might not have another chance like this one."

I touch her shoulder. It's warm and damp. She trembles but is no longer crying. We walk back to Mam-ma's. Everyone is still sitting where we left them except for Mam-ma, who's up and rattling around in the kitchen.

"Uncle Tad, how're you doin'?" I ask.

"Okay," he smiles. "Cal Dawnya, what makes your big head so hard?" Uncle Tad has always loved teasing me, whether it's my name or my hair or my clothes, it doesn't matter. And I only pretend to mind.

I punch him in the arm as I pass his chair on my way to the kitchen. "I'll see you at 7:30, right?"

"Right, be on time. It's a long trip."

"Yes sir, yes sir, I'll be right here." I give a mock salute.

I tell everyone good-bye, go back along the short grass, the sweet paw-paws, the rough hedge and onto the swinging bridge. I skip across and look down for a minute to see the green water rippling below. I wonder if the fish are biting. The bus rolls to a gentle stop; the driver accepts my quarter and carries me back to the holler.

I wake early, add my pajamas to my already packed bag, dress, brush my teeth and wake Daddy. He assures me that he can pour himself some cornflakes and that Zephie is coming over to cook his lunch.

"Don't worry about me, honey. I want you to have a good summer. But," he adds, "you will come back and see me before you go back to school, won't you?"

"Yes, I will, of course I will. Get well, Daddy." I hug him and swallow the big lump in my throat. I hope he will be okay. I don't know this Zephie woman, but I trust she can give him some help.

I catch the bus at 6:30, get to Mam-ma's at 6:50 and walk, once again, over the bridge and begin to brush my hand along the hedge and stop: no car. Uncle Tad's car is not in front of the house where it was parked yesterday. I race up the steps, onto the porch, and bang through the front door.

"Mam-ma? Mam-ma?" I call out again. "Where are they? Where is Uncle Tad? Where is Mom? Where are they?"

Mam-ma comes in from the kitchen drying her hands on her apron.

"Stop your noise. They left before six o'clock."

"What do you mean six o'clock? They said 7:30. It's only seven now. How could they leave without me?"

I stand there in the middle of the living room, still holding my suitcase, my purse dangling around my wrist. I start to cry as I imagine seeing Uncle Tad arranging Mom's bags in the trunk of his car. I imagine her hurrying into the passenger seat. I imagine them driving down the road, down U.S. Highway 119.

I was wholly unprepared to have my mom and my uncle leave without me. For several weeks, writing letters back and forth, Mom and I had been planning that I would spend the summer with her and Uncle Tad. We talked about the possibility of me finding a summer job. I had told all my friends.

Instead, I spent the summer helping Daddy complete a house that he'd been building for Mr. Lewallen when he got sick. I nailed baseboards in place and painted the woodwork and anything else within my strength and ability.

I believed her when she blamed her family for urging her to take off early without me; however, I blamed her for not being strong.

DISHING DIVORCE

JESSICA HILDEBRAND

You quietly asked me, "Do you think I could divorce, too?"

My back was already turned; I was stuffing your forty dollars into my front pocket. We had just finished loading stacks of Corelle dishware from my deceased sister's estate sale into your dilapidated 1990's Dodge Caravan.

Beth told everyone she raised me more than our mother had done. To her I was a child, the little girl she had to take care of when she wasn't doing homework in high school and college. When I was six, she left town to take her first real job in the Twin Cities. Back in Milwaukee, I was expected to get myself ready for school every day: eat cereal, get dressed, and wear the right coat for the weather. My mother didn't do mornings; my father, an early riser, had already left for his studio. He was a photographer, very much a creative type, attending to his own schedule. I was pretty much on my own after that as my brother, who was nine years older than me, found me uncool and of no use. He had wanted a dog, not a younger sibling.

No one thought to ask my sister why, or in fact, *if* she fed, bathed, or dressed me all the time. She had simply taken it upon herself to do these maternal acts. There were photos of her pushing me in a swing in the park across the street from our house, and she would always say, "Everyone kept asking me if you were my child! I always told them no." I was indeed an unexpected child for my parents, who had already felt complete with their 1950s nuclear family. Then there was me. My father always told me I was a gift in his old age. This was how our family handled the sixteen year age gap between my sister and me.

Our mother died tragically, stupidly, in February 1992 from slipping, falling in the snow covered backyard with a bottle of brandy in her hand. She was found frozen to death the next day. Our father died from cancer in February 2003, and one of the many things we couldn't agree upon was which one of us was his favorite, the "daddy's little girl". Was it she, the firstborn? Or me, the caboose kid? Our brother was the only son, a golden child. Squarely in the middle of us age-wise, he was the buffer for all our differences of opinion. Scott took his own life in February 2016. Beth never forgave him for dying, nor me for remaining. We disagreed and argued regularly for six years afterwards; she'd often cry and lament the passing of her "little brother".

You'd annoyed me on Facebook Marketplace since seven o'clock in the morning. You kept texting questions about the condition of the tableware. I was sitting at the top of the second floor condo stairs scrolling through messages while trying to enjoy the cool, early morning breeze that blew up from the open front door. I grudgingly got up and went over to the island counter where I'd stacked the dishes, having recently photographed them for the posting, and looked more closely. Double checked. Yup, everything anyone could want was there: complete dinner settings with soup, cereal and snack bowls, dinner and dessert plates, and every manner of relish dish, serving dish, and a couple of different sized platters, everything my single sister had collected.

Are these still available?

Yes

What color? Are they all frost white?

Yes

Do any of the dishes have a pattern?

No

Are any of them cracked or damaged?

No

How old are they? Do they have lead in them?

This last question I had to google before answering.

No.

Do you still want them?

Can I come later this morning?

Finally, you committed to purchasing the dishes, so I put a hold on them online. Then I spent the next two hours fending off other Marketplace buyers who wanted to scoop up the incredible bargain on Corelle dishware, a veritable starter kit for any new family, and all for only forty bucks.

~

"Why don't you keep them?" a friend of mine asked back when we were going through the kitchen cabinets early on, deciding what to keep, sell, or donate.

"I never liked them, too thin, and supposedly made out of the same material as the nosecones of airplanes," was my snarky response.

Whether this is a fact or not I'm not sure. It was just something my sister said. I believed her. However, they were white, plain, very simple, just like the dishes our mother served dinner on when she was feeling up to it. I remember, years ago now, talking to the photographer who worked with my father at the studio when I was in middle school. He mentioned he thought that my father was very demanding, telling my mother over the phone exactly what he wanted for dinner. I replied, "No, Jeff, he was telling her to make dinner."

"I just don't find them attractive," I answered dismissively.

~

I got your text. You arrived. Finally. At first glance, I pegged you for a woman in her sixties. You appeared overweight, probably eating a heavily processed diet of mac 'n' cheese, white bread with baloney, and too many cokes, I quickly judged. Not healthy, I surmised. A loose, well-worn T-shirt hung over faded, baggy jeans with old tennis shoes poking out. First exiting the car, then quickly turning around to grab something from the front seat, you pushed wire-rimmed glasses back up your nose while walking shyly towards me, clutching a purse close to your chest—a pocketbook, you called it.

You followed me upstairs to see the Corelle dishware arranged on the countertop. I'd stacked them all in small piles of matching pieces, making it appear quite the dinnerware haul. You bent over them, picking up pieces to examine more closely. To my great relief you agreed to buy them, and we both grabbed a stack and started carefully down the stairwell.

~

My sister also drank. And back in 2000, I had to show up at the condo for paperwork my father needed. He was in the hospital. I knocked on the door, walked in calling out hello while I ascended the stairs. They were very steep, eighteen steps straight up. Sitting bolt upright in a chair in the living room, flicking cigarette ashes into a crystal ashtray next to a half full highball glass of liquor, Beth acknowledged I was there for the banker box of paperwork in the corner and snarled at me to just take it. Without saying another word, I grabbed the box then headed down the stairs.

Just four steps from the bottom she jumped me from behind. Surprised, I staggered forward, stumbling across the entry hall tiles, letting the heavy box drop. Scrambling up, I reached for the door handle; Beth grabbed my T-shirt and pulled me backwards. At the same time, I began twisting and turning, trying to release myself from her grip. We exchanged blows as we fell backwards into the hall, both of us swearing. I was able to grab her shoulders and pin her up against the wall. It was suddenly quiet; we stared at each other. We just stood there, face to face, both of us gulping in air.

"What the fuck?" I exclaimed.

That's when I loosened my grip, raising one hand to wipe hair from my eyes. She smiled maniacally. That's when she bit me.

"Would you take twenty dollars?" you asked after looking over the dishes we had moved downstairs, which were now gathering heat out on a table in the open garage. I was desperate to sell the piles of unwanted but still somewhat valuable items like tables, chairs, lamps, and bookcases. My own house was full. I only kept a few family pieces of furniture, a press wood desk and chair, and Beth's vintage 1960s square trunk with brass fittings. Of its era, it was sunset gold with an olive green and red stripe wrapped around the lid. Inside I found sweaters she had knit; they were too small for me to wear.

"No, this is a really good deal," I shot back. I'd already reduced them from a reasonable asking price.

Immediately regretting my curt response, I covered it up by turning up my smile. After a moment, you agreed to buy them and reached into your pocketbook to give me two twenty dollar bills folded together. You already knew I wouldn't budge, but it was worth a try.

You asked how it was that I was here selling all this stuff out of a condo garage, and I gave you the quick overview I'd perfected during the past three weeks of selling items to random strangers who could follow my directions to the last condo on the back row of this quiet neighborhood of townhouses.

"My sister died and I'm cleaning out the estate that I inherited," I replied, hands on my hips. "I'm divorced after thirty-four years of marriage by my choice, mind you, and the best decision I ever made. I have two grown children, married, both moved away with families of their own. I'm the last surviving member of my family." I swept my right arm up and out like a game show hostess. "Hence my digging my way out of the familial hoard.

"My sister," I complained, "had filled the 1,800 square foot condo above us—literally chockablocked it—every room, shelf, and closet with the items of her life, my parents' lives, and my brother's too."

I ticked off these facts like they were accomplishments. I don't really know why I felt the need to mention I was divorced; it happened over four years ago. However, it remained a small part of my psyche whenever I was back in my hometown. Nothing to prove. I just felt like letting everyone in on the fact that I had started over again.

Both of us now carried small stacks of dishes and put them on the seats and floor of the Dodge Caravan. You volunteered you had a family for whom you wanted to cook meals, and these dishes would be "absolutely perfect". You talked about your young teenage son with whom you hoped to sit down and eat at the kitchen table more often. I felt like a shit for judging you earlier.

We slammed the sliding van doors closed, and I said goodbye. That's when I turned and started to walk away. I felt the sun's warmth on my back; it was going to be another hot and humid day. You were standing, one foot in the well of the driver's side, with the door open wide, staring over the van's hood at me sheepishly.

"Do you think I could divorce, too?"

Stunned, I turned around and walked back, standing only a few feet away now.

"How old are you?" You suddenly enquired.

"Fifty-nine, but I divorced at fifty-five," I replied. "Why?"

You proceeded to tell me you were fifty-six and you had a fourteen-year-old son. He was your youngest, having been born a dozen years after the first two you had in your twenties were grown. You had no control over the older ones, you lamented; they were long gone and out of the house.

But this one, you wanted to spend more time with him, to sit down and eat off dishes, not off paper plates, nor standing at the counter. You hoped he would open up about what was bothering him, and this time you would listen.

"So, it's just the two of you then?" I asked.

You shook your head; dank, gray-brown hair brushed your shoulders.

"It's so hard because I have to get work where I can, and my husband sits around the house and drinks all day. He finds fault with everything I do... I'm so tired," you trailed off.

At this point, I asked gently, "Are you okay? Does he get physical with you?"

Looking down at your tennis-shoed feet, you admitted that he did.

"But I don't think he means it," you added, looking up.

"Do you want to leave? Do you have someplace the two of you can go?" I inquired. "Have you told anyone this?"

"No," you whispered, breaking eye contact with me. I took a step forward then stopped.

"There are people who can help you and your son. I can connect you," I entreated. "Back at home as a social worker, I helped women like you take the next step every day."

Suddenly, I felt it: a hard gut punch. Unlike you, it wasn't a physical blow, but rather an uncomfortable feeling deep inside, which brought me up short. Guilt, shame, the unpleasant feeling of being humbled. I had thought myself different from you, better than you; I was wrong. I saw clearly that I was standing there in front of you, whining about selling off estate items, all the while pocketing easy money. That I was doing all this work to serve myself: to sell the condo and keep that cash, too. I would walk away from this a safer woman because I wouldn't need a man to keep me.

You went on saying you made enough money, that you could pay the rent on an apartment for yourself and your son. You'd like nothing more than to come home after work, rest in a big comfortable chair, and do nothing for as long as you wanted. But then you looked me in the eye saying,

"Except for dinner, I'd be making dinner and serving it on those dishes."

With the van door between us now—you on the inside and me on the outside—I asked you to take out your phone, open your contacts, and put my name and number there.

"Call me. I'll connect you with people who can help here. You'll need your own money, your own bank account. Can you do that?"

The concern in my eyes now made you turn away, lowering yourself into the old van's well-worn driver's seat. I stepped back and let you close the door.

You rolled the window down, looked up at me, and said, "Someday."

This statement was full of both hope and promise, regret and despair.

Will you leave?

Will you finally find rest?

Will you make dinner for your son and serve it on those dishes?

The sky was clear blue, the wind had died down, and the sun had grown much hotter. I walked back into the garage, putting my hand on the wad of folded twenty dollar bills, and prayed that someday I would see your area code appear on my phone. I'd answer, and you would tell me you are safe, too.

THE ESCAPE

TERRY CHAMBERS

The boy ran as if his life depended on it ... and if truth be told, it did.

The routine in the Louisville City Workhouse and Asylum had never varied over the forty-five days of Sean O'Malley's imprisonment, but today would prove to be different.

Awakened at five a.m. to the relentless clanging of an alarm, immediately followed by the intensity of an overhead Krieg light piercing down into his dank cell, his routine had begun to feel almost commonplace after having served half of his ninety-day sentence.

Following a quick piss in his cell's corner trough, he slipped into the striped prison-issued shirt and well-worn dungarees and eased the puss-filled blood blister on his right big toe into his boot.

One-two, buckle my feckin' shoe! Grimacing, he laced up his well-worn cap-toe work boot and braced himself for the next twelve hours of pummeling limestone boulders at the nearby Cave Hill quarry. Rolling his bed rags into a hemp pillow sack, he deftly shoved it into the far corner of his bunk, hoping no one would strip him of his meager belongings before he returned from the rock pits at sundown.

Convicted of stealing a five-pound country ham from the smokehouse outback of Roppel's Grocery up on Payne Street, he had been manacled, tried, and sentenced within a matter of weeks. It wasn't like he was a rum runner or something! He'd simply been acting the maggot and done it on a dare from his buddy, Micah O'Reilly, was all.

Unfortunately, His Honor Judge Buckstone Pisterman had no sense of humor about such things and had called him a miscreant - whatever that meant – and further added that he must pay for his crime.

The finality of his situation seared white-hot into his man-child's brain as the city magistrate's gavel assaulted the oak sounding-block on his bench.

BAM BAM BAM

Looking down and over pince-nez eyeglasses teetering on the end of a bulbous nose, His Honor had dispassionately croaked out his sentence. Shackled and with clenched fists, the defiant and unapologetic defendant glared back.

"The Court finds you guilty of all charges and fines you twenty dollars and fifty cents for the purloined pork, and another five dollars for costs and penalties due the great

Commonwealth of Kentucky, County of Jefferson, City of Louisville. You may pay Clerk McShane today or work it off at the Municipal Quarry. Court adjourned."

BAM BAM BAM.

The bailiff called out, "All rise," as the Judge exited the Courtroom in a flurry of black robes.

The boy stared at the now-empty bench and could not breathe. He knew that kind of money was unheard of for a grown man to come up with, much less a lad his age.

Quickly calculating the time he'd have to spend to pay off his debt, not counting the three days he'd already spent in the Green Street jailhouse waiting for this hearing, he felt abandoned. To any strapping Irish lad with things to do, people to see, and places to go, this news may as well have been a life sentence on Devil's Island.

Deputy O'Bryan unceremoniously marched Sean and two other wretches out the rear door of the Courthouse where the Black Mariah awaited. Loaded into the paddy wagon, they were shackled to the iron ring in the floorboards and driven from the town center to embark on this new phase of life. He couldn't have felt any worse if this were his very own funeral caisson making its way along the cobblestoned pavement. Headed down Green Street toward Baxter, the driver repeatedly kicked the brass bell on the floor to scatter the young hooligans running alongside as they jeered at the lawbreakers inside.

Rambling onto Lexington, Sean closed his eyes and thought of his family. He hated this outcome for his Ma's sake but couldn't care less when it came to his Da. He and his old man had never been close, and as he grew older, their indifference to one another was obvious.

But his Ma was another story. He knew she would be crying her eyes out every day until he came home.

Disgracing her was the part he hated the most about all of this.

She would never be able to look her neighbors in the eye again, now that her only son was a jailbird and locked away with the likes of common drunkards, vagrants, and prostitutes. He'd have to think of something to do to make her proud of him once again.

Rounding the bend of the road in front of the American Medicinal Spirits Company, he shuddered at the sight of the massive brick fortress. Having lived a mere four blocks up the way on Rogers Street, he'd heard talk of terrible things that happened to the unfortunates locked within its walls. Now he'd learn firsthand if they were true.

Yes, this morning had begun no different from all the others he had awakened to inside this hell hole, but all that changed as he stood for roll call in the passageway outside his cell. It was then that old Pood Moss stabbed the overseer just above his left kneecap with a makeshift shiv fashioned from a rusty bed spring.

And in that instant, the boy's destiny changed forever.

In the mayhem that followed hauling Guard Metzger out of the cellblock, Guard Tucker had not only kept the gate to the catwalk wide open, but had also left the key to their freedom hanging on the hook next to the door going out into the prison yard.

Without pause, Pood had led the mad scramble out into the yard as twenty-three of his prison mates followed. Heading east, they scrambled up and over the brick wall of the adjoining Cave Hill Cemetery, where they melted into the dark eeriness of the Yankee soldiers' boneyard. Charging past the flagpole just offside the flower-laden lily pond, the fleeing horde tore across the necropolis, jumped headstones, and knocked over flower urns without a thought to the noise or carnage they caused.

Weaving in and out of the shadows along the base of the brick wall running parallel to Lexington Road, Pood's one single aim was to get to the Grinstead Avenue gate in hopes of losing his trackers deep within the wilds of Seneca Park. From there, he would head east, cut through the potato fields spanning St. Matthews, and from there:

FREEDOM!

Unable to scale the outer wall and immediately give chase with their bloodhounds, the sheriff's posse had to instead scurry along the boundary fences of the adjoining

Eastern Cemetery with their droopy-eyed, big-eared sleuths until they reached the front gate of Cave Hill. Once inside, the canines homed in on the task at hand and made up for the lost time. As the pack neared the frog pond near the Confederate field of fallen rebels, their primal howls echoed mournfully across the hallowed grounds.

Often called a nose with a dog attached, these four were some of the finest in Kentuckiana. They were the direct offspring of the legendary red-haired, Nick Carter, a full-bred Kentucky hound named for a dime novel detective. Handled by Captain G.V. Millikin in the early 1900s, he became an American legend during his fifteen-year crime-fighting career with more than six hundred fifty detections that sent one hundred twenty-six criminals to jail. Chasing this walled-in ragtag bunch wasn't even sporting fun for the retrievers now in pursuit.

Once the dogs got their scent, the more able-bodied fugitives knew time was not on their side and cursed their fate as they barreled headlong across the hallowed grounds. The older men struggled to keep up the pace, and as dawn broke they hunkered down into the diminishing shadows of the nearby crypts in the hope the scent of the recently departed would mask their smell.

Far in the lead, Pood knew his was a do-or-die situation and ran like old Scratch himself was on his tail. He'd figured, and rightly so, there was no way he wasn't in for a stiff whoop-ass from the guards for his attack on their friend. But damn, it had felt exhilarating when he hit bone, and that old bastard screamed in agony. And he'd deserved it. After all, he'd been on Pood's ass every single minute of every single day since he'd arrived two months ago, and he was done taking his shit.

Sucking in great gulps of air, Pood galloped past the final few rows of tombstones.

His eyes burned, and snot flew from his nose. The outside gate was near enough now that he could see street lamps just down the hill that led to the entrance and beyond into Cherokee Park.

He grinned and thought about the men and boys he had left behind. So long, suckers! He prayed the others would be caught, in order to slow the coppers down from coming after him so fast. If so, he would be home free and soon heading out the Frankfort Pike.

Who knows, he thought, with some luck, I could be in Shelbyville by tonight and eating fried chicken and mashed taters in Midway by tomorrow. He looked forward to a new start in a new town.

POW! Ironically the first bullet ripped into Pood's leg just above his left kneecap and stopped him in his tracks.

POW! POW! The second and third blew off the right side of his head.

As others catapulted over the cemetery wall, Sean had crouched in the shadows of the gateway leading to Payne and Lexington Avenue. He figured, and rightly so, that the guards would tear off after the larger group of escapees, giving him the time needed to skedaddle in the opposite direction and make a clean getaway.

If he ran now, he knew he'd never see his family again, but he also knew if he didn't git, he risked being brought back for an extended sentence. Worse yet, he might even be sent to the state pen in Frankfort. Quickly weighing his options, he decided to make his getaway and get the hell out of Kentucky by heading north into Indiana across the newly opened City Municipal Bridge. He wasn't sure how he would come up with the thirty-five cents for the toll, but he had always been a very resourceful bloke and would manage that bit of business when the time came.

When the coast cleared in the prison yard, Sean darted catty-cornered across the intersection and jammed his way headlong into the throngs of cattail rhizomes stretching alongside Beargrass Creek's Middle Fork. Breathing raggedly, he jumped down the bank into the waist-deep stream. Even though he seldom prayed, he thought it couldn't hurt to ask St. Paddy to extend a nod in his direction for a wee bit more of Irish luck, so by the time the peelers did a headcount, he'd be long gone, and his trail cold.

Just not as cold as this.

"Begorrah, I'm freezing me feckin' balls off!" He cursed at the icy water that shrank himself up between his legs.

POW!

At the sound of the first shotgun blast, he froze.

"Jaysus, Mary, Joseph, these bulls mean business." His eyes widened in terror as his brain raced to formulate a plan, but his body remained paralyzed.

POW! POW! The next two rapid-fire bursts got both his adrenaline and legs pumping. Taking a final look back over his shoulder toward home, he bulldozed his way through the cold spring water. His thinly soled boots slipped and slid on the silty bottom as he stumbled and sloshed his way downstream. Moving deliberately, he tried to stay up under the tree branches that hung low to the side of the creek to avoid being seen from above as the sun rose.

Around the next bend, the freshwater that had rippled out of the green lushness of the park transformed into waist-deep mounds of gelatinous pools of guts and clabbered blood oozing from the open troughs behind the Beargrass Slaughterhouse. Never having been this far up the Beargrass before, he hadn't known he would be dealing with a boundless flow of putrefied guts, shit, and blood dumped into its waters. The local butchers who frequented Phoenix Hill's pub had always joked that they used every bit of the pig except the oink. The bastards had obviously lied based on what he was now forcing his way through.

The sewage he waded through was sickening, but the

stink was even worse, making him puke until all he had left to offer were dry heaves. Each time he felt the acids rise, causing him to spasm, he was terrified it would cause him to lean forward and swallow a mouthful of the contaminated drift.

Passing the Baxter Street station house bridge, he entered Butchertown with its rows of brick dwellings and wooden shotgun houses. He steeled himself, knowing what he had just slogged through was terrible but that the strings of slaughtering pens, backyard butcheries, packing houses, soap makers, tanners, and coopers would be ever so much worse. The carnage was everywhere along this part of the creek where packs of mangy junkyard dogs grappled and snarled in hideous tugs-of-war over blood-sodden entrails.

Sleep, sleep, grah mo chree
Here on your mamma's knee
Angels are guarding
As they watch o'er thee

Soundlessly crooning this old Irish ditty provided a trancelike mantra that helped him muscle his way through the nauseous offal behind the Bourbon Stock Yards and past the stone bridge at Story and Frankfort Avenues.

By late afternoon he had entered The Point neighborhood and rounding a bend spied the Ohio River. At the sight of the clear flowing stream, his thirst became so overpowering that he was driven to leave the safety of the creek in search of water. Popping his head up and down above the embankment, he surveyed the row of tumbled-down shacks lining the street above him. Overjoyed, he spied a wooden gazebo hemmed in by an overgrown elderberry bush with a tin bucket on a wheeled pulley system attached. It just had to be a well. He just hoped it hadn't gone dry.

Inching his way out of the creek, Sean belly-crawled through the knee-high yarrow and poison hemlock, keeping an eye out for any potential movement from any direction. His Irish luck continued to pay off as it became apparent that the owners of the shacks along this stretch of the river must have decided not to return following the last flood. Lifting the bucket to his lips, he teared up. He had never tasted anything more refreshing than this first swallow, even though the rusty bucket had discolored the water.

Taking three long and delicious gulps of the nectar, he poured the remaining water over his head.

Knowing he needed to get to the river before dark, he eased back down into the cold creek. He tried to formulate a plan, but his mind wouldn't focus. All he could do was put one foot in front of the other and pray that his next step would be the last one needed.

He had never been so exhausted. All he wanted to do was sleep.

Where the mouth of the creek widened into the river, the depleted boy crawled onto its left descending bank. In the distance, he saw a single boat beached along the shoreline. Cradling his head onto his knees, he closed his eyes and moaned. He was soon asleep curled up in the tall reeds along the shore.

When he awoke, the sun had set.

"Hey, you there! What ya doin' hiding in them thar weeds? Ya runnin' from the law or somthin' ?"

Startled, the boy struggled to stand, but his legs wouldn't oblige. Instead, he fell face-first into the cool river mud. He had never been so painfully exhausted and only wanted all of this to be over so he could go back to sleep.

Hanging his head, he hopelessly rose to his knees with his hands raised skyward and moaned.

"Don't shoot! Ya got me. I'm who they're after. Take me in and get your reward."

"Bejappers, laddy, don't be such an eejit! No self-respectin' Pointer would ever be calling the plonks on ye, even if you were John Dillinger hisself! So stop your worrying about that now."

The scraggly old geezer laughed and extended a gnarled hand toward the boy.

"Here now, let me help you up. My, oh my, you look a sight for sure, and for shite's sake, ya stink to the high heavens, you do!"

Pop Ramage laughed as the boy guardedly stared at his would-be captor. The old shanty-boater had been on the river long enough to know that this young'un hadn't an ounce of fight left and was in dire need of a helping hand.

Jerking his head in the direction of the old tug bobbing across from Towhead Island, Pop's voice became gentler.

"Now stop your worrying laddy-o and come on aboard the Saline. Come on and join me for some grub, but first, you'll be taking a good long dunk off her stern and rid yourself of some that there stink. Come along now son, we won't be dining in style, but it'll be hot and there'll be plenty of it."

Sean was too tired to resist, and his belly growled loudly at the mere mention of a hot meal.

"Come on now, boy. Let's get you something clean to wear. You may as well send those rags you're wearing on downriver. If the law finds them below the dam, they may think they have one less ex-con on the run to worry about."

"You're safe now, boy. Trust me; everything is going to look a lot better in the morning." He winked and walked away.

Pop didn't pry about his past or future plans as the two ate in uninterrupted silence.

The only sound to be heard was the clatter of the forks on their tin plates as they each devoured two large helpings of black pudding sausage, washed down with an oversized tankard of warmed Poitín moonshine.

Pop covered the boy with a well-worn, but warm blanket as the mixture of food, alcohol and the rhythmic sway of the boat took its toll. No longer able to focus on anything except the sound of water lapping against the side of the boat, Sean lay his head on the threadbare sofa cushion. It was the first time he'd slept the entire night since he'd left home so many weeks ago.

Following breakfast the next morning, Pop gave the boy six bits, a tin of biscuits, and a pint of milk, to start off on his journey North. Heading toward the city center, the lad turned around once and waved to the old man. Pop smiled and waved back, then went inside his boat.

Hugging the river's shoreline, Sean headed toward the

city center, and by ten a.m., he stood facing the entrance to the Second Street Bridge and looked across to Indiana.

Enslaved people escaping north to their freedom had called the Ohio the "River Jordan." Like them, Sean could not imagine what lay ahead but knew he had nothing to return to in Irish Hill. His life now could only be made better over there in the Promised Land.

Stepping onto the bridge's walking path, he never looked back.

DISTANT RELATIVE

CRYSTAL ADAMS

One minute I was photographing the northern lights and the next everything went black. As my eyes struggled to open, the world around me was unfamiliar. It looked sterile, bright white. The air smelled like bleach causing my nose to burn. Everything around me was blurred as if I were laying in a fog. I felt nauseous and had the worst headache I have ever experienced in my life. As I went to rub the sleep from my eyes, I realized that I couldn't move my arms. I was tied to a table! At this point I noticed that I wasn't alone, and these "people" did not even look human. *Did I hit my head or something?* I thought. As my mind began to rapidly cycle through panic, palpitations set in and it felt like a herd of wild mustangs racing at top speed through my chest. I went to scream only to realize that my mouth had the sensation of cotton stuffed in it from the back of my tongue down my throat. One huge gulp and a deep breath...

"Where am I?"

One of them stepped closer and bent down as he cocked his head curiously. He stared at me for what seemed like forever with lilac-colored orbs. His voice was soft and unthreatening.

"I assure you, we mean you no harm child, please take a minute to collect yourself a bit? Our hearing is more advanced than yours and while we understand that you are upset, your volume is offensive to our ears."

Suddenly anger and surprise replaced fear. My eyes widened, I felt my face heat up as it turned blazing red, and my mouth hung open for just a split second as I processed what this critter had the nerve to say.

"Oh, it is I who should apologize for offending your tender ears. Where the hell am I! Who are you! Why am I here!" I screamed as loud as I could to make my point.

This is when the other one spoke, "My dear loud one, we are not on Earth and if you will calm down, we will answer your questions all in good time." She was petite in comparison to the male. Her hair reminded me of the color of a stray orange tabby cat that I feed occasionally at my apartment. She had fox-like ears and lilac eyes, but her demeanor was different from the male's. Whereas he seemed calm and gentle her general temperament reminded me of that cat with which she shared a hairstyle.

"Lady, Fox-Humanoid, Alien, Bad Dream—whatever the hell you are, we are lightyears away from me calming down! In fact, telling me to calm down is having quite the opposite of your desired effect. I did not kidnap and tie you up... You want me to calm down, do you?"

I paused and managed to say in a more compliant tone, "Untie me and answer some of my questions."

The older male, without saying a single word, carefully and gently untied me. He cleared his throat and told me to remain sitting on the table.

"Lizzy, you are aboard our ship, far from your home. If you become combative, we will have to restrain you again," he said.

"Is throwing her out an option if she screams again?" the female felt the need to interject with a wink.

I rolled my eyes as I weighed my options. In realization of not having any, I chose continued compliance and nodded my understanding to whom I presumed was in charge. I rubbed my wrists as I contemplated what was to happen next. I wondered how they knew my name. They were interesting beings. Not stereotypical "aliens". They were attractive, human-ish I suppose. The male was much taller than me. He had bright white hair and lilac eyes. Their ears really did resemble that of a fox, which explained the advanced hearing.

"My name is Gweux, thank you for the compliment. This is Dr. Kell. We think you are attractive as well and we know your name because..."

"Oh my gosh, you can read minds! That is beyond rude, man, you can't invade people's privacy like that..."

Dr. Kell spoke again, "Like I suggested before, we could just toss you out of the ship and wave as you float by!"

At that point I was tired and unsure if they were going to let me live or not anyways, so I just thought to myself, *Go ahead,* and rolled my eyes defiantly.

Gweux held his hand up to stop her from speaking any further as he cut his eyes toward her with a squint and audible whisper. “Kell, I believe your personal feelings toward Jo may be spilling over. We need to speak in private to discuss whether you can proceed professionally,” he said through clenched teeth.

Gweux’s expression softened as he turned back to me and touched my shoulder. He then went on to attempt to reassure me that they meant no harm. He explained that they were from a planet called Todd outside of Earth’s solar system and asked if I had any questions.

“Yeah, you said the name Jo, do you know my grandmother?” I asked.

The open mouth and doe eyed expressions at my question would have been funny if I wasn’t so suspicious of them. Dr. Kell commented as she typed, “Advanced hearing...inherited.”

They asked me to describe her.

“She is about 6-1 with white hair, her eyes are...” I stopped and looked at Gweux in astonishment, who smiled and nodded for me to continue.

“Her eyes are similar to yours actually, her hair too... Lilac eyes,” I repeated slowly.

Reading my confusion and my mind as I thought to myself, *But I would have noticed if she had freaking fox ears,* Gweux spoke again.

“She pins them under her hats, surely you noticed she wears hats and bonnets at all times?” He said that with a cocked head and a slightly raised eyebrow as he watched me piece together that he knew my grandmother. He explained to me then that my grandmother is in fact Toddan. She was sent to Earth to learn about where the humans were at technologically years ago, her undercover mission obtained the intel that technologically speaking humans were ready to learn about the existence of life outside of Earth, but that humanity lacked the social skill requirements. While here, she met and fell in love with a human. She was granted permission to stay so long as she kept her genealogy a secret.

"My grandmother, Jo?" I questioned.

"She is my sister, and to complete your description she has a rather cackling yet contagious laugh and is unquestionably happy, correct?"

I had to laugh as I nodded and relaxed a smidge. I asked again why they took me, and he explained that my grandmother reached out to them about my constant headaches and often inability to eat. He explained she and I share a genetic defect that could be cured with a blood transfusion followed by a simple surgical procedure. They hoped to complete the transfusion during my anesthesia, but I woke up unexpectedly. They showed me scans and a pathology report.

To say I was stunned would be an understatement. Twelve hours ago, I was a typical human woman with an affinity for the stars. But here we were. My fascinations all of the sudden made sense, and in all my twenty years on Earth no one had ever thought to say a word about Granny's secret.

"My Granny Jo raised me. My mother died when I was a baby," I said.

The feelings welled up; I could feel tears fighting to escape my eyes. As if it weren't bad enough that no one had thought it pertinent to share our family history with me before now, I have a medical condition that is genetic and is curable from that side. I could not help but feel betrayed. No one ever told me any of this. They were all content to just leave me in the dark about it!

As my emotions ran their relay race to see which feeling was going to explode first, Gweux spoke again. He explained that Granny Jo was forbidden to disclose her identity, not even Gramps was allowed to know.

"Well, this is stupid," I said defiantly. "I don't have lilac eyes or fox ears."

"Jo's pregnancy was heavily monitored. Your mom was genetically modified to carry the traits of your human ancestry. The interesting thing with you was you have our ears, and your eyes have similarity to ours as well," Gweux said with a cackle and wide grin.

"Excuse me?"

"Yeah, we fixed them postpartum."

"So, you docked my ears, like a Doberman Pinscher?"

"Sort of, notice they are just slightly pointy on top," he said as he handed me a mirror.

I pulled my red hair back behind my ears to look and sure enough, *Fox-ish,* I thought to myself. As I stared at my reflection, I noticed my own eyes. Gweux said what I was thinking out loud.

"Yes, child, your blue eyes have a lilac tint to them under certain lights."

At this point I started feeling a migraine coming on and the sensation of nausea flooded my being. I felt my body toppling over. I would have fallen to the floor if Dr. Kell hadn't been so quick to catch me. Gweux explained my medical condition in depth. Dr. Kell commented that the combination of anesthesia, hunger, and stress were more than enough to trigger an episode. She gave me an injection of a Toddan pain medication that relieved my headache and lessened my nausea in about fifteen minutes. I asked what the procedure entailed. Gweux explained it to me in detail and answered all my questions. The blood transfusion donor would be my grandmother. She was aboard the ship.

Dr. Kell had prepped Granny beforehand, and she was recovering from the blood draw in another room. Kell brought her in to sit with me. She brought albums with her, and we sat in silence as she showed me photos that filled in many of the blank spaces as to who we are and where we come from. She apologized for all the secrecy. She took off her hat and showed me her ears. *Those ears!* I thought to myself.

I agreed to the procedure. The first step to the process would be a blood transfusion. I was told I would need to take medications prescribed by Dr. Kell for about six months and then return for a checkup. If the checkup was clear, then I would be ready for the next step in the treatment plan.

After the transfusion I felt nauseated again. Granny assured me that I was fine and ready for travel. She said I could rest at her house.

"She is not to be moved until she has rested properly and is able to eat," Kell said.

After the recovery period we returned to Granny's home. I rather enjoyed watching Uncle Gweux and Granny Jo catch up over her fancy International House Coffee. *Apparently, the family "cackle" is inherited,* I thought to myself as I listened to them talk and laugh together in the kitchen.

Kell sat in a chair at the table with them with her back perfectly straight and her feet planted side by side in front of her with her hands on her lap. She did not say a word, not a single word out loud, yet I heard her voice. *I can read minds now?* I questioned myself.

"Quite the show you two are putting on..."

I instinctively distanced myself farther from the kitchen.

"That is enough Kell." Gweux telepathically said to her, flatly.

"Don't tell me after all this time you developed a conscience," Jo snapped coldly with a black-eyed stare while she and Gweux continued the lighthearted verbal exchange about Alaska weather.

Kell smirked, "Conscience, no. But even I would not murder my blood relative to save my own skin."

She glanced in my direction for only a second, but the look in her eyes was different than it was on the ship. She seemed softer now, like that orange tabby after drinking milk.

The conversation carried on for another hour or so before Gweux said they needed to be going soon. Kell said that she wanted to examine her patient one last time and winked at me from the kitchen. They approached me about the exam in the entry hall as I was pretending to walk down the stairs. I agreed but timidly asked for privacy; Granny and Uncle Gweux agreed to that and went outside into the garden. Kell proceeded with my examination in my childhood bedroom upstairs.

She examined me without a word then suddenly looked me straight in the eye.

"I know what you heard in the kitchen. You are right to not trust us. Jo is the one with the illness. And you are being used to treat it."

"So, the roles you described before are reversed?"

"In a sense kid, yes... But they are prepping you to be a body donor for her so she can safely go home to recover fully."

"If you know I know what was being said then so do they," I whisper-yelled in a panic.

She laughed, "Finally, you are quiet."

"They didn't catch it, they need not learn of your telepathy," she said.

"What do I do?"

"Run away, stay as far off grid as possible. Do not take these meds." She handed me what looked like a credit card and explained how I could contact her with it.

"And how shall I protect myself from aliens?"

"By being smart and listening to me. Let's go down and see if you inherited their acting skills..."

I hugged Gweux and slugged Kell in the arm. I told them I was excited to see them at Christmas.

Gweux boarded the ship, Jo went inside. As I headed toward the gate, I glanced over my shoulder one last time at Kell; she winked then proceeded to board the ship herself. I no sooner got in my car when Kell showed up via that device she'd given me in the passenger seat.

"HEY!"

"What is wrong with you?" I asked, startled.

"Ah, did I offend your tender ears?" she asked with a cocked head and a cackle. "Listen, I only have a minute. There is an address in the GPS I want you to go to, and I will meet you there in a few days."

"And then what?" I asked, feeling that worry knot forming between my brows.

"Rest. You will be safe there." With a smirk and that sarcastic wink of hers I have come to expect, she was gone.

I turned the ignition as I programmed the GPS to give me directions. *This is my life, my body. For now, trusting Kell is my only option.*

THE LOBSTER ACCORDING TO GERARD

STEVE CAMBRON

They made way too much of the lobster thing. *Mon Dieu*! It was just an attempt to impress some friends. Me, Theo and some other members of our *Club des Hashischins* were at the Blind Man Cafe, deep into our evening absinthe as was our custom in those days, and Charles said that among the artists, poets were the most exiled of all, Plato having kicked our wretched asses out of his Republic because we could not tell the truth. Henri remarked that it was probably for the better because, "Truth is not always a pretty thing to look at. Who would bother to hang it on a wall?"

Theo said, "*Nous les poets*, we're all fish out of water."

"No," I said. "We're...lobsters, in a crowded street feeling our way back toward the secrets of the sea, while the uncaring world scurries on around us. And like lobsters, we grope through our work one word at a time, combing through the muck and detritus for the treasures lying beneath." Henri adjusted his *pince-nez*, leaned forward and rubbed his chin. Theo halted his absinthe spoon in midair. I had no idea where this was going, but it felt good to be so at one with my words. "And when the lobster moves, his antennae precede him, feeling what is to come before his body gets there in the same way an inspired poet's vision reveals something of the world before others see it."

Honestly, I don't know where that came from. Maybe it was the alcohol, or the lingering effects of the afternoon hashish. Perhaps it was told to me in a dream long forgotten, restored to memory by the confluence of circumstances. There was a long hush. Then Charles began clapping, and the whole table broke out in applause. Victor raised his glass and toasted me with a line I'll never forget.

"There are those who say Gerard is crazy. If this is how crazy people speak, let his madness infect us all!"

Well, what was I to do? Victor Hugo, one of France's greatest authors, had just paid me a supreme compliment. The statement required an act. The act required a symbol. And the symbol required a lobster. *Les bourgeoise* have their precious poodles. Why should a lobster be any more ridiculous than a dog, a tortoise, an anteater, or any other animal that one chooses to take for a walk? Besides, I feel a great affinity for lobsters. They are calm, considerate, and never bark.

The story goes that I rescued it from the lobster nets during a seaside weekend at *La Rochelle*, that I named it Petit Thibault. Well, what else would you expect from a poet banned from the Republic? In actual fact, I stole it from the market early one morning at *les Halles*. There was a big bucket of them on the sidewalk. The fishmonger had gone in to get some more ice. One of the little fellows had climbed over the backs of his friends to get free, a beautiful sunburst of carapace spilling over the side of the bucket. The moment was right. I scooped him up and nestled him under my coat, his wet antenna tickling my neck as I walked. I could feel him moving against my chest like a heart trying to free itself from its cage of bones. Which made me wonder, how much does the heart really know of the outside world it beats so fervently for? He never once pinched me, an expression, no doubt, of the deep gratitude and affection he felt for being saved.

When I got back to my apartment, I borrowed some twine from my concierge, Madame Lefevre, to make a leash —not the blue silk ribbon that you hear about in the now famous version of the story. They also say that I was wearing a cravat and waistcoat. That much is true, because that is what I always wore in those days.

You must believe me, I had every intention of taking that lobster to the Garden of the Palais Royale that afternoon and walking him about on his leash just as the story has it. It was mid-May, the tulip trees were bright pink with blooms. It had rained the day before, and all the flowers seemed to glow. I don't know how much lobsters see or smell but I think he would have enjoyed a walk around the park. I can only guess what the reaction of those *bourgeois* ladies passing by would have been. They would have no doubt gawked and mumbled their disapproval from a comfortable distance. I doubt they would have taken the time to reflect on the deeper metaphorical implications of what they were seeing. I hope, at least, they would have given him the same respect as they give their dogs.

Well, as I said, I have an affinity for lobsters. Should I apologize for that? Besides, I barely had a *sous* to my name. Nothing but stale bread for days. When I dropped him in the boiling pot he made a sound, not easy to describe, like...a sigh from a siren far away begging to be released from the rocks. Yes, I know it sounds terribly cruel. But when you think about it, thanks to me that lobster became immortal, probably more famous than any poem I ever wrote. Certainly more famous than most men. Not a bad ending for a lobster, if I do say so myself.

Later that week at the Blind Man Cafe, I told Theo, Victor and the others what I knew they wanted to hear—that I had taken the lobster for a walk in the park just like I had intended, that that the stupid *bourgeois* promenading around with their dogs were so shocked they scurried off to find a Gendarme. I came up with the name Petit Thibault on my way to the cafe that evening. The blue silk ribbon? Ah! That was a flash of inspiration that emerged in the telling—a touch of the empyrean, just the accent I needed to round out the form. Curiously, no one ever asked what became of the lobster. Maybe they didn't want to know. He had, after all, served his purpose. I told them anyway, yes, down to the last sizzling detail, just as I would have written it. I put Petit

Thibault in a bucket of salted water, boarded a train and took him back to *La Rochelle*, where I released him on a beach and watched him crawl blithely back into the sea under the light of a full moon—an image I borrowed from the moon card in tarot. I had a reputation for doing crazy things back in those days. So, it's not as improbable as it sounds.

~

I know this is not what you wanted to hear. But like my friend Henri said, "The truth is not always a pretty thing to look at." The world is starving for stories, this story needed a lobster, the lobster a name and a blue silk ribbon. The denouement required an ocean and a trail of sparkling moonlight to guide the lobster back into the dark mystery it came from. You want truth? Well, in that case, just imagine what I looked like when they found me that morning not long after, hanging from the window grate in the alley in the dead of winter, frozen stiff, an apron string knotted tight around my neck. They said there was a raven capering around in the snow beneath my feet repeating, *"J'ai soif! J'ai soif,"* the only words its owner had taught it. How ridiculous! That's not how I would have written it. The scene was gothic enough without sticking that damned raven in the middle of it. Way overdone for my taste and owes far too much to Edgar Allen Poe. The most troubling thing about death, I've found, is that it doesn't grant us the courtesy to edit our own endings.

FLOWER BEDS

NATALIE BICKEL

Magnolia Marcou's hair danced in the breeze of the evening. Its wild curls twirled at the slightest movement in the air. The mild temperature begged her to stay longer as she walked along the coast. In just a few short months, the ground would be covered in wildflower blooms. A purple carpet of succulent flowers would line the shore of Pacific Grove, California. Oh, how Magnolia longed for those endless blooms.

Watching the moon dance across the waves reminded her first of her childhood. The long summer days capped with chasing fireflies with her cousins in her aunt's backyard resurfaced. She could hear their laughter and smell the ocean-salted air, an undertone mostly overpowered by fresh cut grass. As the moon continued to shape shift, her memory rushed her forward to the year before—a flashlight chasing her footprints across the sand, running after her. Her heart began to race as she immediately tried to come back to the present. An underwater sensation, or maybe it was better to describe it as a feeling of inversion that collided into confusion, began to numb her. Nolia, as her cousins called her, felt this way most of her waking life—muddled, muted, yet transfixed by the unnatural sensation.

She paused for a moment on a driftwood log propping her feet covered in laced up boots, knowing that winter wouldn't last long and she'd be able to feel the sand in between her toes again soon. Besides, January would be here in less than a month, which meant magnolia trees had begun to showcase her namesake, the branches lending space for rare white flowers.

The wind was growing more fierce, whipping across her face as she sat solitary, causing her hair to shift furiously, incapable of fighting back against it. As she made her way home, she thought about what the morning would bring. Tomorrow's local Saturday morning farmer's market would be bustling, and she planned to be there bright and early.

Magnolia walked the streets, which were a little more empty than usual on a Saturday morning. The colder weather kept people in bed longer. In Monterey, the winters were tolerable, and she enjoyed the crisp feeling in the air of the season.

"Nolia! Wait up!" A voice yelled from behind her. It was Harper, a close friend she'd found about three years ago.

"I forgot you were coming," Magnolia stopped on the side of the street, away from the forward motion of the crowd.

"I wasn't sure if I was. I woke up early in a panic, thinking today was Monday, so I just stayed up." The words rushed out of her like they were past due. "Anyways, where did you sneak off to last night? I got worried when I passed by your place and your car wasn't there."

Magnolia hesitated. "Oh, I decided to make a pit stop on the way home. I needed a few groceries. I've been out of oat milk for two days now."

"I thought that's why you were going to the market today?" Magnolia shrugged. "Nolia, please don't tell me you went to the coast alone."

"Why would you think that?"

"I know it's your favorite place, even after what happened last year… But it just makes me nervous."

Magnolia focused on the booths that were up ahead, but a car's headlights took her back to the memory of the frantic flashlight again.

"Nolia?" Harper asked, noticing her friend's distracted state.

"I didn't go. I wouldn't," she responded, quickly trying to assure her friend of her lie, which seemed to work, as Harper's attention was transferred to the first booth offering coffee.

The two sipped as they walked along the road, but Magnolia felt preoccupied. The reason she came to the market was for fresh flowers, and, well, she did need oat milk, but now that wasn't going to happen. She started coming up with another lie, thinking of a way she could buy the milk anyways, when the booth with flowers came into view, her excitement returning. Magnolia didn't know where her love of flowers came from; maybe it was a subconscious way she paid homage to her name and to her parents for giving it to her. But, as she approached the buckets sparsely filled with flowers, she suddenly missed the feeling of being kissed more than she wanted to be surrounded by blossoms.

"We don't have many to choose from today. With it being winter, the retirees seem to get here and clear us out early."

Magnolia glanced up at the man working the booth, barely hearing his words. She started thumbing a stem, admiring the indigo blue color of the sprouted flower. "Do you have any more hydrangeas?" Magnolia stretched her neck to see if any were hiding at the bottom of the bucket labeled accordingly.

"Unfortunately we're out. If you get here early next week, I'll try to save some for you..." He trailed off, waiting for her to finish his sentence with her name.

"Magnolia," she said, extending a hand.

"We don't have any of those flowers either," he joked, shaking her hand. She smirked and the freckles across the bridge of her nose became more noticeable to him. "I'm Will."

"I'll take these." Magnolia handed Will a small bouquet of most of what was left. He wrapped it in light brown tissue paper and tied it with simple white yarn.

"What will you do with your flowers, Magnolia?" he asked as he handed her the finished product.

"I'm making flower crowns for a party tonight."

"Nice. Is the party in town or at the coast?"

Magnolia watched his lips as she spoke to her. His demeanor made her feel instantly safe, but that was an instinct she wasn't sure she could trust. "It's my niece's birthday, so it's outside of town a bit." She flashed a small smile, noting that Will seemed to hope for an invite.

"Ah, well, not the party I envisioned, but I'm sure they'll love your crowns."

Harper had caught the tail end of the conversation, catching up to the booth after grabbing some homemade candles. "Well, it's actually my cousin's daughter, so she's not technically my niece, but I don't have any siblings so we just call her that..." She was starting to ramble, which she could tell by looking at Will's expression of amusement. "Would you want to come?" The words exiting her mouth surprised her.

Harper whispered, "What are you doing?"

"Uh, yeah, why not?" Will chuckled.

Magnolia fumbled in her purse for the handmade invitations her cousin had made last week. "Here." She shoved one in his direction. "Bring more flowers if you can."

Will nodded as Harper basically pulled her away. "What in the hell did I miss? Do you know that guy?" Harper sounded rushed and almost annoyed, but Magnolia felt nothing but peace as she admired her new bouquet carefully tied in a bow.

"You're here early," Sarah seemed to let out a sigh of relief as she opened the door for Magnolia. The house had clearly been freshly cleaned, which was comical since a group of eight-year-old girls was about to reinstate chaos into the space. However, Magnolia had seen how uppity the moms in

Monterey could be, and she knew Sarah would earn their favor, translating to little Frankie making more friends.

"How can I help? It looks like you've got everything already in top shape." Magnolia lightly touched the flower power napkins as she noticed the cake, which was one giant pink flower.

"Most of the party will be out back. Did you bring the flower crowns? I can show you where to put them." Sarah pushed the panoramic glass doors, which took most of her body weight to open.

Magnolia followed her outside into what looked like a fairy land, but that's how it normally looked, birthday party or not. Sarah and Tom's yard was the mossiest shade of green. The two could have easily been mistaken for designers, with their patio set up making visitors feel almost cozier than when inside the house. The warm glow of Edison bulbs hanging on cedar posts, an outdoor fireplace made of charcoal colored bricks, Moroccan pillows, and Adirondack chairs gave it a novel ambiance; not to mention the grand lure of the cypress trees interspersed throughout with their tall bark bases leading up to outstretched evergreen arms, which were only visible when tracing them all the way to the sky. Magnolia noticed the table set with party decor and began carefully placing the flower crowns at each place setting. The flowers at the market had added great color, but she had had to incorporate some of her own stash at home to give them the "wow" power she knew her niece, Frankie, would love. She made sure to put the one with blue ribbon, Frankie's favorite color, at the head of the table.

The doorbell rang, startling Sarah. "The girls aren't

supposed to get here until half past six. Who is here an hour early?" She asked no one as she rushed to the door, touching every pillow and accent in the living room on her way. She glanced behind her one last time before opening the door. Her confusion must have shown, because the person on the other side of it cocked his head to one side, almost like a dog trying to understand the human language.

"Hi, I'm Will. I believe your cousin invited me to help with decorations for a special niece?" Will held up two brown bags with fresh flowers sticking out the top of each.

"Magnolia?" Sarah yelled her name as a question without greeting Will.

"Oh, hey! You found more flowers!" Magnolia couldn't help but smile at the guest she'd forgotten she'd invited.

Sarah looked quizzically at the two of them. "May I?" Will moved forward to enter the home as Sarah slowly created space for him.

"Maybe we can put a few flowers on the cake, and then the rest we can put out back somewhere," Magnolia offered, more so to Sarah than to Will. Sarah approved, a little more emphatically than Magnolia expected after the way she had greeted their unexpected guest. Will started trimming down stems as he placed bright colored blooms of pinks, blues, whites, and purples around the cake. Magnolia took inventory of the rest of his floral loot. "I bet we could intertwine the rest with the strung lights outside, leaving some for a centerpiece," she thought out loud.

"I'm going to go check on Frankie," Sarah said, but then lowered her voice so only Magnolia could hear her. "Are you sure you're okay to be alone with him?" She made sure to make direct eye contact with her cousin.

"Yes, I'll be fine." Magnolia mimicked her intense gaze. Sarah didn't appear fully satisfied, but slowly she made her way upstairs to find Frankie. Magnolia led Will outside and the two began dispersing the remaining flowers. "I'm surprised you came," Magnolia said, tying twine around a peony.

"Yeah, well, my options were slightly limited."

"What do you mean?" Magnolia stopped working, internally guarding herself in case he was trying to insult her.

"That invite, correction, the invite from hell you gave me...was *covered* in glitter," Will said. "I figured it'd be best to go where the glitter originated rather than head into town." He smirked at her.

"I know what you mean. It kind of looks like you went to a festival three days ago and still haven't showered." Magnolia noticed a few pieces of glitter hanging onto his shirt, glinting off the outdoor lights.

Will chuckled. "I'm going to be finding this stuff for months, I swear. Just one day of having it in my house, and I keep finding it in my hair, my clothes... I think a small speck actually made it into my food today."

"Well, thanks for coming. This is a huge help. Sarah is clearly a bit stressed about it all."

"Honestly, I didn't have any plans, and this sounded fun —something out of the ordinary." He paused, smiling as he finished tying the last dahlia near a bulb above. "Your cousin did seem a little uptight. Who knew eight-year-old parties could have this much pressure around them?"

"It's more so the moms of the eight-year-olds," Magnolia corrected. "Appearances mean a lot here. And when they matter this much, people talk."

"What do you..." Will started, but was quickly interrupted by a glitter covered, "flower power" slogan-wearing, small girl whose personality didn't match her size.

"Aunt Nolia!" She shrieked as she rushed into her older cousin's arms.

"Happy Birthday, Frankie!" Magnolia said, picking her up and twirling her.

Frankie looked over at Will, crossed her arms and simply stated, "No boys allowed. This is a girls' party."

"Frankie, this is..." Sarah paused as Will inserted his own name. "That's right. Will was just helping us decorate. He brought you some beautiful flowers."

"Are you Nolia's *boyfriend*?" Frankie taunted while she kept her eyes locked on Will, her head craned back to see his face that seemingly skyrocketed above her.

Will laughed and leaned over to Magnolia. "Nolia, huh? I figured you were a 'Maggie'," he said, ignoring Frankie's question.

"Definitely not a 'Mag' or 'Maggie'," Magnolia assured him, feeling the heat rise to her cheeks.

"Well, Frankie is right. This is a girls' party, so I'll head out," Will said, grabbing the bags once filled with flowers, now holding only pieces of stems and blooms that weren't quite full.

"Thanks, again!" Magnolia yelled, as Will nodded in her direction before shutting the front door behind him.

"Who the hell is that guy?" Sarah asked now that they

were alone. Frankie examined each flower crown as they spoke.

"I met him yesterday at the farmer's market. He worked the flower stand," Magnolia answered.

"Just promise me you'll be careful. After what happened..." Sarah trailed off.

"I know, I got it. I'll be safe," Magnolia responded briskly. "Now let's get to partying." She raised her voice enough so Frankie could hear her, which then turned into jumps and excited screams.

~

December had ended, and almost just as quickly January and February had followed suit. Magnolia had gotten into a winter routine. She would head out for a run most afternoons when it was the warmest before grabbing an apple cider from the cafe close to her apartment. She felt steady when she had something to look forward to every day. After Frankie's inaugural party into her eighth year of life—or at least that's how serious Sarah had made it feel—Magnolia hadn't seen Will. She'd gone to the farmer's market a few more times, mostly to look for fresh blooms with the thought of him a minute fragment of her attendance, with no luck of finding either. Winter, while mostly lush in the West Coast, wasn't producing what she'd hoped.

Today, on her way home from her run, she would make a different stop. Instead of relishing in the sweet taste of cider, Magnolia planned to grace the entrance of a cactus shop. Her blooming pincushion cactus was thriving, but the lack of fresh flowers made her want to fill the center of her tables with more. With large windows letting in ample amounts of both warmth and sunlight, her cacti always thrived.

As she slowed her pace to a brisk walk, her heartbeat and breath slowly started to match the new rhythm. The bell rang above the door, noting her entrance. She was first drawn to the blue columnar cacti, its spiral twists enrapturing her attention when a familiar voice disrupted her trance. She clenched her hands into fists, her grip so tight her fingertips started to go numb. Magnolia walked around the cacti, hoping to be hidden by them. Every step felt like she was moving in slow motion, flooding her with panic. Knowing the desert plants didn't fully conceal her, she held completely still as she looked for the body the voice originated from, searching for *him*.

Magnolia couldn't remember hearing the bell ring after she'd entered, meaning he'd been here first. She turned her back to where he was standing based on his voice, the view of her still mostly blocked by the tall cacti as she held her breath and closed her eyes. It felt like twenty minutes had passed before she heard the bell ring muffled by his voice again. Then the door shut, and it was silent. Magnolia stood frozen for a while longer, feeling the confusing inverted, underwater sensation. Another voice slowly coaxed her out of her trauma-induced state, the ringing in her ears subsiding.

"Nolia? Is that you?" It was Will. Her eyelashes fluttered open and shut, and she could feel where her silent tears had run down her cheeks. "Are you okay?" His brows cinched.

"Pincushions," was all she could mutter. "I'm here for

pincushion cactuses," she repeated, wiping her cheeks quickly and shifting her body away from Will. "You know, the small, potted spherical cacti that bloom little pink flower crowns?" She asked, making sure Will understood her, hoping he'd wipe the look of concern from his face.

"Yeah, we have some that are already blooming, some just starting to sprout, and some that just finished a cycle," Will said, trying to make eye contact with Magnolia. "Here, I'll show you," he said when she didn't respond. A few more customers entered, taking Will away from her as Magnolia made her selection, wanting to escape quickly. Will rung her up, carefully placing the small pots in a compostable cup tray. "Hey, would you want to hang out sometime?" he asked.

"Maybe." Magnolia's words were coming out short.

"We could go to the coast?" Will offered.

"No, not the coast." Magnolia sputtered, air constricting in her lungs.

"Okay, how about drinks at Flimby's?" Will tried again. "Tomorrow night?"

"Sure. I can meet you around 7." Magnolia looked at Will briefly, shifting her petrified gaze from her desert plants to him. She did her best to force a small smile before turning to leave. She practically broke back out into a jog to get home, her heartbeat and breath sharper than when she was sprinting before.

~

Magnolia ran her fingers through her hair for what felt like the twentieth time. She questioned Will's intentions, wondering if they were genuine. She was a pretty trusting person considering what had happened last year, which everyone in her life seemed to constantly remind her of and therefore wouldn't let her memory fade. If she had asked Sarah, Harper, or any of her close friends, they would have told her to stay home, but something about Will drew her in. His demeanor expressed a comforting calm that Magnolia couldn't quite understand. It was almost hypnotizing, but in a way that made her feel safe. She looked at herself in the mirror, gave a steady nod to her reflection, and marched out the door refusing to turn back, her peripheral catching the coffee table where the pincushions' fresh blooms were opened.

Magnolia parked her car on the street a block away from Flimby's, the only parking she could find. As she got out of her car, she heard her name. It was Will's voice. "Man, parking was tough to find tonight!" Will said, catching up to her. He paused, the tension in her body clear from her rigid stature. "Are you sure you want to do this?" He asked, turning to fully face her.

Magnolia took in a breath, not so deep that it inflated her belly, but deep enough. "Yes. I need some answers from you."

"I feel the same," Will said as her wild curls billowed around her from the evening breeze. He touched one near her cheek. "Come on," he said, lightening the moment with a grin.

Magnolia felt her chest decompress the farther they walked. Her shoulders relaxed, and the excitement of possibilities rushed to the surface. The two were seated at the outside bar covered by a canopy shade, which wasn't necessary this time of day other than to block the wind that had suddenly picked up. After ordering their drinks, Will leaned on the bar, shifting so he could naturally look at Magnolia rather than the bartender.

"So, what happened..." Will started to say when Magnolia cut him off.

"When did you start working at Agave and Vines?" she asked abruptly.

"All right, you can go first, I guess," Will chuckled. "I work three jobs. There's the gig at the farmer's market, part-time at Agave and Vines, and my favorite with FishCat Nature Reserves. That one pays the most, but still not enough to live in Monterey."

Magnolia, while interested in getting to know Will, needed clear-cut answers. "Did you know the man that was in your shop yesterday? The man that was there when I was there?"

"Nolia, I'm not trying to chastise you, but you've gotta be more specific," Will said.

Magnolia played with her nails as she talked. "I got there around 1:30 in the afternoon." She paused, as if trying to pull out the memory that was already fading, her mind creating a block around the painful moment. "I think he was the last customer you rang up before coming to me, but I don't know that for sure." Her breaths were coming out shorter and shorter with every word.

Will sat for a moment as if replaying the afternoon, trying to locate the customer, almost like a game of *Where's Waldo?*. "You were the only person I recognized yesterday," he said matter-of-factly.

Magnolia looked directly into his eyes. "You mean it?" she asked, sternly, her hands now balled into fists.

"I promise you. No other customer sticks out to me from that day. I just remember finding you in...some sort of a fog?" Will suggested, his eyes lined with concern, which Magnolia would no longer meet.

"Okay, then. Tell me more about your conservation job. It sounds cool." Magnolia quickly changed the subject as she simultaneously unclenched her fists.

"Wait, you're not going to tell me who that guy was?" Will pushed back.

"Fine," she said, a sharpness returning to her voice. "I'm pretty sure that was my ex-boyfriend. I thought he'd moved away a while back, but clearly, he's here again."

"Did he hurt you?" Will's voice was quiet.

Magnolia felt like breaking into tears, but instead swallowed the feeling. "Let's leave it at this for tonight. I have a restraining order against him, and you saw the way I reacted when I heard his voice. That's all I can give you right now."

Will brushed a wild strand of hair away from her mouth before shifting his hands into hers. "You don't have to tell me anything you don't want to, but I'm really glad you came to the shop yesterday. I wanted to find you again after Frankie's party, but I didn't know where to look." He paused. "And whatever the hell that guy did... I wouldn't ever hurt you, Nolia," he said, sounding like he'd known her for a long time.

"Somehow, I know that, too," Magnolia said, a smile reaching across her face at Will's gentle nature.

"Our drinks have been empty for about twenty minutes, but I don't really want to leave, yet. Do you?" Will asked.

"No," Magnolia replied.

"Would you want to stay for dinner?" he offered. Magnolia nodded as Will grabbed a nearby waiter's attention, the two moving to a table. "You know, I'm kind of glad you said no to going to the coast tonight," Will said, looking over the menu, "but, why did you?"

Magnolia smirked at his first comment, and again swallowed to relieve the tight feeling in her chest. "I'd rather go when the blooms are there—in April."

"It's a date," Will said.

The orange wings of a monarch fluttered past Magnolia's cheek, almost landing in a stray curl, a telltale sign of spring. She sat with her toes in the sand instead of boots on the same driftwood log she had graced her presence with in December. Today was a stark contrast to that evening. The sun illuminated every grain of sand, casting a light that made the beach look like a land of crystals. The Pacific Grove blooms had finally arrived, a blanket of purple succulents lining the coast, making it feel like a mystical land. But the biggest difference from that night was that Magnolia wasn't here alone, causing the air to feel lighter and filled with warmth, the inverted feeling no longer lingering.

Will mimicked the butterfly's motion, twirling a strand of hair around his finger before moving to her cheek to pull her in for a kiss.

"Nolia," he whispered. "I see why you wanted to wait until April."

She smiled at him, a good man who loved and cared for nature, who cared for her. Magnolia was falling for Will, and most everyone in her life seconded that notion. Yet, he didn't know her full story. She'd only told him a portion of it on their first date. The horrible memory didn't belong here anymore, not with the view of the breathtaking coast before them. It didn't fit here with her blooms, and so it was time for her to release it.

"There's another reason I didn't want to come here with you," Magnolia started. "This place is one that makes my heart flutter, both from its unexplainably gorgeous wildflowers and from an almost tragic night." She paused, unable to look at Will, who she felt shift to give her his full attention.

She watched the waves crash to the shore as she spoke. "My ex, who I mentioned before, was ill. We dated for a few months, but he made things feel like we'd been dating for much longer. Every small conflict, every differing opinion felt intense—like if I didn't change my mind, he would make me feel crazy, as if my thoughts were alien. I think it all came from his past. People had a pattern of weaving in and out of his life. His parents divorced and neither one wanted custody, so he stayed with an aunt who didn't care what he did. He had no rules, which I think turned him sour. I even noticed that his friends dipped in and out, bailing on double dates on several occasions." Magnolia took a breath and watched a paddle boarder gracefully balance on the water's surface.

"I know what you're thinking," she said. "How could you be attracted to that kind of person? In the beginning, he wasn't that person. It was as though he put on a mask of openness to everything I valued, and then turned each one of those values against me. He would say that I chose to spend too much time with my family and friends whenever he was supposed to be my favorite person. I think I was somewhat blinded to how deeply he hurt inside because he'd already convinced me that I was the problem."

Tears started to sting the backs of her eyes, and Will put one of his hands on top of the one of Magnolia's that was resting closest to him on the log. "One night, I canceled on him. He was making me feel like I was upside down in my own body. I wasn't happy anymore, so I went to Sarah's house to talk things over with her. That's when he called begging me to meet him, and said we could just go to the coast and have a relaxing stroll. I agreed to go, even though Sarah insisted I stay."

Tears were rolling down Magnolia's cheeks in a steady stream, but her voice remained stable as she spoke. "When I got to the coast, to this place, he was waiting on the sand for me. He seemed off. His eyes were filled with anger. The sunset was starting to fade away. As we walked farther down the beach, neither of us spoke. Once the sun was completely gone, he started asking me questions about who I was with, if I was cheating on him. The day before, I had been at a bookstore and ended up in the same aisle as some guy. We briefly talked about a book he was holding, and then the man moved on. He claimed he'd seen me with another guy yesterday, and that's when I realized he'd been watching me when we weren't together." Magnolia closed her eyes. "I pleaded with him that none of it was true. I told him I wanted a break, and that's when he pulled out a knife. He raised my hand, the one he was holding, and sliced my arm. I shoved him as hard as I could, which thankfully released his grip, and I took off running as fast as I could back towards my car. He chased me the entire way, a flashlight bouncing off the sand, hitting my heels when he gained speed."

Will sniffed, a tear rolling down his own cheek. "I don't remember the rest. Somehow I made it to my car, made it back to Sarah's, and she took me to the hospital to get stitches and to make sure I wasn't cut anywhere else. Shock took over my body, and that part of the story is gone for me."

Will took both of her hands in his. "Thank you...for telling me. I can't believe... I don't understand how... You are worth everything," he sputtered.

"You don't have to try to say anything to make it better. I know it's a lot to process, and I've made my peace with it," Magnolia said.

"Where is he now? Did you ever see him again?" Will asked.

"Not until the day at Agave and Vines. I got a restraining order and heard from some of his previous friends that he had moved across the country. They knew something wasn't right with him either, but didn't realize how bad it was until the incident."

"Are you sure it was him that day?" Will asked.

"No. I didn't fully see him. I was hiding behind the tallest cacti. I just heard his voice, and then things got a little blurry."

"Nolia, I would never do anything like that to you. I hope you know that."

"I do. Looking back over the situation, I see exactly where

I went wrong. I can see the moments where I was too trusting, and the moments where red flags were flying high, and I chose to ignore them."

Will kissed her again. It was a kiss that held immense love, even though neither had spoken that word aloud. They embraced for a long while, only the sounds of ocean waves, overhead seagulls, and the breeze dancing past their ears filling the space. "It wasn't your fault," Will said when their faces broke the connection, allowing space in between them again. He stood up, extending his hand for hers. She grabbed her round-rimmed sunglasses from her shirt, where the temple was hooked, before obliging Will.

They began to walk along the path when she whispered, "You didn't judge me."

"I would never," Will said. "But, I do think we should judge our favorite blooms," he said, noticing a smile expand across Magnolia's face. As they walked along the trail, they pointed out the biggest blooms, the most colorful, and the uniquely shaped ones that stood out among the rest. "You know, you remind me of these flowers," Will said. "They have this wild nature about them that's untamable..." Magnolia ran a hand through her hair that was mimicking Will's point. "And they thrive in unexpected places," he finished.

Magnolia took Will's hand in hers, feeling inexplicably calm, walking next to someone who got her completely. Her steps were lighter. Even with her expansive love for the blooms, she hadn't adored them like this before. Will stopped, his back to the ocean, so his view was that of Magnolia in the foreground of a sea of magenta.

"Hopefully we can start to fade your past memory here.

We'll replace it with new ones, just like this—stupidly happy ones." Will put his hands on either side of her face, feeling Magnolia nod slightly against his touch before kissing her to let her know the weight of his words.

Their kiss connected them in inexplicable ways, but it was cut short, as the crack of a gun, the only thing that could have pulled them away from each other, erupted. Magnolia's body flinched hard against his as another shot rang out, impacting her back.

"She belongs to me!" Will heard from over Magnolia's shoulder. He blinked a few times, his vision blurred from shock, only to recognize the man who was in Agave in Vines that day retreat with his weapon.

"Will," Magnolia said in a constricted, hushed voice, which was all she could muster. He felt himself collapsing with her, somehow laying her down on the carpet of wildflowers first before crashing to the ground beside her, the pain in his abdomen overtaking his ability to stand.

Magnolia felt Will's fingers traipse through strands of her hair in uneven, broken movements as his breath shortened. Her gaze shifted towards him, reaching for his other hand, barely making connection at the same time their eyes did. With glimpses of the fuchsia flowers surrounding them, the life drained out of her. Magnolia Marcou was where she'd always wanted to be—among the wild blooms of Pacific Grove, California.

KENNETH

ROSANNA STAFFA

I was working as an acupuncturist in L.A. Small office, clean and airy on Wilshire Boulevard. I checked my patients' meridians at the acupuncture points on their wrists, twitching like butterflies under my fingertips. I listened to the language of the *qi* flowing under their skin. I detected dreams of fire and muscle aches. It was the kind of work that required quiet and concentration. Healing seemed to even soften the light in the room.

It was the dead of August heath, with no rain in sight and nobody walking around. I saw them everywhere on milk cartons. The disappeared kids had freckles and glasses. My child would never be found. Miscarried babies are not real, someone said. A grainy image from a hospital security camera of me walking in pregnant was all.

Friends said they knew how I felt. I did not know how I felt. *Bereft* is a word someone used. I looked it up in my Collins Italian-English dictionary. *Privo*. *Senza*, without.

Outside the grocery store at the corner, I noticed a woman in a long skirt walking in circles, whispering to herself, like the nuns in my childhood in Italy. I saw men shuffling barefoot near bus stops, phone booths, and bodegas. They looked disoriented, as if someone had dropped them off there with no explanation. Hands grasped the air, feeling invisible shapes.

The Tao Te Ching held a belief that we were all connected by the same vibrating *qi* energy. The man at the corner trying to sell me a stolen watch, the old woman with a yapping poodle, we all shared the same vital force. And even a presence that was gone was not truly gone but was actually right there; their energy still existed, if in a different form. The baby might be the shape suffused with moonlight I saw against the ceiling in my room.

On a Wednesday morning, early in the day, I sat on my front stoop and scanned the Classifieds in *The Recycler*, a free weekly. There was a palpable hope to the listings' desires. Guitarists were sought, dogs rescued, bicycles offered. Life was going full blast. So many were just one click away from what they wanted.

A post caught my eye: a free detox clinic in Santa Monica sought an acupuncturist volunteer. Two days a week. It was urgent. The ad seemed crazed, a note scribbled in a panic. I had heard of the place. It was mostly for the homeless and Vietnam Vets. None of my colleagues considered volunteering there. The despair of a want nobody listened to touched me to the deep. I dialed the number. The man on the phone said yes to me immediately, Italian accent and all.

He only asked if I was experienced in using ear acupuncture for detox. I was.

The first morning I showed up at the clinic too early, with beginner's anxiety and the rustling of doubt. The lack of traffic made the city look abandoned. There was a livid light in the sky, and I noticed the power lines crossed by the flight of dark birds screeching.

A taciturn line of shivering addicts, mostly quite young, had formed on the sidewalk. I went to stand at the back of the line, as I had no keys yet. I stood tall with half fear, half swagger. I was overwhelmed by the scent of feet and male sweat. An older woman walked up and down the line, digging her fingernails into her hands, whispering a name. She was backlit by the early sun, a wavy silhouette. Back and forth she went with her hypnotic lullaby-like murmur. I wanted to tell her that whoever she wanted to find so badly, possibly a son, clearly was not there. Knowing the truth was a start. Refusing to understand only prolonged the agony. When I was bleeding in the shower, I wanted to be anywhere but there, knowing.

There was only a light breeze pushing dry leaves around, but I could not stop my body from twitching. I reminded myself that I should not flake out, not now.

A massive man in front of me, tattooed and in a tattered T-shirt, turned and inched closer. He towered above me. He had a shaved head, scars over his skin, and deep-set eyes. He observed me for some time. I stared back. I could feel my heart pulsing close to the ribcage.

"It's going to be fine," he said. I felt exposed.

"Oh, yeah." I tried to sound hardcore. "I know."

"Hang in there." He leaned close, paying attention. I realized he had noticed my shakes and agitation and was being kind to a fellow addict in withdrawal, worse off than him. "It's safe here. No reason to be scared."

"Well, I'm not."

"We all are."

We locked eyes. It seemed that he gave me a gentle nudge. I nodded, felt I could do well here. I told him I slept badly, it affected me. In truth, I had had strange dreams as of late. Idiotic dreams that startled me out of sleep. Like, I bought a helium balloon, tied it around my wrist, and lost it on a Ferris Wheel ride. I started telling the man I had not had a good night's sleep in a while, but I'd do fine. I liked his trust.

"Is your accent French?" he interrupted.

"Italian."

"Cool. You freaked me out for a moment." He was breathing faster. Half kidding, but not really. His chest heaving, he turned away to stare at the front door. After a bit, he sought my eyes, and the way he looked at me made me see he was okay and he cared for me to know. I looked back, feeling better too, like we had confessed something to each other. We shared a little laugh. We would be all right, after all. He said that he had served in Vietnam, where French was used.

"I freak out," he said with gap-toothed warmth. He kept looking at me; he seemed sorry for me, and it was okay.

"We all freak out sometimes," I said, echoing him.

"The wait is something, isn't it?"

"Yeah." It was.

"No kidding, but it's short." A little shy, he told me that Henry, the acupuncturist who would open the door, showed up rain or shine. He drove an old car, we had to be patient. He would arrive, he always did.

"Sure." I nodded as if I knew. Maybe that was all there was to say. But I didn't stop. I felt I should come clean with him, who had nudged me toward a safe place. "I am the new acupuncturist. It's my first day here: no keys." The man stared straight at me, saying nothing for a while. He eyed me suspiciously. "I look young, but I have a lot of experience as an acupuncturist. I trained in China."

"Wow. Look at you."

"Nothing fancy, a small clinic there," I said. "That was just something I truly wanted. You know, being good at what I did."

"That's cool. I bet you are." He must have registered a flicker of apprehension in my eyes. "You might even be better than you think."

A battered white Honda arrived with much clatter. Everybody started shifting in place, seeing the car make its way.

"See? Henry is here," the man mumbled. "I wasn't bullshitting you."

When the driver of the Honda parked and jumped out, I raised my hand to wave. A moment later, Henry was by me, a thin man with bushy hair and glasses, wearing a crisp white shirt. His eyes had deep melancholia, and I looked away, not wanting to risk getting sucked into them.

"I thought you wouldn't come," he said. In fact, I had arrived early, afraid I'd change my mind if I lingered at home. I was a bit spooked by his precise intuition. "It's been a problem for months. People saying yes and not turning up." He spoke in a blunt tone, the way private people do to invigorate themselves.

He unlocked the front door. We walked through a narrow hallway lined with a handful of offices. The walls were white, naked like in an art gallery waiting for the paintings. Henry let me into a small room. A table was pushed toward the back with a few rows of metal chairs facing it. There was a box filled with notecards on the table, a desk lamp, and pencils in a cup. That was it.

"Here it is. Works?" Henry asked. He eyed me with trepidation. I nodded. Everything in the room appeared faded and metallic, even the light. At that moment I'd forgotten how I had gotten myself to this place and why. The strange hope that responding had given me. I was simply there, staring at the barrenness with a rising sense of confusion about what I expected to find here.

"Disposable needles, yes?" I asked. Of course, but I didn't know what else to say. He showed me the boxes of acupuncture needles that filled the drawer and the packets of alcohol swabs. The room had the quiet feel I imagined when drowning. I hoped to make it through the day. I thought of the man who had spoken to me outside and took a deep breath.

I asked Henry if the tall man standing in front of me in

line outside was a regular. I was surprised; I didn't ask questions lately, as I didn't want anything. But I was curious about the man's story.

"Kenneth, yeah," Henry said after a pause. "You are alarmed by him? I get it, but he is never a real problem." He didn't say he was no problem at all. "He served in Vietnam. He has PTSD."

"He told me. They speak French in Vietnam, yes?"

"Yeah." Henry had a frown and assured me we could call security if needed. They were bouncers. No guns. If patients ever caused trouble, they would not be allowed to return, and everyone wanted to be back. This place was the end of the line for them. That was it.

"My accent freaked him out," I said, "that's all. I wish I didn't have an accent. It's not like I need it."

"It'll be no problem here. We keep talking to the minimum."

Henry's head turned, in military precision, to the door he had left open. The patients were trickling into the room.

They picked up their cards, marked them, then found seats. They shuffled about like churchgoers at a service. Kenneth and I exchanged a slight nod. He had a smile of encouragement. The others looked at me but did not make eye contact. The only woman seemed to have used up all her words and needed to sit quietly with others. She emanated a sense that she knew tomorrow wouldn't be any different. I averted my eyes.

I was not used to a full room being so hushed, waiting. Henry signaled it was time to start. I marched briskly to the table to get the supplies and to energize myself with a sense of purpose. He took needles out of the drawer, and I did likewise. I stuck them between the fingers of my left fist, as usual. The routine gesture kicked in my confidence.

"I predict earthquakes," a man with chipped glasses whispered to me when I walked by. "It wasn't the drugs."

Henry started his treatments from the back. I watched myself move in the space, apprehensive about making mistakes, ruining everything for him, who had been so glad to have me there. Kenneth was sitting quietly. I went to the front row.

"I'm getting a Game Boy," an older patient with long matted hair said out loud. "I'm getting a Game Boy."

"No, you are not," someone shushed him.

"I'm getting a Game Boy," he repeated.

A man stood up. He had a smirk. "Shut the fuck up," he said.

Henry gestured to him to sit back down. He did not.

"Every day the same shit."

"Joe," Henry said. Anything could have happened, but nothing did. Joe sat down. The old man kept silent, twisting his mouth.

My heartbeat had gone wild at the exchange, but my hands were steady. I looked at the row of men waiting for me.

I concentrated on the ear of my first patient to determine the exact location of the points to needle. It was always like making out a new map. He was a young man sitting with his arms crossed, his mouth set. He stared straight ahead with a fierce expression, letting me know I did not have to feel sorry for him here in this crappy place. It was his choice. I thought we had more in common than he imagined. I said, "Breathe in," as usual before insertion and, "Breathe out," when the needle was in. He did, and his posture relaxed. I sensed the needle release the *qi* and hush his mind. His compliance in getting ready for the next needle told me that he trusted me. It gave me a thrill. For the patients in this room, it was here and now or nothing. My memory stopped dipping into the past, rustling for something, telling me the same story over and over. I was simply there, working. My mind grew energized.

I went to the next patient and then the next. When I returned to take the needles out of my first patient's ears, he simply got up and left. The familiarity of the rhythm and the haze of the silence in the room were soothing. Kenneth was dozing off, waiting for his turn.

It was then that the woman stood up and crept to the front of the room, dragging her feet. I had a stab of remembering myself walking out of the hospital. The detox clinic now seemed again a basement, desolate.

At the front of the room, the woman let herself down on the floor, then rolled on her back, arms spread.

"Goddamn," someone snickered.

I went to her.

"What is it?" I asked in a low voice. The other patients were getting agitated.

"My back hurts," she whispered. "It never stops. Never stops." She remained on the ground staring at the ceiling, arms flung wide like a supplicant.

Henry was finishing a patient's treatment and gestured to me to intervene fast. It was clearly urgent.

"You need to get up," I said, warm but efficient, like I'd

faced this all my life. There was no reaction from the woman. Her eyes looked at me with such authentic pain I summoned back my energy.

"Well, no worries," I said, bending towards her. "We'll deal with this once you sit back. I'll give you my hand to get up."

"Why this goddam pain?" she said.

A few patients stood up. One clapped. I was a bit frightened.

"Why? Why?" she repeated.

"I'll help you. You can do this. We can talk when you sit up again."

No pain would lessen by getting up and sitting on a chair, but I could only stick to the task at hand. I disliked insisting but I kept at it, as friends did when pressing me for a walk on the beach after the miscarriage. All I had wanted to do was flail on the floor like this woman when they did, refusing any attempt at relief. There wasn't any, that much I knew. But there was something reassuring in carrying out a simple task, as I started to realize. I could give the woman that. We would do this one thing together. The idea grew on me.

"Hold on to my hands. You can do this. Get up." I grabbed her hands. She did not slip them free, just kept looking at me. We both held on. There was nothing else I could do, was there? This was it. We remained locked in eye contact. Encouraged, I pulled harder. "Get up. Now. Right—now." I repeated it loud and crisp. She did. I let go of her hands and watched her go back to her chair. She settled in with a soft whisper that could be singing or praying. She looked calm.

Things might be going in the right direction after all. I felt hopeful.

But now I saw that my sharp tone had startled Kenneth out of sleep. He was up, wobbly on his legs. He looked around with a moan, seeming cornered. He jumped up, waving his arms.

"What is it?" I said. He looked trapped in a scary place he was the only one to know.

"Kenneth." I had trouble drawing breath. "Kenneth." I told him that everything was fine. He was not listening to the words, just watching my hands move. He started mumbling fast to me. Clipped words, in a menacing tone.

Henry signaled that he was heading to call security. I gestured not to, but he started going to summon them. I put myself between him and the door. I asked Henry to wait. This I could do.

I was as freaked as Kenneth seemed, but I went to face him. A Chinese master had taught me that a person facing you tends to synchronize with the rhythm of your breath. I regularly breathed in-out. The master recommended repeating the name of the person to center them and bring them back.

"Kenneth. You are safe here," I told him. He was. We would make it, me and him. We all would. I wanted him to. I needed him to say that yes, there was hope. "Take a little walk now, Kenneth, and come back when you feel better." I told him I would be there, waiting. I promised, "It's all right, Kenneth." I knew it wasn't necessarily so, but I wanted it ferociously. "I'll be here waiting," I repeated. I saw he was straining to hear my words. He put one palm over his eyes. I kept my tone even, speaking in a reassuring voice. I said to just take a walk and I would wait here for him. He looked at me. I thought I saw him nod. He started going, each step tentative. It was steaming hot but he looked cold. I watched him go until he walked out the door.

I went back to work. I picked up more needles from the drawer and Henry came by me. I expected him to say something generic and encouraging that would irritate me.

"It's always like this here," he said instead. "It's not easy for me, and it's been years. I'm sorry."

I didn't know how badly I wanted Kenneth to trust me until Henry signaled to me to get centered on the work without looking at the door. I sneaked looks at it anyway. After a small group of patients left and the room was empty for a moment I went to a chair and lowered myself into it. I heard the rustling of life outside. Some shuffling, a burst of talking. People living their life with not much going but enough hope to go on. I strained to hear Kenneth's steps approaching. I wanted him to listen to life for something missing, as small as it could be, and want it badly enough to return.

At the end of the workday, only a couple patients were left. One seemed to be a student and had a backpack full of books. He noticed me looking at them and said he was an actor. He liked reading plays. He told me plays spoke of the soul. They were the work of God. He seemed transfixed by the sound of his own words. It's then that I saw his eyes were fixed, his clothes threadbare. He was on his way to an audition, he told me. I saw him filled with hope and apprehension. He saw he affected me.

"I like Beckett," he said. Beckett understood the silence, he explained. Desire. I wanted him to say more. But his attention had already shifted. He scratched along the inside of his leg.

"Hope, you know," he said after a while. "No harm in it."

I nodded, thinking otherwise. I kept glancing at the door, a knot in my chest. I was disappointed and then white-knuckled hopeful, listening to each new step approaching. I waited. I wanted Kenneth to walk back in. His trust in the little I had to offer here meant everything to me.

By the time I took the needles out of the actor's ears the light outside was shifting. He was the last patient. I saw that Henry was growing restless with my hesitation at finishing up. He had a sigh and a look that showed he knew I was determined to wait for Kenneth to return.

His eyes had a warmth that told me he liked that I wanted this so badly.

It was closing time. One more patient came in, and Henry treated him anyway. I saw it was a courtesy to me, still standing looking at the door. It was a peculiar feeling, wanting again so strongly. I simply did, and that was it.

It was then that Kenneth reappeared. In the dimness of the dark hallway, I could only see his shape, and behind him, the nowhere he had left behind. He went to a chair and sat quietly. He gave me a little signal with his hand to tell me he was ready, and I picked up the needles for his treatment.

When the workday ended and he was gone, before heading out Henry and I stood for a moment by the desk. It's strange what memory holds onto, but this was it: Henry was silent, taking his glasses off and looking at me.

"Still want your key?" he asked. "Fine if you think this place is not the right fit."

A small halo of warmth was floating up from the desk lamp Henry had clicked on. I said that yes, I wanted the key. I waited for him to find it in his pocket.

"I can't promise you it gets better, but it does. Somehow."

It's been years since I kept going to the detox clinic as a volunteer, but what I remember so distinctly is that moment, me and Henry alone, facing each other at the end of my first day. I knew he saw me precisely the way I was, broken and feeling the first stirring of hope. There was risk and pain at the clinic, and there was Henry who, like Kenneth when I was waiting in line, saw I could do it and would.

NIGHTSHADE

JEANNE HAMMOND

Travis came up the wooden porch steps listening to the crickets saw. He liked the sound, and that of his own stiff boots scuffing the wood. The uncovered porch was where he sat and waited for it to get dark—and for the peace and quiet of the woods to settle over him. Mostly, he was on the lookout for ghosts.

He'd seen a few. All people in the flesh, so far. They'd appear at dusk, just before the light by the road came on, when the long driveway was a patchwork of shadows. Last week, an old raggedy man had walked into the woods with a beer keg and venison shank. Another time, Travis came up on a middle-aged woman sitting on the stump next to his woodpile. She was in a daze, barefoot and cradling a pair of deerskin shoes.

He figured these folks weren't hurting anybody. If he noticed them, it was because he was keeping a lookout for his Pop, thinking he might still show up and want his old house back after twenty years. Travis had been living in it, and he had a wife now. And some nights he feared she'd walk out of his life as easily as she'd walked into it.

Six years ago, Mercy had been passing by on the road in front of his house on foot, pulling a pink roller bag. He'd seen her from the porch and walked down to talk to her when she sat down on the concrete culvert next to his mailbox. She was heading up the hill to stay at her friend's, she'd told him.

"I recognize your house. My Ma worked for your father some years back," Mercy had told him. Travis had said he wouldn't know, because his father had left there when he was eight.

"Ah, maybe Ma made it up," she'd replied.

"So at least your father didn't run away with my Ma," Mercy had said with a teasing smile. "But we definitely should get a blood test 'fore we get married."

Then he'd invited her up to the porch for a drink of water. "I wanna big life," she'd told him. "All these trees yours? The house too?" She took it all in, her face all aglow. She'd reminded him of Christmas with that look.

They'd been married for almost six years now, and he still came out to the porch each night and sat in the chair he'd made from some railroad ties and pallet boards. He leaned back against the chair's stiff back, tucking his hands under his head. He liked to watch moths and stink bugs and skeeters flitting about the lightbulb before finding the bug zapper. The *Szzzit—szzit!* of insects meeting their end soothed his nerves, maybe because he listened to a louder version of the same sound all day at the sawmill. He was thinking how much he liked the smell of cut wood when he heard the *thud—thud—thud* of the boy's head against an inside wall. Mercy was inside with the boy, trying to get him to sleep. Travis and Mercy had an understanding that, if after an hour she wasn't able to get Buddy settled and into bed, Travis would try.

He eased himself up in the chair and unlaced his boots and left them just inside the door. He was a few steps up the short hall when the banging stopped. He opened the boy's door just enough to see Mercy sitting on the narrow cot, her slim waist twisting to lean over the five-year-old whose moist face grimaced as she smoothed his hair. Buddy's eyelids fluttered and slowly closed. After a few moments, Mercy slowly stood up and stepped back from the cot. Travis noticed her ribs rising as she drew in a breath.

He let his own breath out slowly, noticing how nice Mercy looked in her belted, blue-striped dress. His mother had also liked to wear dresses. He liked that Mercy wore her dark hair long. He watched her until she moved past him, out into the hallway. The screen door slapped shut behind her and she swore. Thankfully, the boy stayed asleep.

Travis went outside and found Mercy lying with her knees up under her chin on the porch swing. He sat back down in the chair he'd made since there wasn't room to sit next to her.

"Night air's good for ya," she said. She kept her eyes closed tight, like she was pretending to be somewhere else. Travis leaned over his right chair arm and nudged the swing.

Mercy's legs stiffened. "I don't wanna to go sideways. I wanna go forward," she said. Travers drew his hand back, wondering if anything he could do would make her eyes light up like Christmas again. He wanted to go to bed and have her hug and kiss him, but he could feel that she was all closed off to his touching her. The boy took everything out of her it seemed.

"I've got the first shift tomorrow," he mumbled, his hands resting on his knees. He stood up expecting her to lie still, but she sat up and grabbed hold of his hand.

"Trav, you gotta ask Marcus for a raise. He owns that sawmill, now his Daddy's gone. He can afford to pay you more, I'm sure he can. You got to ask him tomorrow." Travis stood aloof, wondering what good ever comes from asking.

She said, "I worked it out for Buddy to start school. School opens up next week. And he's got special needs, Trav. 'Course you know that. To go to school, he needs a Special Ed aide. And I found someone!"

Travis was surprised that Mercy had gotten the boy into a school. The boy hardly spoke.

"He'll be able to get speech therapy," Mercy added. She said the last two words like she'd rehearsed them.

Travis didn't have a clue what a Special Ed aide cost.

Mercy said, "The state pays for the time the aide's with him at school. We pay her twenty dollars a day to go with Buddy on the bus."

"We pay her a hundred a week, just to ride with him on the bus?" Travis asked, rubbing his beard along his left jaw.

Mercy sat up straight and inhaled deeply. She didn't meet his gaze but looked out at the dark road. Porch light puddled in a small circle by the door.

"I can't take him myself, Trav. You're at the sawmill. It's all

I can do to get the clothes washed and meals cooked. The school's eight miles. I'd have to hitch home after dropping him off, then hitch back to pick him up. It's pay for the aide or get me a car."

Travis saw some sense in what she was saying. If Buddy could go to school, he needed to go. Travis just wasn't crazy about asking Marcus for a raise.

Marcus had been two years ahead of Travis in high school and had been a jerk back then too. When Marcus inherited his father's commercial sawmill six years ago, he became Travis's boss. In rural Fleming County, Kentucky, jobs were hard to come by. Travis hadn't minded working for Marcus's father Jed so much. Working for Marcus was another story. He knew that one way to get Buddy to school would be to drop him off himself and leave work early to pick him up. But he'd have to negotiate a shorter work day, and he couldn't imagine Marcus approving that. Even if Marcus did, he'd cut Travis's take-home pay.

Travis went inside and walked as softly as he could to the back bedroom, where he stripped off his clothes and let them fall to the floor. When he rolled onto the bed, the springs squeaked. All he could think was, *God, I hope Buddy doesn't wake up.* Travis loved his son; he just didn't know how to quiet him without pinning him down or frightening him.

~

The next morning Travis woke up late. He could hear Mercy in the living room coaxing the boy to stop throwing his blocks by naming the numbers on each one.

"I'm gonna be late. Headin' out," he said after gulping coffee. Mercy appeared and handed him a sandwich.

"Don't forget. You ask Marcus 'bout a raise. We got to know today if Buddy can start school next week."

Travis's empty stomach tightened. She was really pressuring him now. He thought there might be someone who could take Buddy on the bus who wouldn't cost so much. He wanted to check out if what Mercy was saying was true—about the cost.

Taking a bite of the sandwich, he grabbed his father's old briefcase under the small table by the door. His clearest memory of his father was his strong, friendly voice saying, "I'm heading to the office, Son. You and your mother have a good day!"

He had few memories of his father—other than that one. He remembered his mother pressuring his father on his way out the door. "We don't need a hundred-acre woods. Man from the sawmill would buy 'em up quick. We could sure use the money."

After his mother had passed away, Travis had checked the deed and learned his father had put the land into a trust or conservancy. Travis couldn't have sold off any property even if he'd wanted to. Mercy hadn't brought it up.

Travis got close to the truck and laid the other half of the ham sandwich on the hood and fished for his key in his pants pocket with his free hand. The briefcase wasn't one of those hard, sleek narrow boxes with latches that popped.

Instead, it had buckles and was roomy enough for his cellphone, work gloves, caliper, compass, pack of cigarettes, and a couple Red Bulls.

Travis walked into the sawmill ten minutes late, without his briefcase. The only time he'd ever carried it in his boss Marcus had made a joke of it. "Hey, guess the IRS is auditing us today," he'd said. "Better give Mary a heads up." Mary was the sawmill's bookkeeper.

This morning Devan, the older man who fancied himself a preacher, nodded hello to Travis. The two other guys, Ned and Charlie, were busy loading logs into the rig for the large circular and didn't seem to notice that Travis wasn't at his post yet. Travis grabbed an orange hard hat from a peg and walked out onto the mill floor pulling on his work gloves. He liked the noise and the physical part of his work. The sawmill had a big open bay, so it was kind of like working outside, in the fresh air and half-light.

Logs the size of tree trunks were forklifted onto a conveyor that fed them one at a time onto a hydroelectric lift, which captured each log lengthwise, adjusted to its girth and moved it, end first, toward the thirty-six-inch circular saw. The log was then pushed lengthwise along the bright, purring saw blade. After each pass, the lift's chassis would move the log a little closer for the next cut, so each board of the run had a uniform thickness. After each rough-edged board was sliced off the log lengthwise it was sent down a second conveyor belt to the edger. There, each of the cut board's rough edges were shaved off to make the board the right length and width—whatever dimensions the boss set.

Travis mostly worked the large circular saw that he and

the guys called “Mad Max”. Travis liked focusing on getting each log sliced up, however many passes it took. The task was repetitive—he could have done the job in his sleep, except for all the noise. He had to listen for any variation in sound that might alert him to a problem—a log jamming or some mechanical issue with the saw or rig.

Travis was just starting the third log when he noticed Marcus heading his way. The boss was easy to spot. He was the only man in the mill who was clean-shaven and wore a pressed shirt. He was what his Dad might have called a “fancy man”, like the salesmen or realtors that would come by the house when he was a boy.

I'd like to grab his neck and squeeze it like a chicken, Travis thought, feeling sweat wick down the arms of his flannel shirt. Knowing he could overpower Marcus was some comfort. As he waited for Marcus to make his way over, Travis thought about what Mercy wanted him to do and wondered whether this might be the right time. He half-watched the rig setting up as he waited for Marcus and sweated out his resentment.

Travis thought, He's always ragging on us guys. *He treats the women here a whole lot better.* Travis knew for a fact Mary, Ruth and Celia had each gotten a generous raise, a so-called “incentive package” last Christmas. Ruth and Celia drove the Bob Cat around the lot and kept inventory.

Travis had worked at the mill for twelve years and still made twenty bucks an hour. It added up to almost forty thousand a year, and it should have been enough. But for some months now Mercy had been asking him when he was going to make more money. "We got Buddy now. He's got special needs, Travis."

Mercy always knew what she wanted. He supposed that was a lot of what had attracted him at first. She had enough ambition for both of them. But after Buddy was born, all she seemed to want was more money. She still dressed up, but her eyes never rested, never lit up.

Travis had powered down the saw by the time Marcus reached him.

"You got a problem, *Arch*?" Marcus asked him. He gestured with his hand to keep the saw spinning.

Travis hated being called "Arch". His last name was Mackin. He wasn't sure how he'd gotten the nickname Arch; he guessed it was because he liked to bend over and then stand up and stretch his arms up toward the steel rafters once or twice a shift.

"No. No problem," Travis said, restarting Mad Max. As the chassis was loading, Travis took off his gloves and dried his hands on his shirt and waited for the log. Marcus didn't move on but stood next to him. Travis could smell his aftershave.

"Arch, we're movin' the sawmill to West Virginia in two months. Consider this your notice," Marcus said matter-of-factly, practically under his breath. That appeared to be all he'd come to say. He turned and walked back toward the office.

Travis wondered why he'd been singled out for the news. Must have missed the announcement by coming in late, he thought. He would have to tell Mercy.

That evening when Travis got home, Mercy wasn't at the house. He guessed she had gone up the road to her friend Bella's for something. Travis could hear Buddy playing in his room quietly, so he decided to go up to the attic. He'd been thinking about his gun. He'd hidden it up there after Mercy had said she didn't want it in the house. The only light was what filtered in through one small window. The last time he was up there, hiding his gun, he'd had a flashlight and had found some old photographs. One was of his father in his twenties standing with his mother next to an old Ford sedan. He couldn't recall his parents ever standing together, so the picture haunted him for a while. He'd found a half empty box and dropped the gun in, taped and marked it with an X, and shoved back under the far eave. It was right where he'd left it.

Squatting down, he opened it, and with one hand felt around under his father's folded shirts. When his hand grazed something sheer and filmy, he realized that some of his mother's dresses must be in the box too. He pulled his hand out like he'd been stung. Feeling the shirts and dresses reminded him his parents' bodies had once been real to him. Their absence now triggered a strange feeling, a yearning that confused him. He felt numb to the loss of them—his mother dead and his father gone.

When he stuck his hand back in and continued to stir through the fabric for the Colt and finally grasped it, he sat back. The memory of his parents standing opposite each other on the driveway now seemed to play like an old movie reel as sunlight streamed in through the little half-window and backlit all the dust in the air. His father was pointing a shotgun at a blonde man who was running for his truck. His mother was pointing the same Colt pistol Travis now held in his hand at his father.

The memory was so clear he supposed it had to be true. His mother had been unfaithful. He closed the box.

He went back downstairs, pistol in hand, and grabbed his briefcase from the floor in the kitchen. He slipped the gun into the center section then buckled the briefcase flap. He would pick up some cartridges for the gun—and cigarettes—tomorrow.

Travis put his briefcase up on the top shelf in the hall closet just outside his child's bedroom door. Then he opened the door and saw the boy sitting cross-legged on the floor, leaning over his lap and rocking back and forth. Buddy was making deep-throated warbling sounds, his splayed fingers fluttering like hummingbirds above the plastic action figures laid out in front of him. The boy didn't touch the small toys, just agitated the air above them as he rocked back and forth.

"Hey, Buddy," Travis said, nodding. He slowly closed the door and stepped back out into the hallway just as Mercy came in.

"What's going on, Trav?" she asked him. Her dark eyebrows arched as she stood looking at him. He wanted to ask her the same thing. She was dressed up, with lipstick and earrings. He stared at her then walked back toward the bedroom. He thought, *If she follows and lays down with me, I'll tell her. She didn't.*

The next morning, Travis woke early and found Mercy in the kitchen.

"So what did he say, Trav?" she asked, handing him a mug of lukewarm coffee.

"I didn't ask him," he said. But before Travis could tell her the sawmill was moving and that Marcus had given him notice, she threw a bagged sandwich at him and walked away.

When Mercy came back into the kitchen, she was dressed and holding Buddy by the hand. Travis remembered she'd told him she was going to take Buddy to meet his teacher. The elementary school was less than a mile from the sawmill, twelve miles from the house.

"Bella's gonna drive me and Buddy," she said. "I ain't in no mood to ride into town with you." Buddy stood quietly, sucking a juice box.

Travis shrugged. He was relieved not to have to drive her and the boy.

Right then, he would have walked more than a mile to have a deep, slow drag from a cigarette, any reason to draw air into his lungs. Something about the way Mercy was acting made him anxious. He jumped in the truck and drove to the Walmart, which was not exactly on his way to work. After he'd picked up the cartridges and cigarettes, he sat in the parking lot, lit up, inhaled, and telephoned the Kentucky Department of Education. A woman answered, and he asked her if the state would pay for an aide to ride with a special needs kid, if the kid's parents were out of work.

"Aides ride the bus with any special needs student at no cost to his or her parents—whether or not they are out of work. There's no charge, either way," She told him.

Travis thanked her. He was sure this was something Mercy already knew. She would have called and found out. He finished his cigarette and cranked up the radio. He'd have to roll through some stop signs to get to work on time.

~

The morning shift at the mill passed quickly. By eleven o'clock, he'd cross-cut six huge logs. He was stretching his back and arms when he noticed Mercy in her blue-striped dress up on the landing outside Marcus' office. Travis wasn't that surprised that she'd lied to him about money. But coming here, to talk to Marcus without telling him, really took nerve. Travis thought briefly of running up and catching her, letting her know that he'd called the Kentucky Department of Education that morning. But he was just hurt enough not to bother. Let Marcus tell her the sawmill is moving. He walked back to Mad Max, shaking his head.

For a while he watched the whirring teeth of the saw blade cut through the golden hardwood like it was cake. After the log had been sliced away and the planks conveyed to Devan over on the edger, there was a lull, while the forklift deposited the next load of logs. Still agitated by Mercy's being there, Travis took off his hard hat and, keeping his head down, walked back over to Marcus' office to see if she was still talking to him. He saw her head at waist level through the glass door. She was kneeling in front of a seated

Marcus and rocking back and forth with a pouty mouth, like she was begging. Travis saw Marcus's hand slip up under her hair along her neck and pull her head into his lap.

Travis felt the half-sandwich he'd eaten in the parking lot rise from his stomach. Then he heard Marcus's flat, thin voice. "How 'bout I take you with me instead?"

Travis teetered where he stood, pummeled by the thudding sounds of bumping logs, the shirring of the motors driving the saws. He felt his mind leave him, and all he could think to do was run outside and grab his gun. He fully intended to shoot Marcus dead. But when he got to his truck and opened the cab door, he thought of the other guys inside, especially Devan, a man who looked out for others, who'd always had his back with Marcus. And he thought of Buddy.

But having seen his wife laying her head in another man's lap had whipped up such a storm in his gut, he could hardly stand up. He thought of the wind trying its best to topple a tree and steadied himself. No matter what, he'd stand—straight-backed, aloof, and strong.

He went back inside without his gun. Mercy had done what she'd done. He hadn't the heart to kill any man in anger, so there was no sense in waving his gun around. He would get back to work before any of the guys had to cover for him. With luck, none of them would have noticed he was gone or that Mercy was there.

But when Travis stood numbly next to Mad Max, he couldn't forget what he'd seen, and his stomach twisted and torqued with the pain of seeing Mercy kneeling before another man—without shame. Travis realized it was shame he felt. And then he noticed an odd shaped log riding up under the rig.

He leaned in to push it aside with his hand, which he knew no one should ever do, and his heart raced like crazy. The thrill of his hand coming that close to the blade's whirring teeth was electric. For the moment, he couldn't remember anything but the surge of panic he'd just felt and the rush it gave him. Soon he was moving both his hands in and around the moving blade, just letting them dip and glide near it as if over the strings of an instrument, jamming to the rhythms and vibrations he heard from the saw, the belts, and the lifts. He was caught up in the moment, a moment so different from the lulling hollowness of his shame. He desperately wanted that shock of this kind of living, of being caught up like a fish by an angler's flicking wrist, a boy's fluttering hands, or the shadows of insect wings. And it was then he got too close, and his life blood spattered, his heart gushed out where his hand had been.

Almost a year later, Travis sat in his chair on the porch and looked out past the road, at the dark, ember-topped trees behind the pines. He'd stopped looking for ghosts. Maybe because he'd become one. Mercy had left him and taken the boy with her. She'd said, "Buddy talks to me more than you do, Trav. I can't take your spooky quiet no more."

He'd made sure she got his worker's compensation checks. And she got money from the government for Buddy too. So she got more money than she'd ever gotten before.

Most evenings he'd just sit and rub the stub of his wrist under the eggy white of the porch lamp and rising moon. He wasn't mindful of any thoughts passing through his head, just the breeze coming up and moving through the trees. This particular night he was absorbed watching the trees' shadowy tops rearrange themselves when he noticed a man on foot walking up the overgrown driveway.

The man walked with a bowed back, and his white hair looked like a comet's tail in the moonlight. His beard was darker, a wispy gray. The man came as far as the porch steps and looked up at Travis with a soft openness that seemed almost childlike. He was dressed in deerskin.

"Son, did I catch you at a bad time?" the man said. His eyes seemed to absorb everything at once: Travis's missing hand, the screen door that needed to be rehung, the scuffed work boots by the door. The hacked-up firewood.

The resonance of the man's voice was familiar. Travis stood up and stared at the man. It wasn't a ghost. It was his Pop.

"I heard you was here all by yourself. I thought it was 'bout time I came outta them woods and gave you a hand."

His father scaled the porch steps and sat down beside Travis.

"Give me your hand, Son," he said. Travis leaned over and reached under his chair. After a while he lifted his arm and extended his prosthetic hand. His father clasped it hard.

"You've been through more than most, Son. A man in pain has two choices. He can either wound others or wound himself. You chose the second. 'Spose I chose the first."

PHOBIA

ERIN WEDEMEYER

You clutch the blood work orders from your gastroenterologist as you wait for the doctor to enter the room. The floor is cleaner than usual, your eyes locked on the sheen of the tiles from the bright rectangular light in the ceiling.

The last time you went for blood work, something strange had happened. You were fine until you sat in the seat, then tears formed and burst from your ducts within an instant. They streamed down your cheeks without control, though you certainly wanted them to stop. The nurse's eyes widened, and she assured you it wouldn't hurt. You *knew* that, and in your head, you told yourself that over and over. Yet when she missed the vein in your left arm you had whined, and the tears didn't stop until you left the lab.

You *do not* want to humiliate yourself and act like such a child again.

Your partner had driven you to that last lab appointment

and greeted you in the waiting room. They said they had never seen your pupils so dilated before and think the situation started some sort of panic attack.

Your mother said it was all in your head and you had to stop psyching yourself out. She hadn't been there, but you had called her on the phone afterward. You believe her for two main reasons: one, she has a medical degree, and two, you desperately hope she is right. If it's all in your head, you can rid yourself of your embarrassing fear by the next appointment. *I'll take every precaution possible, and I'll be in and out. This time won't be like last time,* you think. *Right?*

You're yanked from your thoughts by two light knocks on the door.

Your primary care doctor enters the small square room, opening the door wider than usual for her baby bump. She smiles. It's genuine, unlike most of those you see from fatigued practitioners. You pry your lips open to return it. Her smile fades as her gaze shifts to your hands.

One of your thumbs paces back and forth on the gray counter you sit next to. *Why am I such a baby? It's just a tiny needle,* you think. *I got a tattoo without a single tear!* You stop your thumb by clasping your hands together. Your fingertips turn white.

"Hey, how are we doing?" she asks as she sits onto her blue stool. She scoots back a few extra inches and turns to you.

"I'm all right," you manage to say.

"What brings you in today?"

You pry your hands open and hand her the paperwork. "I need to get some lab work done."

She takes the papers and reads, her green eyes shifting left to right. "You know you can just go to LabCorp to get these done? You didn't have to bring them to me."

You stare at her short, dark hair, pulled back into a ponytail, to avoid looking into her gaze. "Well—I—I kind of, like, freak out, I guess," you say. "I don't know why." You think about sitting back in the tan chair instead of sitting so erect, but all you do is drop your shoulders slightly. "I just haven't had good experiences at the other labs, so I wanted to see your lab."

She nods. "Well, I can certainly arrange that for you." She turns to her computer and talks herself through the process as she searches for the requested tests in the system.

You wait, and although you have nothing critical to do after the appointment, you combat an urge to rush her. Your body itches to leave as soon as it can.

"Okay, so I've set up all the requests in our system and have sent them to the lab," your doctor says as she swivels around carefully. Her white coat, hanging down behind her, flows with the motion.

You nod, a quick, rigid nod. Your throat is tight and dry. You'd like a drink of water.

"Is there anything else I can help you with before I send you over?"

You suck in a sharp breath. "Oh, I can't—" Your voice cracks and you pause. You're now aware of your heart as it pumps a little harder. "Can we schedule the lab for later?"

She pauses. "Oh, sure thing, honey." Her tone has changed, as if she's a mother pigeon and you're her frail child in a nest made from cigarette butts, straw wrappers, and a few twigs. You could almost see paintings of bubbles and vibrant cartoon fish forming on the plain white walls.

As your doctor turns to the computer, your eyebrows scrunch. The mouse clicks and a box opens on the screen. "What works best for you?" she asks.

"Fridays." Your temples are hot.

"How's this Friday? What time?"

This Friday is only three days away. Your first thought is to push it back a week to give yourself time to prepare. *A whole week to prepare for a stupid little needle?* you scoff. "That's fine," you force yourself to say. "Later the better."

"Alrighty! I've got you down for Friday at 3:30."

"Sounds good."

After your doctor leads you to the door, you scurry out of the building, avoiding eye contact. You look down at your flurrying feet, thinking, *Relax, damn.* There's an ache at the back of your head from your tightened neck. *It's not even happening 'til Friday for Christ's sake.* The green tile below your feet changes to concrete, then to asphalt.

You look up to find your car. Once you're behind the wheel, your body locks up. You sit and stare at the dashboard for a few seconds, maybe minutes. Your nails dig into your skin. Although you're not exerting energy, your heart still pounds. You heave a deep breath in through your nose. It leaves your lungs as a heavy sigh. You drop your shoulders and open your folded arms. *All you have to do is sit there. It'll be two minutes tops. No crying. In and out.*

The day before your lab appointment you begin your caffeine hiatus. Caffeine shrinks veins, and the last thing you want is the phlebotomist missing yours. *Another necessary precaution*, you think as you stare at your cup of water, wishing it was coffee. You're not sure you'll have the energy to make it through work.

You let your responsibilities distract your mind from the appointment throughout the day. You don't want to think about it. You *shouldn't* think about it. It will just lead to you freaking out over nothing.

As you're looking in the mirror at the end of the day, a memory flashes in your mind. You left the lab with four Band-Aids, having given out twice. The phlebotomist had missed your small vein the first time.

Your tiny bathroom now feels minuscule, as if there was only enough room for you, the mirror, and your dread. The dread takes up most of the space. A whimper escapes your throat. *Pathetic*, you think and grip the sink countertop. *Why am I like this?* The yellow light deepens the shadows of your heavy frown. *Quit making a big deal about it.* You wrench your fingers off the counter and whip around.

Like a hamster on a wheel, your heart races.

~

For the six hours leading up to the visit, you drink an entire water bottle every hour. *A quarter of the bottle every fifteen minutes,* you remind yourself. The hydration should deter another four Band-Aid incident. You hope that fact will keep your fear at bay so you can compose yourself. It seems to, at least for those six hours and the car ride to your appointment.

Yet as you walk toward the door of the building, you feel it creeping in. There's a stinging in your inner elbows, and you find yourself wanting to cross your arms. *Stop it! There's nothing to be afraid of*, you think, but your heart disagrees, ramming against your ribcage, anticipating, dreading. You fight the urge in your arms by clenching your fists. The back of your head throbs. *In and out, in and out. Sit still, and don't cry. Sit still. Don't cry.*

Your partner opens the door for you. "It's okay," they say.

I know.

You inch towards the glass window of the office, your legs so tight it seems like a waddle. You haven't removed your stare from the receptionist, mainly because every movement seems to take triple the energy it should, but you're also avoiding the intrusive stares of the other patients in the waiting room. "I'm here for a blood draw," you say, voice soft and restrained.

The receptionist looks you up and down. "They'll take you back shortly."

Pajama pants and a sweatshirt keep you warm, but not comfortable. While you wait, your leg bouncing, your partner talks about the pictures on the wall. They're trying to distract you, which is both soothing and humiliating. You lock your eyes on the frame of the middle image, a flock of birds.

The white door swings open, and a woman calls your name. You spring up as if your legs are a coil, but the tension in your body does not ease. Your arms cross during the action, your fists still clenched. *In and out. Don't cry. Two minutes tops.*

As you're brought back, your partner walks beside you, petting your shoulder. Your breathing is as rapid as your heart beat.

"We're going to have you sit in one of the rooms instead of the lab, okay?" the woman says.

You saw her lips moving, and you're certain you understood her in the moment, but you already forgot what she said. You nod. Thoughts pour and crash through your mind like Niagara Falls, but you're not sure what they're about. You're angry with yourself for acting so childish, for making this more work than necessary. At the same time, you're trying to relax your muscles. Mostly, however, all you can make out is fear, intense fear.

You hear your partner say something to the phlebotomist as you enter the room. You sit down in the padded chair, but it feels as if it was chiseled from stone. You focus on the white light in the ceiling and roll your sleeves up. Your lips are tight.

The phlebotomist enters, holding the tray with the tubes and the needle to the side in an attempt to keep it out of your view. You see it in your periphery. You can now hear your heart in the veins of your ear canals.

"My, you're so tense it's all the way down to your toes," he says. Braids at the top of his head restrain the tight corkscrews that reach for his shoulders. He pats your ankle. "Try to relax and take deep breaths."

As you alleviate the tension in your body as best you can, your thighs tremble (your toes uncurl too). *Stop!* you think, but you don't fight it too much. You'd rather focus your energy on preventing your bicep from flexing; you don't want to restrict the blood flow. If you could concentrate on relaxing your arm and controlling the trembles at the same time, you would. The phlebotomist glances at your legs and frowns.

Do not *cry,* you tell yourself. Your fingers squeeze the side of the chair. *It'll be over in two minutes.*

Your partner cups their hands around your eyes, like the blinders for a thoroughbred. "I'm here, okay? Just look at me."

You focus on their pupils. It helps a little, gives you something calm to try to focus on instead of the race in your mind; Venipuncture Panic has winning odds 1-5. At least, you think your mind is racing, but you still can't make out about what. Your brain simultaneously feels like the infield during the Derby and a black hole.

When you hear the cap pop off the needle, tears burst from your eyes. *God, I'm being so ridiculous,* you think. Your lips are weighed down by your self-hatred, though the frown only adds to your outward childish appearance.

You wish you knew why you acted this way. You wish you knew how to stop it. If only your embarrassment could work with logic to beat the panic. *Why can't I stop crying?* Your body stiffens.

The needle punctures your skin. It doesn't hurt, as expected, yet your weeping doesn't end. "Relax your arm, hun," the phlebotomist says.

"Hey, you gotta breathe," your partner says. They stroke your cheek and take a deep breath.

You hadn't realized you weren't breathing, but your restricted lungs confirm such. You try to breathe on your partner's count. All the while, you're still trying to dam your tear ducts.

"Yeah, this is a panic response if I've ever seen one," the phlebotomist says.

His voice is distant, drowned out by the thunder of Venipuncture Panic's hooves, but a small part of you hears him. The acknowledgment of your fear instead of the usual phlebotomist's disdainful coddle is enough to ease the fight against your bawling.

It's been seconds. It feels like hours. You're too focused on remembering to breathe to pay attention to anything else. Your heartbeat drowns out the other sounds of the room. The smell of disinfectant ceases to exist. The slight sting in your vein numbs. But despite this loss of senses, you're hyper aware of movement: the nanometer change in the needle as the phlebotomist adjusts his grip, the sweat sliding through your hair, and the brief departure of your partner's gaze.

"What will you guys be having for dinner?" the phlebotomist asks. The movement of his lips catches your attention more than the sound of his voice.

Your partner looks at you. From their expression you can tell they're urging you to respond. If there wasn't a whale on your chest holding its tail up in triumph, like Shamu when she glides on the stage, you would. Your partner answers for you, saying, "Pancakes."

Your lips quiver as you strain to push the whale back into the water. It's a task that would be easier achieved with your whole body, but you don't dare flex your arm. "With turkey bacon," you say between gasps and sobs. Your tears are enough for even the whale to swim in. They run down the sides of your face into your ears. It sounds like you've joined the whale in the ocean.

"Mmm, I love bacon," the phlebotomist says.

The lack of pity in his reaction stirs something within your mind. It seems to have given the racer a mild tranquilizer, but its hooves still pound against your skull.

A few more painstaking second-hours pass. You think your partner and the phlebotomist continue to talk, but you're not certain. Your gaze is too focused on your partner's eyes to see their mouth moving, your mind too concentrated on breathing, and your ears are drowning in water.

Only when the phlebotomist removes the needle do your senses, mostly, return. Terror reduces to fright. He applies cotton and a bandage. "All done."

The corners of your lips turn up. After your partner removes their hands, you take as deep a breath as possible, a couple seconds longer than any breath you've taken in the last five minutes. You sit up. Tears still slide down your cheeks.

After slowly slipping off the chair into a stand, you turn to the phlebotomist. "I'm sorry," you say, wiping under your eye. "Thank you for not missing my vein." Your voice shakes.

"Don't apologize!" he says. "This is all part of my job, and I love my job. You can't help having a phobia." He smiles, a near replication of his I.D. badge.

You stand there, frozen, with his words ringing in your ears. *Phobia...* The word clears the darkness in your mind, revealing a dirt track. Venipuncture Panic now runs with reason, kicking up turf, instead of stampeding about a black void. *I guess I can't help it.* Your fists unclench.

Your partner holds your hand and guides you out of the room toward the waiting room. You stare at the floor just like your last visit, avoiding the practitioners' gazes. You know they're questioning why there are tears soaking an adult's cheeks after a blood draw.

Their thoughts anger you. You want to explain yourself, to tell them that you can't control it, but you keep your lips sealed, more concerned about leaving the building.

Your partner pushes on the metal sheet for the door's handle. The door creaks as it swings open. You release your grip on your partner's hand and hold onto your inner elbow, grasping the bandage as you scutter through the waiting room and down the parking lot.

When you finally get to the car, you slump over onto your partner's shoulder. You need a few minutes of comforting strokes and assurances to calm your nerves and embarrassment.

Venipuncture Panic crosses the finish line: first place, though there wasn't any competition. Like you, the horse is exhausted yet antsy, chest heaving.

"I wish I wasn't like this," you say.

"You *can't* help it, love," they say, still gliding their hand up and down your back. "Trying to fight it is just making you more stressed and tense."

More tense, you think. A sigh parts your tight lips. You sniffle. *It's over,* you think. *It's okay. You're okay. You can relax now.* You blink for what feels like the first time since you were last in the car. There's no longer a pain in your chest.

"Plus, people *can* overcome phobias, but it doesn't happen overnight," they add.

"That's good," you say.

"You may have hypothyroidism," the endocrinologist says. Her eyes are hazel. "But we'll have to do some bloodwork to be sure."

Your breath catches. After collecting yourself, you say, "So, I actually have a phobia of getting my blood drawn." You can tell the endocrinologist doesn't believe you from her emotionless countenance as she nods. You shift your gaze to her blonde hair and leave it there. You can't really blame her. There's a lot of people that say the word without knowing what it's like. But *you* do, and you'll take the necessary action to make it at least bearable, though you're not going to trick yourself into believing it will eradicate it. "Could you please print out the tests so I can take them to my primary and get them done there?"

For a brief moment, there's uneasy silence between the two of you. "Sure, I can print those out for you since you've got a problem with needles," she says.

You hold in a sigh. Irritation, not fear, fuels your pounding heart. "Great." Although you do appreciate that she's printing the request for you, you wish you had the cogency to tell her a phobia isn't the same as "having a problem with", psyching out, being childish, and everything else you've heard.

RAMBLE ON

HOLLY HINSON

Led Zeppelin kindled a fire in me that begged to be tended. It was the soundtrack of my becoming.

Robert Plant was desire and fantasy. The quintessential rock god. Enrobed in snug jeans, his lean frame, gyrating hips jutting, shirt unbuttoned, tousled blond curls flashing as he strutted and commanded the stage. His keening, semi-orgasmic moans and melodies awakened something primal in me. And Jimmy's galloping, rolling guitar licks commanding my hips to move. With five older sisters, the band had already stopped touring by the time I was introduced.

In 1979, I left every midnight showing of the concert movie *Song Remains the Same*–enervated, on fire, only to return to my lonely room. I stared at the ceiling, wondering what it would be like for someone to sing for me, to dance for me. Robert performed for legions of fans at enormous public arenas, but I imagined this sacred bond between us, a secret only we shared. At the end of the night, after the ferocity of his performance, he wound me down and the raucous rock would turn into a loving ballad. What would it be like to have someone croon to me mournfully, magically? To be cradled in loving arms, head resting on a strapping bare chest, my man's tender caress stroking my hair, gently pressing a kiss to my forehead, tracing the line of my lips.

I wanted a whole lotta love. Way down inside, I needed it. My hunger was endless.

The creek behind the house of my youth smells of earth and moss. I take my journal and climb onto a rock that juts out over the water, my throne. Idly, I bask in the sun like a lizard and listen to the gentle gurgling of the brook. I daydream of a boy who will come along and see me on my cliffside perch, gaze upon my infinite coolness, and fall instantly in love. He will demand to read my musings. I will at first demure, then hand over my dog-eared notebook. He will declare me a genius, and we will read the poems and journal entries and talk about what they mean, talk about life, talk about dreams and desires, just talk, and maybe kiss a little, but gently.

I wasn't sure I was worthy of something so magical. I wasn't meant to have anything so pure. What I had known so far of love was secret and sinister and made me feel desperate. I knew more than I should have about the needs of men, and I was already damaged goods. My father's unseemly desires for his five-year-old daughter, and the Sunday mornings spent "cuddling" in his bed when Mom and the other girls were at church, had taken away my choices, and sullied me. "This is what you shouldn't let boys do to you," I could hear his voice in my head.

Men wanted my body and I wanted affection, and to belong to someone. Being used and discarded was the price of admission. I didn't understand then how I already knew so much about what men wanted, and being vilified for pleasing, bringing pleasure. Mockery. Mortification.

Chuck Russman, my date to the freshmen winter dance, is tuning the radio in his car and stops on Styx when he passes me the flask. "Want some rum?" he asks, and I nod, tipping the silver container up too fast, splashing rum on the front of my magenta formal. My friend had fixed us up, but I am uncomfortable. He is from the Catholic boys' school and not from the neighborhood, and that means he is probably too good for me, even though I am a Catholic school girl, too, but I never felt that was me. In his Toyota, we are kissing, and he is stroking my knee when I instinctively drop my head to his lap. "What are you doing?" he asks, shocked. I quickly lift my head and realize my mistake. The shame rises.

I can smell the formaldehyde as soon as I open the back door to Mr. Paul's Biology class, and today there is a new transfer student sitting on the lab stool next to me. With her dirty hair, disheveled uniform, slight body odor and glazed eyes, she is not a typical preppy Catholic school girl, and the class is making sure she is aware of this. She wears combat boots with her uniform skirt, and I smile at her in recognition of a fellow rebel. We will become good friends, because she doesn't judge. She doesn't care that I got caught with a joint last year and suspended and that hanging out with me might get her in trouble. We bond in our pariah-ness, our distaste for those other mf-ing Catholic bitches, and our love of Zep and all things hippie. I trade my sister's hand-me-down fringed leather poncho to Maria for her Led Zeppelin III album.

~

I meet Dudley, my first real boyfriend, at a band jam in my friend John's basement. I immediately connect with his freckles, crooked smile, little brown mustache and gentle personality. A drummer, he is humble, humorous and unflappable. He is a much nicer guy than I deserve. His friends have opinions.

"Who?"

"Not her, man. She's slutty."

"Haven't you heard her nickname, man?"

A deadly whisper, "*Headjob Holly.*"

~

Yet Dudley cares for me and defends me. He is a rare teenager, a self-possessed, independent thinker, and cares not a whit what anyone else thinks. He likes my fire, my weirdness, my eagerness to embrace life, my too-bold actions, my too-loud laugh. He is shy, but he writes me love letters and quotes Led Zeppelin lyrics. "If the sun refused to shine, I would still be loving you." I can feel the borrowed but caring words warm me, and I can imagine Robert Plant's soft voice singing to me as I revel in the romance. Dudley is my muse and my man. We never sleep together.

~

There are parties back in the woods at the place we have dubbed The Pit, a shallow crater where we built bonfires. It is a good 15-minute walk of deep bush-whacking following the old trails behind the fire station, virtually impossible to navigate after dark. If you were shown the way, or if you got too high or drunk, you would get lost. I learned this the hard way.

Its seclusion guarantees that, for a handful of us, The Pit is ours. Tonight, we are away from adult admonishments, we are free and invincible and goofy. We use colored chalk to paint rocks with hearts and flowers and skulls and cross-bones and use them to decorate the perimeter of The Pit. We make pentagrams with sticks, pretending it will keep intruders away. We get out the Ouija board and play by fire-light, trying to scare each other. We drink and drug and our dramas play out. Tempestuous Lisa to freewheeling Rachel:

"Did you really think I wouldn't find out that you kissed Brandon, what the fuck? We were supposed to be friends?" A little shove.

"Whoa, hold up," says Rachel. "Brandon said you guys were on a break, and he kissed me. I was the kissee, not the kisser."

Brandon, of course, is conveniently absent. There are hookups and breakups every weekend.

We play cassette tapes in a boombox, and I hear Led Zeppelin telling me the story of me in all the shades I am becoming—in brash, pulsing, empowering beats; in lacy, lyrical whispers, in audacious tales of plainspoken men and women with no regrets, in mournful, my-woman-done-me-wrong blues, in twangy, mystical folk, and complex story-songs with lyrics I dissect endlessly. Comfort and pain and seduction. Sublime. And I dance, a one-woman whirlwind of buttocks and breasts and flying hair.

~

Maria and I are laughing in the hall. I have put orange shoelaces on my sneakers as a minor rebellion against the dress code, and we are waiting for a teacher to notice, even though it means a detention. As we enter the art room, I glance at the shelf of clay objects the class has fired in the kiln and are drying. Mine is a ridiculously inept dolphin that is so disfigured it's hard to tell what it is. Maria's is easy to identify, though. She has made a bong. I am bowling over with laughter.

"Holy Shit, how did you get away with that?" I ask.

"I told Ms. Raidt it was a flower vase," she says. "It could be—potentially," she says, drawing the word out.

"That is so fucking cool," I say.

"No, you are so fucking cool," she tells me, punching my arm just a touch too hard. Maria has told me in no uncertain terms she is a Holly fan. I am lifted by her comments on the daily—you're so smart, you're so funny. She laughs at the limericks I create, and we develop a catchphrase for the preps who occasionally taunt us as potheads. We sing it like a cheer, raising our voices as we say, "AWWWW fuck 'em!"

Glenn King is the name of my doom. One of my best friend's brothers, he is about four years older. GQ with his wavy dark hair, sexy green eyes, and arrogant smirk—exactly the bad boy recipe I can't resist. In my sister's boyfriend Tim McBride's moldy old basement, we are drinking Boone's Farm Strawberry Hill, and I have taken half a Quaalude from my friend's mom's prescription. We are playing spin-the-bottle when it lands on Glenn. Suddenly, he is kissing me, and I am transported to a dream. I am kissing him back with a loss of inhibition when I awake from my reverie and bolt from the game, but it is too late. I am flushed and sick staring at the many witnesses to my betrayal. Of course, Dudley finds out. He is a laid-back guy, but he has a code, and I have broken it.

"Please, Dudley," I weep. "Glenn means nothing to me, it was stupid, I'm sorry I love you. His brown eyes are nearing tears. I'm begging you, Glenn's an asshole, and I don't even like him."

"Then why?" Dudley asks, and I can't articulate it. It is done. I am exactly the girl everyone says I am. The one boy who had seen through my image, my artifice, who saw my value, is gone.

~

In sophomore year, my school friend Maria ran away from her abusive home—and school—with her biker boyfriend. One day she was in class, and the next she simply disappeared. My Holly fan was gone. I still imagine her wild brown hair and the fringes of her jacket dancing through the open window of a VW van adorned with Grateful Dead stickers. She is free but a little scared. In her tough girl shell, she is laughing and drinking anyway. When I've talked to old school friends about her, they don't remember her at all, as if she only existed in my mind.

After Dudley left me, it felt like nothing mattered anymore because the boy who had confirmed my lovability was gone. I punished myself with self-destruction. I was back to the smart, socially awkward, too-loud, inept girl who was the butt of jokes. Nights behind the Rose Bowl bowling alley with joints and pills and wine to sweep away the snorts of laughter, the names, the rejection.

I've now been alive long enough to forgive myself for the things I did looking to belong, looking for love, yearning for an expression of self. I can cringe and laugh and marvel at the sweet girl, the rebel. I know her essence is still way down inside me, and sometimes it rises.

Those ugly memories linger, but I can see that girl in my mind's eye now, and she is not bad, she's just a kid, big-hearted and worthy of compassion, of consideration. She has value. She is beloved.

SUMMER PEACHES

NELL CAMPBELL

"You have to make your own magic." Tilly's mother had drunk deeply of the girlboss bullshit early and was addicted. "There are no wishing wells or fairy godmothers. You have to make the most of every opportunity. Turn that chunk of coal into a diamond!" The platitudes and self-help mantras were exhausting. Her mother wanted her to move in the right circles, with the right people, in the right places, all the time. And her daddy would just smile when she came to him frustrated by the meticulously full social calendar her mother mandated during the school year.

"Summer's only a heartbeat away," he'd remind her. "Your mama means well, and she knows how the real world works. We wouldn't have made it this far without her and we'd smell like sheep all the time."

Daddy's family was cash poor but well-heeled in the way those things are reckoned even today, but they started off as soldier-pirates. That's how Tilly liked to think of them. Among the first European settlers to cross the Appalachians, Daddy's great-great-great took payment for military service in the Revolution in land that wasn't the fledgling government's to give. By and by they'd clung to it and worked the soil-booty for so long now that Alden's Acres was celebrated as a Pioneer Century Farm. One that Grandmama converted to raising sheep after Papaw passed. A paradise of rolling green fields dotted with trees and patchy forest nourished by the jagged creek that bore the family name once maps were drawn up.

Her love for it built up with each visit like silt in that creek bed. Tilly wished she could live her whole life on the farm instead of just a weekend here and there and ever shortening summers. But Tilly's father had brushed the dirt from his boots and wanted none of it. So, Tilly's regular bedroom was in a house too big for its lot. Neighbors so close she had to pull her window shades at night.

At Grandmama's, a girl could stand naked in the magic that was moonlight, as she did just now. Tilly swayed a little before the wide-open window letting the night air cool her skin still warm from the day's adventures. The owls never called her indecent. The bats and frogs paid her no mind. Certainly Peaches, the lemon beagle who Grandmama said was just Tilly's, didn't wake up from her spot on the bed and scold her for the brazenness of a moon bath. The cool light made it almost possible to feel the activity of her every cell.

Most of the time she felt like she existed along a veneer, on the packaging of a life rather than the actual thing itself. Her school with its just-so uniforms and her curly red hair always pulled in a tight ponytail. Events Tilly was shepherded to with the daughters of her mother's own friends. And the horror of cotillion classes; those even her daddy believed silly. Who thought pairing random sophomores together and making them learn ballroom dance after an hour of formal dining was a good idea? An idiot, that's who.

Five days a week, ten months a year, her world was spun sugar. Fancy and meant to delight, but it dulled her appetite. But here there was rhubarb compote spread thick on dark bread, and Tilly needed a balance of sweet and tart. The complex, dirty delight of these hills and trees, not the brightly colored and packaged-for-your-convenience sweet.

Tilly sank down on the soft cotton quilt. Here—under her hand, this creature's velvet ears and pink tongue, this was the center of the real world. Peaches was the best dog. Affectionate and exuberant, hungry to explore each new day in a way that was the only honest way to be. Days that satisfied her beagle always satisfied Tilly, too. They were one heart—girl and dog on a Middle Tennessee farm at the end of a summer day almost too hot to enjoy but for the relief of wading for crawdads in the creek. Moonlight filled the room up for dreaming and Tilly crawled into her narrow bed. She tucked her feet under the beagle's soft belly and fell asleep smiling. This summer was going to be magical and not a right person, place, or circle to be found. Everything the other ten months of the year was not.

~

From the rise of the back porch Tilly could see a dog-shaped speck trotting out beyond the near field to the tree line. She'd lingered over breakfast with Grandmama and had insisted on washing all the dishes and wiping them dry rather than leaving them on the drain board. If her last week on the farm didn't start, then it couldn't end, could it? It seemed fitting that the early August skies threatened storms just as she herself was brewing with unsettled energy.

"Peaches!" Tilly called out over the sheep when she was done, but the beagle didn't come running. The grass was unmown except by the cropping of the flock beyond the yard. Grandmama let the rambles ramble except for a patch close to the house, a mote of green, clipped neatly for company. Thinking the dog was obscured by grasses, Tilly picked her way down the slope and up again, leaf hoppers arcing across her path like dancers before a queen. She looked and looked and finally, as she came closer to the creek, she saw a beagle shaped sprawl under a huge tulip poplar just ahead. A sharp metallic scent on the morning breeze caused her nose to wrinkle. The hound's sides were heaving, her tongue wide and flat as it lolled, an external expression of her heartbeat with each pant.

"Hey, sweet girl! Whatcha doing way out here?"

Peaches confined her tongue behind her teeth and lengthened her neck, ears alert. Tilly was close enough now to see what kept the dog's attention. A soft, gray body lay still, the hound's paw across its neck. The dog released her tongue again to pant but watched Tilly approach with her head turned slightly away. Suddenly Tilly was struck that this was not her lemon beagle. No, the markings weren't quite right. And this hound held itself differently. The dog looked wary, as if concerned what Tilly would do next.

A distant whistle came from across the creek. The dog in front of her whined but didn't rise. They stared at each other, and Tilly wondered if the dog was as confused by her as she was by it. The same long series of whistled tones came again, closer now.

"Jack! Come here... Come on now... Jack!" a boy was calling.

"Are you Jack?" Tilly asked the dog and was answered by a cocking of the beagle's ears to one side. "He's here!" she called out toward the bank and soon a face appeared among the leaves. "I don't think he'll come, he's protecting his kill from me," she said.

"His kill?"

"A rabbit—I think. It's too big to be a squirrel."

She could see all of the boy now as he sat down on the far bank and took off his shoes. He looked young, but he was probably about her own age. He had that long look about him that most boys in her class did. This boy hardly needed to roll up his jeans to cross the creek. They didn't look uncomfortable, but he'd clearly grown up not out since he'd gotten them. His longish brown hair was covered in a worn ball cap, and his tan skin was the coppery warmth of a summer spent outside. She had the fleeting thought that this boy's mother probably never badgered him into reapplying sunscreen at the pool. Actually, this boy didn't look like any of the boys at her parents' club or her cotillion class. He looked unburdened by that world. He flashed a white smile at her as he climbed through the brush and up the near bank.

"Got you a rabbit? Good boy!" he said as he knocked the leaves off his hat and pulled it back on low over his forehead. The dog nudged at the gray body with his nose and smiled up at the boy. "I'm Clint, who're you?"

Of course you are, she thought. A perfect name for him. She loved alignments like that. His name wreathed his body like salty butter on sweet corn. But she couldn't voice that thought out loud, not in company. She answered, "Tilly Alden."

"Oh! You're Mare Alden's little one?"

She scrunched up her nose a little. "I guess so? She's my grandmother."

"Huh. I ain't never seen you around before. You new?"

"No." It came out more indignant than she intended. "I've been here all summer."

He snorted a little. "That's new." But the smile he gave her was disarming. "What are you doing way out here? There's a storm coming you know. And you don't look like the kind of girl who hunts rabbits."

"What does that mean?"

"Hey, no offense, it's just, those shoes just look awfully fancy for crossing creeks."

Tilly looked down at her sparkly blue Kate Spade Keds. They were her mother's concession to Tilly wanting casual clothes for this summer outside town. Her mother would think she'd ruined them; she'd replaced the ribbon laces with plain white shoelaces as soon as she'd gotten here. The glitter was nearly worn away on the inner right heel where she always scraped her foot climbing the big sycamore. Still, compared to the ratty sneakers that hung from Clint's hand they looked—resplendent.

"Yeah, well..." No words came to mind as he looked at her curiously. She kicked at a mound of dirt and stepped quickly away when red ants erupted from the remains of their neat home. "I hunt," she blurted. "Have you seen another lemon beagle around? I thought Jack was Peaches when I came down the hill."

"Nope, but I'll help you hunt." He winked, and she knew he didn't believe she'd ever hunted a day in her life. "I bet Jack can find her. They're littermates you know. They like to visit." Clint picked up a stout fallen stick and Jack sounded no complaint when the boy affixed the rabbit to it so easily that Tilly could tell that he'd done the same thing a million times. Tilly knew Peaches had come from a neighbor's litter, but she hadn't seen any other dogs around all summer other than Grandmama's Aussies. They were happy in their work and rarely left the flock.

"I've already looked all her usual places."

"Did you check the down by the quarry?" The boy was stuffing sock feet back into his shoes. "Jack heads that way sometimes cause there's a deer trail that goes down to the pool. He thinks he's a might hunter, ya see."

"The quarry? Is it close?" She looked at the darkening sky to the west as the breeze picked up.

"Not too far. Come on, we'll show you."

How had she never been here before? She marveled as she followed the boy and his dog down an overgrown deer path which opened up to reveal a deep gash in the terrain. They'd been walking a good while and the smell of rain was potent. She was beginning to change her mind about following the boy and his dog so easily when suddenly they were there. Kudzu and Virginia Creeper cascaded down from the rim, and trees framed the entire thing with a green fringe that gave a lush privacy to the hollow. It was amazing. But there was no sign of Peaches.

"I don't see her."

"Oh, this isn't really it yet." Clint looked back over his shoulder at her and waved her on.

They descended to the quarry floor and followed Jack up to an enormous, stacked stone column, a remnant of abandoned industry. As she came around the column a cool breeze sent a shiver over her skin. It had to be twenty degrees cooler here than at the top. She wished she'd known about this place during that awful stretch of heat in mid-July, but she had a few days yet to explore. A delightful trickling sound added to the refreshment of the air, and Tilly stopped to touch the cool water that sprang from the earth. It widened quickly, becoming a narrow stream that led them, as if they were welcome guests, from the rocky edifice to a deep pool hidden from the world.

"Is that your girl?" Clint motioned to the form curled up under a lone tree on the far side of the pool.

"Peaches?" she called. The dog rose and sprinted around the pool on a narrow, nearly invisible ledge. She bounded up and jumped, leaving muddy paw prints on Tilly's rosy capris, and now everything she'd brought from home was marked by the season. Her mother would insist she throw it all out, expensive garments ruined by Tilly's carelessness and her filthy animal.

"How did you get all the way down here?" she asked. The dog pushed against her hand until Tilly knelt on the ground and gave the full ear and neck scratches that the nuzzling signaled. "My sweet girl..." she murmured into the beagle's soft fur.

"I knew we'd find her," Clint said. He'd picked up a handful of rocks and was skipping them across the water's surface. Peaches gave her a lick and took off after Jack, both noses to the ground at the edge of the pool. She watched the matched hounds tracking who knows what until she heard a thump that wasn't another rock in the water.

"Since we're here, I'm going in," Clint said, dropping his second shoe and tossing his hat down after it.

Tilly stared frozen in place as the boy stripped off his t-shirt and jeans. Finally, her brain flashed a warning that she was far from the farmhouse with a boy she hardly knew and she didn't have her phone. She didn't get the sense he meant her harm. He'd been helpful, he was a neighbor, and his dog was Peaches brother—they were practically related.

"Don't you swim?" he asked, hopping on one foot to shuck off one sock and then the other.

"Um...yeah?" But she couldn't do that, could she? Suddenly the cool, sheltered paradise felt like a million degrees, and she wanted nothing more than to follow the boy into the pool. "But the storm..." She looked up, to give herself a moment to think as much as anything, and saw only blue, not a cloud in sight.

"What storm?" he said, ending her examination of the sky. He stood for a moment with his fists at the wide elastic band of his navy underwear, the son of a pirate. His body was thin, with ropy muscles that pulled under skin that was tanned above his boxers and pale below. Clint gave her a smile like summer lightning as he turned away. "Well, come on then."

A laugh escaped her. Her mother would not approve. Heck, Grandmama wouldn't either.

She sat on a flat stone and untied her sneakers.

~

Clint wasn't paying attention to her as she attempted to unzip and unbutton as if she did this type of thing all the time. At least, she didn't think he was. As soon as he dove in, the boy swam to the far side of the pool. Now he floated, long limbs outstretched, a star boy in a wide darkness lit by the sun. She hesitated with the last button, but he remained still. The boys at cotillion were always peering surreptitiously at the flesh of girls revealed by their party dresses. At school looks were different but omnipresent. Tilly was rarely noticed in either situation. Still, she could usually feel the graze of their regard.

This strange boy seemed to have forgotten she existed. Even the dogs had finished their exploration and retreated to settle against each other in a patch of grass. The breeze had stopped, and the sun was directly overhead. She'd feel the sun's attention tomorrow for certain. She should call for Peaches and come back tomorrow with a towel and the right SPF.

She dropped her clothes and tip-toed to the edge.

The water was pleasantly warm against her calves as she slipped a foot through the mirrored surface. She could do this. She pulled in her stomach and raised her arms over her head. She rose up on her toes and tipped, as elegantly as she could manage. Then, when it was too late to change her mind, the pool revealed a chilly heart that took her breath. She shot up to the surface, spluttering.

"Just lay back and float."

Tilly's heart raced to hear Clint suddenly close by. How had he swum over without her hearing?

"Really. The sun only warms the top bit. It's like whipped cream on banana pudding, you know? I mean, it's all good, but that top layer, mostly cream with a hint of banana? That's the best."

She pulled her legs up to her chest. That was better.

"Not a fan," she said. His body was churning up colder currents as he treaded water next to her.

"Seriously? Everyone likes banana pudding." His foot brushed her knee as he folded his legs and then stretched back out on the surface. "Just lay back."

She leaned back and let herself go until she reached an equilibrium of sun warmed thighs and hair drifting sleek around her ears. She felt like Ophelia in that painting in Grandmama's library, except Tilly was very much alive.

"I don't. But you're right, this is perfect."

"Of course, I am." He flicked water at her face. "What kind of fancy shit do you like then? Strawberries and caviar?"

"God, no," she giggled. "That would be nasty. Strawberries and cream are good, but I like peaches best."

"I should have guessed that." He paddled his hands and glided closer. "Who names a dog after fruit?"

"It's a great name. Who names a dog Jack?" She paddled away.

"You're right. It's odd, but he looked like a Jack to me."

"Well, she makes me think of being here and peaches are perfect, so she looked like a Peaches to me."

He dropped his legs and looked at her then. She felt his attention and lowered her legs, too. This close, and without his ball cap hiding them, she could tell his eyes weren't brown but a deep green. She felt the path of his eyes from her face to the drops of water running off her hair onto her shoulders.

"You don't look like a Tilly to me."

Her breath caught.

"You look more like… I don't know. Something more," he said.

Now her heart was racing. She never told anyone her real name. Her mother had insisted on the nickname after conceding to Grandmama's wishes to give her the family name.

"Tilly is what everyone calls me. I'm not telling you my real name—it's too awful."

"Okay. Come on, not-really-Tilly," he said, and started swimming away. "You're gonna love this. It's like you and your little hound were meant to be here."

Tilly followed Clint across the pool and, as they came closer to the far side, saw the stones were cut away in semi-regular chunks rising out of the pool like steps. And the ledge was more than the narrow strip she'd thought; it was a mossy beach.

"We can lay out here and follow the ledge back to our clothes once we're dry." He navigated the quarried treads out of the pool with practiced ease. The water sheeting down his body narrowed into mesmerizing rivulets as it poured from his hair and the hem of his boxers.

"This is unreal," she muttered and forced herself to look away at her own hands, pushing the water away in little circles as she held herself in place. It was ridiculous to be here, but here was the only place she wanted to be. Tilly swam to the ledge and sat on a submerged tread with only her shoulders exposed. "You must come here all the time."

"I do." He had moved farther away and was reaching up into the leafy branches of the tree. He jumped, and the branches shook with his attack. "Got 'em!" He turned with a wide grin and Tilly saw a small yellow fruit in each of his tanned hands. "The last good ones of the year."

"What are they?"

The boy made his way back to the lip of the pool and shook his hands off after dunking the fruit in the water. "Not really sure, but they taste like peaches."

He must have seen her skeptical expression, because he laughed a little. "They're not gonna hurt you, I promise. I eat them all the time when they're ripe."

Clint set the fruits on a smooth stone, where they looked

like the perfect centerpiece on a table set for some nature goddess or fairy queen.

"But they don't keep. I've tried bringing a few home to save for later, but they only taste right fresh off the tree." Clint sat on the far side of the little table and stretched his legs out in the sun. He leaned back on his elbows and closed his eyes, face glowing in the sunlight.

"Mmmm. We'll let the sun warm them on the stone a little and then feast," he said and laid flat, putting an arm across his eyes. It was like he knew she was reluctant to come up out of the darkness of the pool. Watching his arm for movement, she scaled the slippery rocks. The grass on this side was soft and grew through a springy mat of mosses that were delicious underfoot. The shade from the tree would be just enough for her to dry and not burn. It really was perfect.

"I know, right?" he said with another charming smile. She must have sighed out loud.

As they lay near each other with eyes closed, Clint told her ridiculous things he'd done with Jack and got her to tell stories of the dumb things she'd done back home. They ate the fruit, and it was the most luscious thing she'd ever put in her mouth. He was so easy to talk to. He asked interesting questions and laughed in all the right places. Each time she looked over at him he was smiling, but his eyes were closed. Soon the sun was no longer directly overhead, and the treetops that fringed the quarry cast shadows across half the pool. They'd fallen into a long, comfortable silence, and Tilly was sure Clint had fallen asleep when he spoke.

"You said you'd stay here if you could. Do you really want to?"

"Who would ever want to leave? I suppose we have to go home eventually since we ate the last fruit, though." She tossed the blade of grass she'd been twirling at him.

As she reached to pick more, he laid a hand on her wrist, stopping her. His fingers were gentle, but the touch scorched. She pulled away and tried to hide the embarrassed flush she could feel spreading across her face and chest by scanning the rim of the quarry.

"But...we probably should go. I mean, it's getting late." It was only now occurring to her that this wasn't a dream, and someone really could catch them lying in their underwear in the moss. "Everyone has to go home, right?"

"I know a way you could come back any time you needed to, but you'd have to really want it. And you'd have to trust me enough to tell me your real name." He reached out and ran a finger along her jaw, pulling her gaze back to him.

A shiver traveled along her spine, and she leaned in before her brain caught up and she pulled back. "I...um. What do you mean?" The question slipped from her lips as a whisper even as her brain was a frozen mess. "We've just met..."

"No. Not that." He dropped his hand and pushed his hair out of his eyes. "Jeez, what do you take me for? I'm no pirate. It's just... You said you hate all the things you have to do back in your world, and I know how you can get back to see Peaches, whenever you want."

"That would be—wonderful, but I don't have a car or anything. I'll be back next June..."

"Right, of course," he said, and looked away.

If she could choose, she would stay, roaming these hills

with Peaches and now maybe Jack and Clint, too. "I would, you know. But my mother would never let me."

"She doesn't need to know," he said, and sat up cross legged and facing her fully. She scrambled to do the same. "Look, Tilly, I'm serious." There was a firm set to his mouth so different from his easy smile. "I like you. You're funny and smart and we share a love for proper dogs. Won't you tell me your real name?"

"Why do you need to know? It's so ugly. I'm probably going to change it officially when I'm old enough."

"Do you have a heart name, then? There are ways to use hidden names, but the art lies easiest if we use the name given at birth."

A very unladylike sound erupted from her. "The art?"

He smiled with a patience of years in his green eyes that didn't match his face.

"Yes, a charm really. A trifle." He reached behind his back and then held out a third golden fruit, but this one was swollen and ruddy about the stem dimple.

"What the hell?" She stared at it in his hand, trying to make sense of what had just happened.

"It's more like heaven than that, I promise—see?" He took a bite, and as soon as his teeth broke the skin the aroma filled her head and her mouth watered. "Take it."

She did.

Tilly traced the monogram on her floral duffel bag as she rode in the backseat of her father's king cab. That the letters spelt OAK was the only thing she'd ever liked about it, until now. Now her name was a safety hatch. Her mother was still talking about all the things she'd missed and all the other things she'd been signed up for when school started back on Monday. Apparently, her junior year was going to include an impressive layer of civic-minded volunteer work to add even more luster to her bespoke education.

"Ottoline Kenner Alden! Are you listening?" Her mother looked at her in the rearview mirror. "Get that trash out of my sight."

"Yes, ma'am. But it's not trash, it's art." Tilly pressed the carved pit to her lips and then let it fall down her shirt on its silver chain.

"Honestly! Why your mother let her buy such a thing I'll never understand. It's gross." And her mother went on while her father kept his stony eyes on the traffic heading back into town.

He'd taught her how to form each strange word as he carved her initials into the woody heart of the fruit. She'd practiced stringing together each syllable and inflection there on the ledge above their pool with more concentration than she'd given any French lesson. Tilly pressed the pit against her sternum. She knew his true name and he knew hers, and with the promise of the charm she would slip back to the mossy paradise for a few hours with the new moon, when only the stars would see. She could be her whole self under the sky, arms wide, so she could make the artificially flavored weeks ahead of her bearable. She'd never wished the moon away before, but now the dark couldn't come fast enough.

THE VOICE

LEAH PUGH

"Hey, Shrieker! What are you going to do for the talent show?"

A cold shiver raced down my spine as I forced my voice to remain calm while removing the last two books from my locker.

"My name's Olivia. And I don't know, something. Why do you care, Camilla?" I smelled the onions she'd had on her burger from lunch and felt the warmth and moisture from her breath on the back of my neck as she stood behind me. *Elch! I hope she hasn't burned a hole in my spine.*

"Oh, please, sing for us!" Camilla's soprano voice was filled with mock earnestness. "We all enjoyed it last time. At least, what we could hear over everyone laughing." She threw her head back and laughed.

My face burned as I remembered how I'd tried to sing "You Raise Me Up" at the last talent show. My voice kept cracking, and after just one minute of singing, the entire auditorium roared with laughter as I fled from the room. Luckily, only one of my parents witnessed my humiliation as the other was home with a sick child. However, Camilla wasn't about to let me forget that awful day. She dubbed me "Shrieker" and taunted me practically every day.

"Hey, excuse me for interrupting this endearing conversation." Sassi, fellow geography classmate and next-door-locker neighbor, stood next to me. "Camilla, you *do* know singing isn't the only talent exhibited at the talent show, right?"

Camilla stared at the small girl in disgust. "I have absolutely no idea what just came out of your mouth."

"Maybe if you didn't sleep through English class so much, you might learn a few new words," Sassi shot back.

Camilla's makeup-caked face turned a bright shade of pink at getting called out. "Well..." she stammered, "if Olivia showed some real talent, she wouldn't have been the laughing stock of last year's contest, now would she?"

The nerve of her! I slammed my locker door shut, threw my backpack over my shoulder, and turned to leave.

She blocked me, holding up a certificate encased in a picture frame. "Check this out! I won first place in Dallas's Next Top Singer juvenile competition this past weekend." She pushed it in my face.

"How immature can you get? You're fourteen and waving that thing like a five-year-old!" I shouldered my way past Miss Perfect and ran down the hall to the double doors leading outside.

Why'd God give Camilla the most beautiful voice in the world, and I got a voice that sounds like nails on a chalkboard? It's not fair!

I stood at the base of the steps, waiting for my bus to take me out of this miserable place.

"Olivia, wait up!"

Looking over my shoulder, I spotted Sassi hurrying toward me. She halted abruptly next to me, trying to catch her breath.

"Next time…wait the first time I call you!" she panted. "Some of us have dwarfism and aren't lucky enough to have your long legs."

"Sorry, I didn't hear you call me the first time," I mumbled.

"I wish my talent could be entered into the show." Sassi adjusted her black, lopsided ponytail.

"And what talent is that?"

"Keeping my mouth shut and not saying what was *truly* on my mind just now."

I chuckled. Sassi was known throughout the entire ninth grade for her brutal honesty. She'd been working on curbing her tongue for the past few months, but she wasn't always successful. Luckily, today was a better day for her.

"What happened to you two?" Sassi looked up at me. "You guys used to be good friends."

"*Good* is too liberal a word. Just friends." I stared at the line of buses waiting to take school kids home.

"Well?"

I sighed. "I don't know, Sass. She got better at singing and, for some reason, out of all her friends, decided to rub it in my face. I know her behavior after last year's talent show didn't help things any. I don't need those kinds of people in my life, and I stopped hanging out with her."

"But she still torments you," Sassi said. "So, I guess keeping your distance isn't working."

"Some days yes, some days no."

"Well, at least I won't have to suffer through listening to her caterwauling next week. My parents chose that day to visit my grandpa after school. So, my ears will be spared. Here's my bus. See you later."

She'd barely gotten into her seat when the window was down and she was shouting something at me. "I think you should enter the talent show, Olivia! Find something you're good at and go with it! Bye!"

"Maybe..." I spotted Camilla getting into her mom's fancy convertible, singing some stupid pop song.

We made eye contact, and she once again held that stupid award up before her mom drove off. My temper simmered, and I almost shoved my way to the front of the line to get on the bus. I fumed the entire ride home and didn't feel any better when I arrived at my front door.

Great! Mom's car is in the driveway. Which means she's not out shopping and is going to ask why my face is longer than a crocodile's nose...

A creaking sound interrupted my train of thought. I went around to the back. Stella, my ten-year-old sister, sat on one of the swings, her shoulders drooping. I walked across the crabgrass to her. She didn't look up as I sat in the swing beside her. I gently touched her shoulder, and she jumped. When she saw it was me, she smiled sadly.

"Hi," she signed.

I didn't miss the tear stains on her face, nor her red puffy eyes. "Hi. What's wrong?" I signed back.

She sniffled and looked down at the ground as she signed, "Russell made fun of me again today, all because he can hear a little and even speak. I can't do either."

My temper shot up as big-sister-protective mode kicked in. I put my arm around her shoulders and pulled her as close as the swing's chains allowed me. She snuggled against me as I stroked her mahogany brown hair before tapping her arm to get her attention.

"Why can't you just tell the teacher?" I signed.

"I have, and she's told him to stop. He still makes fun of me behind her back." Tears filled her dark blue eyes. "Why was I born deaf? You're lucky you have a voice."

"You have a voice, too. It's just that not everyone can hear it like Mom, Dad, and I can."

"Huh?" She frowned in confusion. "I can't speak at all." She opened her mouth, and a grunt came out.

Sadness tugged at my heart; it was all I could do to keep my tears at bay. I took her small hands in my slender ones.

"The voice isn't the only tool a person can use to express their thoughts and feelings." I tickled her fingers. "Some people use their hands, facial expressions, or even body language as a way of speaking."

She cocked her head like a curious sparrow and stared straight up at me. "How does using these," she wiggled her fingers, "give me a voice? Or even my facial expressions?"

"Because with your hands and facial expressions, you're able to tell people what you think and feel. Like yesterday when you burned yourself. That little dance you did while waving your hand around in the air told Mom something was wrong. And whenever you want the rest of Dad's eggs, you sit next to him and look from his food to his face until he gives you the eggs."

Those blue eyes turned a shade darker, telling me that Stella was pondering what I'd just said.

"So, you're saying I do have a voice..." She paused her signing. "Just not everyone can hear it?"

"Exactly." I nuzzled her nose. "And it's a very beautiful voice."

"Olivia," Mom called my name.

I looked up to see her standing in the doorway. I tapped Stella's shoulder and signed, "Hey, look, there's Mom. I wonder what she wants."

"I made snickerdoodles," Mom signed.

Stella was out of the swing before Mom had even finished signing *snicker.* "Hooray!" she signed in delight.

I laughed and shook my head. "Just try to save some cookies for Dad."

Instead of tearing for the kitchen like I thought she would, Stella gave me a great big hug. "Thanks for telling me that I have a beautiful voice. I want you to know I think your voice is beautiful, too!" She gave me another hug before scampering off to the kitchen.

Those kind words should've made me smile, but I could see Camilla's spiteful face leering at me and hear her yelling, "Shrieker!" thus souring my sister's otherwise nice comment.

Well, we'll see who the 'Shrieker' is, now won't we? Grabbing my backpack, I raced to my room and closed the door.

Dropping to my knees, I pulled some karaoke CDs out

from underneath my bed. I had just a week to practice for the talent show, and maybe with a little luck I could perfect my voice and redeem myself!

"Why am I so nervous?" I rubbed sweaty palms down my pant leg. "It's not like I'm going to perform for live TV or anything." I hit the record button, then the play button, took several deep breaths, and started singing.

Fifteen minutes later, after doing at least three recordings of "Real Gone", I felt pretty proud of myself.

I actually sound good! I eagerly pressed the play button.

What I heard sounded like someone singing with a tin bucket over their head because their nose was congested.

"This can't be me!" I skipped to the next recording.

It sounded the same, and the third one was worse because I tried to sing with a country accent. Hot tears stung my eyes as I deleted all three recordings, turned my boombox off, and shoved my CDs back underneath the bed.

"No more!" I wiped away the tears. "I'm not going to sing ever again!"

"Hey, Shrieker, are you looking forward to tomorrow?" Camilla sneered.

It'd been a week since my horrible attempt at singing, and I hadn't tried since then. I was not in a good mood and felt like punching Camilla right in the face.

But instead, I sighed, "Leave me alone."

"You know, even though you only have twenty-four hours to get ready, I can give you lessons."

I shot her the most ferocious frown I could muster, but that didn't faze her. Instead, it made her laugh.

"Face it, Olivia. You'll never be good at singing, and you know it! It's a talent that one has to be born with." She tossed her thick, red hair over her shoulder. "Fortunately, I was lucky enough to be born with it!"

"Unfortunately, it seems to be the only thing you were born with," Sassi piped up.

I hadn't even realized she was at her locker until she said something.

"What's that supposed to mean?" Camilla cried.

"Leave Olivia alone, Camilla. She's not bothering anyone. Especially you. For that matter, *why* do you insist on tormenting her?"

"I'm not tormenting her, only offering to help her with her singing."

"You didn't answer the question, but who cares. Remember what I said the other day? Singing *isn't* the only talent in the world."

"But it gets peoples' attention." Grinning smugly, Camilla whirled around and sashayed down the hall, singing "May It Be". Students and even a few teachers stopped whatever they were doing to listen to her with looks of obvious adoration on their faces.

White-hot jealousy surged through me. I was in such a horrible mood that I sat by myself at the back of the bus so I could let my anger and hurt fester without any interruptions. Tears threatened to run down my face, and I kept my head bowed so no one would see.

The ten-minute ride home felt like it lasted for millions

of years, and I was never so glad to see our front door as I was now. I rushed inside and went straight to my room. Without bothering to take my shoes and jacket off, I fell lengthwise on my bed and cried a river.

I don't know how long I lay there crying before I felt something tap my arm. Thinking I was imagining things, I ignored it. But the tapping persisted.

"What?" I yelled, jerking my head up.

Stella stood in front of me. A plate of snickerdoodles and a glass of milk sat on a tray she held tightly in her hands. Concern was etched into her face, and I knew without her asking that she wanted to know what was wrong. She set the tray on my nightstand, sat beside me on the bed, and wrapped her chubby arms around my shoulders. She hugged me for about a minute before letting go.

"You held me when I was crying, now it's my turn," she signed.

Fresh tears filled my eyes and spilled down my cheeks, plopping onto my lap. She pulled a wrinkled tissue from her pocket and wiped the remaining tears off my cheeks.

"Thanks," I signed.

"You're welcome. Want to talk about it?" She tossed the tissue in the wastebasket.

I don't know why, but I found myself telling her about how I'd embarrassed myself at last year's school talent show, how Camilla was continually making fun of me, and how I wasn't going to tomorrow's talent show.

"This was the show I missed because I was sick, right?" she signed.

"Yep." *Believe me, you didn't miss a thing!*

"What would you do at tomorrow's talent show?"

"I want to sing, only I can't. I'm horrible."

"What do you mean? I like it when you sing. It's pretty."

I held back a snort. *Yeah right!* For once, I was glad she was deaf. She wouldn't have to bear the humiliation of knowing that her older sister couldn't carry a tune in a bucket!

"Would you sing something for me now?" She put on puppy eyes.

I sighed. "Oh, all right."

She chose the song "You Raise Me Up".

Oh great! The song that started this whole mess with Camilla.

However, I couldn't say no to "singing" her favorite song. The instant I started signing, all of my anger, hurt, and frustration melted away, and peace wrapped around me like a warm blanket. I forgot everything else, and at the end of the song, Stella stood up and waved her hands excitedly, the deaf way of cheering.

"I told you that you have a beautiful voice," she signed.

"Huh?" I frowned, confused.

She took my fingers and wiggled them. "A voice isn't the only tool a person uses to speak."

I stared from my fingers to my sister and back again as realization dawned on me. My brain replayed the part on the bus where I was complaining about Camilla. And then fast forwarded to something Stella had said that same day.

"Why'd God give Camilla the most beautiful voice in the world, and I got the raw end of the deal?"

"So, God really did give me a voice...just not everyone can hear it?"

I have a voice, just not everyone can hear it, I thought.

And finally, Sassi invaded my thoughts: *"Singing isn't the only talent exhibited at the talent show."*

"And next up, we have Olivia Grant." Mr. Jopin's voice caused beads of sweat to break out on my forehead.

Why does our principal have to have such a booming voice? "Take it easy, girl. You can do this," I whispered to myself.

But *could* I beat Camilla? I mean, after all, she'd just dazzled the entire room with "Someday".

"I'll be posting this on Youtube," Camilla hissed as I walked past her. "It'll have one million hits by nightfall!"

I didn't even look her way as I walked onto the stage and up to the microphone. Taking a deep breath, I looked down at the principal and assistant principal sitting in the front row. The cage holding the butterflies in my stomach burst open, and I almost hyperventilated from the nerves. I scanned the audience until I saw my family in the second row, middle seats. My parents gave me little waves while Stella gave me a big smile and thumbs up.

"You'll do great!" she signed eagerly.

Her little antics made me smile and helped me calm down so I could focus once more.

"What are you going to be doing, Olivia?" Ms. Angie, the assistant principal, asked.

"I'm going to be doing 'You Are Loved' in American Sign Language," I signed, watching for my younger sister's reaction.

She had no idea I was doing this. All she knew was that her older sister had entered a talent competition, and she was coming to support said sister. When she realized I was signing her second favorite song, her jaw fell open in surprise. Mom had to reach over and close it for her.

I nodded to the guy in the sound booth just as panic grabbed a hold of me. Fear of a repeat from the last talent show began to play with my mind, making my throat dry. I started to tremble, but at that moment Stella and I made eye contact. She gave me a huge smile.

That broke the spell, and taking a deep breath, my fingers began to move. A little shaky at first, but the longer I went, the more fluent my motions became. I was no longer competing against Camilla, nor was I trying to prove myself. I was signing for my sister and her alone.

The song ended all too soon, and I remembered to bow. As the last note died away, a silence settled in the auditorium, and panic once again gripped me. I heard a snort from stage right and instantly knew it came from Camilla. I became aware of a rushed 'tapping' sound a split second before something, or rather someone, almost bowled me over.

"Oomph!" I grunted.

Stella had gotten out of her seat and rushed me on stage. In a good way. She squeezed my waist until I could barely breathe. She looked up at me, her eyes shining brighter than a pair of sapphires, and she wore an ear-to-ear smile. She gave one last extra tight squeeze before letting go.

"Thank you!" she signed. "Thank you, Olivia!"

All of a sudden, the audience began clapping, and I

noticed for the first time that Ms. Angie had tears running down her face.

"That was beautiful, Olivia." Her voice was choked up.

"I liked it," Mr. Jopin said. "Where did you learn to sign so fluently?"

"And what made you choose *signing*? A good portion of the other girls were *singing*," Ms. Angie added.

"Well, I have a sister who was born deaf." I smiled at Stella, still standing beside me. "And she taught me that there's more than one way to sing."

THE WIND RIDERS

JOHN BEECHAM

"Get to work, kid. You'll be in the sky soon enough."

"You really think so?" Petyr asked, his eyes lit by a smile.

"Only if I'm lucky," Griff grunted. He shuffled away as Petyr pushed a clump of down feathers into a small pile.

Petyr's Rites of Initiation were only a few days away. If he succeeded, he would become a Wind Rider, and spend his days soaring above the Urth. He would fight enemies of the fae, hunt for food, and search the realm for treasure and adventure. But if he failed, the village would not accept him as a Wind Rider, and his elders would find another role for him to fill. Something more mundane. One that might involve a broom, pick or shovel instead of a sword and shield.

That won't happen, Petyr told himself. *I'll earn my feathers one way or another*. He'd been preparing for his rites ever since he was a little boy. Petyr knew the names of every bird that lived near his village, knew how they flew, the kinds of food they liked, where they put their nests, and when they were active. He knew what their eggs looked like. Even the names of all the great Riders were etched into his mind, since he'd begged the Story Master to tell him their legends over and over.

What still formed a doubt inside his mind was that for all his knowledge, if he wasn't fast enough, clever enough, and *tough* enough to show at least one bird that he was worthy, he'd have his feet stuck to the ground until the end of his days. It was enough to make him feel sick.

"Hey, feather-head," a voice spoke, interrupting Petyr's thoughts. "This is for your boss."

Petyr looked up to see a girl about his age holding a scroll out to him. It was a piece of parchment, rolled and sealed with a red wax stamp.

"My name's *Petyr*," he told her, taking the scroll in his hand. He leaned his broom against one of the thick wooden posts. "I'm going to be a Wind Rider soon, so you ought to speak to me with some respect."

The girl picked out a fluffy down-feather that had gotten caught in Petyr's scruffy brown mane. She had blonde, braided hair and green eyes that sparkled with mischief. Her face was as round and pink as a peach. "I'm paid to be efficient, not courteous." She blew the small white feather from the palm of her hand and it landed on the tip of Petyr's nose. "And I have other deliveries to make." With these words, she turned on her heel and walked away from him, a canvas messenger bag swaying from her shoulder as she did.

"Wait! What's your name?" Petyr asked as she left.

"Bianca," she spoke as she turned her back to him and kept walking. "Now be a good feather-head and get back to your chores, Petyr. And don't forget to give that scroll to your master!"

Petyr watched for a few moments as she went on her way, following the ruts of the mouse-carts along the village's main road. *What a strange girl,* Petyr thought as he ran a finger along the scroll. He examined the red seal holding it closed, and saw a capital letter A for Aderyn, the name of his village. *It's from the elders,* Petyr realized. *It must be about the Rites of Initiation.*

He knew Griff would scold him if he gave him an unsealed scroll, so he walked over to where his master was standing, making marks with a quill on a parchment he held. "Excuse me, Griff," Petyr said, "but this came for you."

"Yes? What is it?" Griff peered over half-moon spectacles, put down his parchment, and snatched the scroll from Petyr's hand. He broke the seal with a flick of his thumbnail and flattened the scroll as he read.

"What does it say?" Petyr asked, his curiosity piqued by Griff's knitted brow, white beard twitching as he mouthed the words on the scroll.

"Village business," Griff growled, tucking the scroll into a pocket inside his shirt. "Preparations for tomorrow. Nothing you need to concern yourself with. Now get back to work."

Petyr nodded and finished sweeping all the feathers and fluff that fell to the ground. He carried them over to the hearth that led to a chimney rising out of the center of the aviary and put them in the fire to be burned. It made an awful stink, but it was the easiest way for them to rid themselves of this kind of waste. Then he had to clean up the bird droppings, an even messier job. It was placed into barrels for the farmers outside the village to use for their crops. As disgusting as this job could be, Petyr was so used to it it no longer bothered him. *Better to have a full belly than let all that treasure go to waste,* was how Griff put it to him, and he often heard the stable master's voice in his mind as he completed this task. It seemed strange to Petyr that the plants ate bird droppings for food, but also quite interesting. He loved to learn new facts like this. Sometimes, they came to him quite by surprise. These facts were much easier for him to remember than where he had put his hat, for example.

The rest of the day passed slowly. Petyr's mind was full of thoughts about his Rites of Initiation, and he had a strange feeling in his belly. It was hard to figure out if it was a good feeling or a bad feeling. Finally, he decided it was a bit of both. He was nervous and excited at the same time. Petyr still felt this way when he got home and climbed the rope ladder up into his family's space in the maple tree.

Petyr's family shared this tree with a few other fae families, not to mention all the birds, squirrels and other animals that lived in it. Parts of the tree had been hollowed out to make room for them, but it didn't mind. Its spirit had spoken to one of the village priests many generations ago and had given the fae permission. Most fae lived in trees like this, or in other plants instead. Inside, it was very dark, but fae are able to see even where there isn't any light. In darkness, people, animals and other things all give off a very dim glow, at least to the eyes of the fae. Fae were very comfortable living in trees, especially Petyr's family. They loved their maple tree very much.

"Hello, I'm home," Petyr called out.

"Petyr's home!" a tiny voice returned. It was June—his little sister. Right now she was scribbling on parchment with a piece of coal.

"Does that mean we can eat?" she asked, putting down her drawing.

"Yes, June," their dad spoke. "Petyr, come on over and take a seat once you've put away your things." He put out dishes of acorn butter and berries for everyone. There was also a plate of cicada meat on the table for them all to share.

"I'm starved," Petyr said as he scooped up a bit of acorn butter.

"Not until we're all seated, Petyr," Petyr's mom reminded him. "I know you're hungry, but that's no reason to forget your manners." Petyr's dad and June sat down too, and his mom nodded at Petyr, letting him know he could begin.

Once they were all settled in, Petyr's family began speaking around the dinner table. "What kind of bird are you going to chase tomorrow?" June asked.

"You're not supposed to think like that," Petyr explained. "If you get your hopes up for a pigeon, but end up riding a sparrow, you might be disappointed. I'll be happy if I can get any bird at all. Not everyone participating in the Rites will be able to."

"There's plenty of work for everyone in the village," his dad said. "If you find a bird, we'll be very happy for you. If you don't, Mother Gaia will find other work for you to do." Just then, Petyr imagined himself with a lined face and white beard pushing his broom around the aviary. It was not an image he liked.

"Gaia bless us, I just hope that everyone is safe tomorrow. You'll make us very proud, Petyr," his mom told him, "no matter what happens."

"Is Griff ready?" his dad asked.

"Oh yeah," Petyr spoke through a mouthful of acorn butter and then drank some water to speak more clearly. "He's been through the Rites of Initiation so many times, I can't even tell if he gets excited for it anymore."

His mom grinned. "I'm sure he does. He might not show it. But I bet he's almost as excited as you."

Petyr chuckled, then remembered something. "A girl came to the aviary today to deliver a message. It was for Griff, and had the village seal on it. She was a rather rude girl, but she told me she was in a rush and didn't have time to be polite. Her name was..." It took Petyr a moment to remember, "Bianca! That's it. Bianca. She had her hair in a long blonde braid. And she called me 'feather-head'."

June giggled, and that made Petyr laugh too. "I know Bianca," June told him. "My teachers told me Bianca used to get in trouble at school. They use her as an example of how *not* to act."

"Hmm," his dad rumbled. "Well, I'm glad you both know how to behave yourselves. Most of the time." Then he winked at his wife, and they began laughing too.

The family ate the rest of their meal together, and Petyr tried to relax and enjoy himself. He knew that if he got his wings, he might not be able to spend as much time at home as he was used to. When he climbed into bed that night, he still had that nervous feeling in his stomach. So he said a short prayer to Gaia, and that helped a little. Then he heard an owl hoot from somewhere outside the tree. Petyr sighed and fell asleep.

~

The next morning was cold and rainy. Petyr could hear the raindrops from inside the tree, fat globs of water hitting the leaves and splashing into puddles. He held a warm bowl of oatmeal his mom had made him, seasoned with honey and cinnamon, full of chopped, dried raisins and little bits of acorn to give him energy. Steam rose in lazy curls. Petyr grasped it and breathed it in as if he could store its warmth inside of him. He ate by himself and focused his mind on the Rites of Initiation, the trial he was finally ready to face now that the sun had dawned on his twelfth year.

As delicious as his breakfast was, he had trouble finishing it. His stomach was tight and tingly. Every swallow made him feel his nerves slightly more. He took some deep, calming breaths, but they were little help. They eased his mind somewhat but couldn't chase the butterflies out of his belly. He knew that he'd be a Wind Rider soon. Or not. And it was the *not* that was bothering him so much. *Gods and Goddesses, let it be so.* His bowl was half-eaten, and he left what remained on the kitchen counter.

Once he'd finished his meal he climbed down the rope ladder, its wet fibers squeezing into his fingerless gloves.

Petyr wore a red cloak over a blue tunic, and both were nearly soaked by the time he reached the ground. *It's no matter. If all goes right, I'll be warm and dry tonight, dancing around a bonfire and singing songs.* He would not let his mind consider any other possibilities as he trudged through the woods.

He soon found a few of the other initiates already at their meeting place, a small round hill in the forest near Aderyn. Petyr recognized them. They were other boys and girls his age, and they had grown up in the village together. Their breath came out in clouds of steam, chilled by the wet morning air. Drops of rain fell from their cloaks and pooled at their feet.

Petyr's eyes met those of another boy, Andrew, and they nodded at each other. Andrew had been one of his best friends at school, but they saw less of each other now that those days were over. He was fidgeting, his fingers twirling the knot of his cloak. Petyr sighed, his anticipation getting the better of him. His cheeks puffed out, and Andrew must have thought this was funny, because he gave Petyr a weak smile. Petyr winked, and for a brief moment a sliver of humor broke through his anxiety. Then Andrew looked away and Petyr did too.

Instead, he rubbed some small wooden beads his mother had given him last year for his birthday. The beads hung off his belt and had runes carved into them. They were meant to calm him, but perhaps the magic in the runes had worn off, because his guts still felt hot and prickly. *It's all right. I need my senses sharp.*

Then the first thin rays of sunlight spread through the

morning fog. As if parting a curtain, the high priest and priestess of Aderyn appeared, each bearing a wooden staff carved to show a bird's talon clutching an apple. Beneath cloaks of gleaming green mallard feathers they wore white robes. Each carried a lit torch hissing steam and smoke in the drizzling rain.

Petyr and the other initiates knelt in the muck on one soggy knee and bowed their heads.

"Greetings to the young and brave," the high priest spoke.

"Rise, initiates," the high priestess called to them.

Their white robes make them look like ghosts in the fog. He heard them begin to chant:

On wind and wing
Ye each may soar
Together sing
On every shore

Above every tree
And mountain tall
Your eyes shall see
And take in all

May beak and blade
Flesh and feather

In sun and shade
Be strong together

Let both your souls
Your minds and deeds
Burn like hot coals
The fire feeds

And when your lives
Have run their course
Return together
To Spirit's Source

When the blessing was finished, the priest and priestess lowered their torches into a silver censer. The censer was a shallow bowl that they used to burn sacred objects. For this ceremony, it contained a lump of coal, twigs for kindling, a small pile of feathers, and a few drops of sweet-smelling oil. This way, the prayers offered in their chant could rise high enough to reach Mother Gaia, and the other Gods, Goddesses, and spirits that the fae held sacred. The smoke smelled strange and gave Petyr the urge to rub his nose, but he resisted.

The rhymes the priest and priestess sang reminded Petyr

how his soul and mind would have to meld with a bird for him to actually bond with it. He'd had bits of practice with the birds of his aviary and those in the forest surrounding his home. "Please raise your wing," and, "Could you leave a few worms in our garden?" Things like that. The feelings they shared were more important than words. But to truly bond with a bird, the bird would need to want to bond with him too. And he'd only have a brief moment to convince them. If the bird rejected him and flew away, it would almost be impossible to find another one before the Rites of Initiation had finished.

But now it was time for him to rise and join the line of other initiates who approached the high priest and high priestess for their final blessing of the ceremony. Each one stood and bowed their heads as the priest and priestess dipped their thumbs into the warm ash. One by one, the initiates received their blessing, the ash rubbed on their forehead in the shape of a feather. Then they stood to the side with their heads bowed until they'd all been smudged between their eyes.

The rain stopped. A strong breeze rushed through the clearing, and the clouds parted, revealing a red and purple sunrise that had finally come. The high priest and high priestess joined their voices and cried, "FLY!"

The initiates scattered into the woods, each running in a different direction. In the weeks leading up to their Rites of Initiation, every one of them had spoken to each other and decided which course to pursue. It would do nobody any good to be stumbling over each other as they searched for a bird to bond with. Instead, they would spread throughout the forest to improve their chances for success. *Gaia, give me wings,* Petyr prayed as he sped north. In a few minutes, his lungs burned and his legs ached, but he would not slow. Not until he reached his destination.

And suddenly, there it was, towering above him: a great, big holly tree. Its pointed leaves drooped to the ground, inviting him up into its branches. Petyr leapt and grabbed onto one of them, pulling it down with his weight. He wriggled himself on top of it and walked toward the trunk as if on a balance beam. Some of the leaves scratched his face, but he ignored them, pushing himself past their needled edges. Finally, he reached its knobby trunk and began to pull himself up. His feet and fingers found holds in each little groove as he pulled himself higher and higher.

As he climbed, Petyr caught a bright streak of red out of the corner of his eye. A cardinal had landed in the holly tree a few branches above him. The bird had not noticed him, so he crept to the other side of the trunk. The challenge was to move slowly enough that the cardinal didn't see him. But if he was *too* slow, the cardinal might fly away before Petyr got his chance. *A male. Females have brown bodies but red crests and tail feathers.* He scanned his eyes for any female cardinals nearby but couldn't find any. *Good.* He kept climbing.

The cardinal minded its own business, eating small seeds from old holly berries still connected to the tree.

Petyr lunged from his perch in the holly tree and wrapped his arms around the cardinal's chest. The cardinal cried, "SKWAAAAAK!" and flew from the branch to escape what he feared was a predator. Petyr reached out to the bird's heart, sending him a feeling through his mind. *Calm. Friend.*

Petyr. This was very hard to do since Petyr was nervous too. He felt the cardinal give a jolt at his words, and then they flapped clumsily all the way down. Twigs and feathers flew everywhere. Petyr didn't let go. He could feel the bird's fear spilling into him, even the rapid beat of his heart as he held onto him.

Once they hit the ground, Petyr finally released him, hoping the bird wouldn't immediately fly away. Instead, the cardinal cocked his head and looked at him with a beady black eye. *Please. Bond. Friend. Petyr.*

For a moment that stretched long and deep, the black eye lingered on him. It felt as if the eye wasn't merely looking at Petyr, but deep *into* Petyr. Part of him wanted to hide from this gaze, but he knew he mustn't. Instead, he stared back, both of his eyes looking back into the cardinal's right one.

Then the bird scuttled around to the other side, and Petyr feared the cardinal would leave him but soon realized he was gazing into him with his *other* eye, the left one. Head still cocked with his crisp red crest pointed back at the holly tree.

Daig, he heard a strange voice in his mind. It sounded like the word "die". Then he realized it was coming from the cardinal.

Daig?

Daig. Name. Flame.

Daig is your name?

Yes. Then he bowed his head and back.

He wants me to climb on!

Petyr pulled himself onto Daig, gripping him where his body and wings met, and perched on the cardinal's back. It felt natural to him, as if he and Daig had been made to fit together. Almost like they were one being.

Then there was a rustling in the leaves behind them. *Squirrels?* Petyr wondered.

NO! Daig's voice flooded his mind. He felt Daig's fear too, turning his blood to ice.

Petyr glimpsed a cat's yellow eyes glowing between tall blades of grass. Before he could even think of what to do, she pounced. Her claws reached out, but Daig ran out of the way with Petyr still on his back. He lost the tip of one of his tail feathers as Petyr pulled his blade, a short sword tied to his belt. Then Daig ran even faster, struggling to fly with Petyr's weight on his back. The ground slowly fell below them, inch by inch. The cat pursued, hissing and screeching.

Petyr and Daig crashed through twigs, leaves, roots and even a few spiderwebs. The cat they had stumbled upon was still right on their heels. She'd pounced almost without any warning and wouldn't give up. *Foolish cat,* Petyr thought. He knew that he and Daig weren't easy prey, but cats didn't always make sense. *The chase. The kill. That's all they think about sometimes.* All he could do was hold on to Daig's chest, grip the bird's body between his legs, and hope he wasn't hurting him.

Friend of yours? Petyr heard Daig's voice in his mind. Already it was getting easier to communicate.

Never met her before in my life. Petyr sent the thought back to Daig. *Why are we still so close to the ground? Can't we fly away?*

Behind them, the cat growled and spit as it jumped over a fallen log behind them. She seemed to be getting closer.

Three razor sharp claws flashed behind them, but Daig dropped lower to the ground and the claws flew over their heads.

I'd love to fly. I'm not used to the extra weight on my back. It's hard to get any space to pick up the speed I need to go any higher.

Well, think of something!

I have an idea. Then Petyr felt his weight shift to the left and fell from Daig's back. His stomach lurched as he tumbled off, so he said a prayer to Gaia to keep him safe, and both of Daig's talon's clutched his arms.

What's going on? Are you going to take me back to your nest and eat me? He looked back at the cat behind them. Now she looked a little lower and further away.

Don't tempt me. They were pulling further away from the cat, but she wasn't giving up. Petyr felt helpless—he'd imagined himself riding his bird, not being carried along by him.

Wait! I know this path! You're leading her back to the village!

Don't you want to stay alive? We don't have any other choice. This path has the most space for me to fly. And don't be fooled by the cat. I think she's toying with us.

What do you mean?

Before Daig could answer, the cat made another lunge at them. Daig escaped her claws but was hit by one of the cat's forearms. He lost his balance in the air and went tumbling to the ground. Petyr rolled alongside him. The ground was more open here, and he realized they were on the edge of Aderyn.

The cat came out into the open. Her fur spiked on her back. *Her hackles*, Petyr remembered the word.

Nancy, Petyr heard Daig's voice in his mind. *Her name is*

Nancy. She is well-feared in the woods of Aderyn. It was good to bond with you, Petyr. I'm sad our time together will be so short.

No, wait! He stood before Daig with his short sword pointed at the cat. Nancy flexed her claws and poised to strike.

At that exact moment, Petyr felt a burst of wind and saw a yellow blur move in front of him. He heard wood shatter as Bianca swung a long wooden staff in the path of Nancy's paw. The cat reared her back paw and licked a spot of blood that had formed where Bianca struck her.

"Run, both of you!" Bianca told him.

"What about you?" Petyr asked as he climbed onto Daig's back. "We can't leave you behind!"

"I can take care of myself," Bianca told him, then turned back to face Nancy.

Daig took a few steps and launched himself into the air, Petyr holding tight onto his back. He tried circling around and diving at Nancy. The cat ducked her head and in that moment a different bird swooped in and picked up Bianca. This bird was a blue jay with a white breast and black crest. She was bigger than Daig.

"Let me go!" Bianca cried. Then the bird dropped her and swooped down to catch Bianca on her back.

"Hang on!" Petyr called. It was hard to be heard in the wind. "She wants to bond with you! Let her."

Bianca nodded and held onto the blue jay's back. Now two birds and two riders were circling Nancy.

A group of villagers had formed on the edge of Aderyn. Petyr could see them whenever Daig turned in their direction. They carried pitchforks, hammers, staffs, and other objects that could be used as weapons. A pair of guards led them, their swords drawn. None rushed to their aid. The townspeople preferred to watch this spectacle rather than be involved.

Let them cower, he heard Daig's voice in his mind. *They can't help us. If they tried, one of them would become cat food after Nancy dragged them into the woods.*

What can we do? Petyr asked. *How can I help you?*

I need you to focus. Focus all your mental energy on Nancy. Look at that patch of white fur on her chest. When I tell you, imagine a ball of fire leaving the space between your eyes and hitting her right there. Are you ready?

Ready? Petyr asked.

NOW! Daig screamed in his mind, and Petyr felt a rush of energy come from his body, a wave of heat that cascaded from his whole being. He watched a small ball of fire erupt from Daig's mouth. It flew right at the white patch of fur on Nancy's chest. Petyr saw the flame spread for a moment, and then the fire went out. A patch of pink skin was now visible beneath her fur.

"UH-REA-REARGH!" Nancy howled. She sped at both of them and reached out her claws. Daig rolled all the way over in the air and dodged her attack. Petyr felt like he could fall off his bird at any moment and held onto Daig even tighter. He even held his breath.

Now it was Bianca's turn. She and the blue jay were flying around Nancy and staying just out of her reach. Then Petyr saw something that amazed him. A sharp icicle flew from the blue jay's mouth and struck Nancy in the chest, right where her skin was now bare. Nancy swiped her paw at the icicle and it landed on the ground.

But she's not even a Wind Rider! Petyr exclaimed.

She is now, Daig told him.

She raised her hackles again all the way down to the tip of her tail, which now appeared twice its usual size. Nancy howled and spat but then turned and fled into the woods to lick her wounds.

The townspeople cheered for Petyr, Bianca, and their birds. Their cheers sounded like a gentle roar.

Daig and Petyr ended their flight. Bianca and her blue jay landed next to them. Somehow, she still looked calm. Petyr dropped to the Urth, his legs still wobbly. He had never been so happy to stand on solid ground in all his life.

UNBORN

THOMAS UKINSKI

She waited in the womb.

She'd been conscious of Her surroundings since She was a ball of cells. She realized She must control Her growth to remain small in the confined space, though Her internal organs rapidly developed. Tumbling in the amniotic fluid in the darkness, fed by the placenta through an umbilical cord, Her brain seethed. Amid the wash of blood and pounding of the greater heart, She listened to the voice vibrating through Her mother's bones. She perceived the baffled resonance coming from outside Her mother's body and construed the noise as language. The meaning was all so clear! She identified the low frequencies of the father's tones as the most familiar speech. Her parents discussed Her many times. She heard Herself described as a poppy seed, a kidney bean, a parasite. She understood that Her tail should have disappeared, but it did not. Fetuses were supposed to spend most of their time in sleep, but She remained awake, Her senses on high alert. She knew the names of everything, and when bright light penetrated the uterus, She could perceive shapes and contours and knew what they were. Flashes of memories not Her own stabbed at Her.

Her mother's distress was especially evident when She stretched and kicked. She did it repeatedly on purpose. Mother tensed and moved in agitated motion at every reminder that She was within. Jolted about, She noticed Her flailing limbs and accidentally scraped Herself with long, sharp nails.

One day, Her mother said, "I don't know if I can do this, Art. I don't want it."

"I understand, Regina," responded Her father, Art. "We can fix it. This thing is an anomaly. Dr. Geherin said so."

"But why is it unnatural? I worry about what we used to do. All the seances, Ouija boards, Wiccan ceremonies, sex magic. Could those be the cause?"

"We stopped doing them before it was conceived."

"What about residual effects?"

"'Residual effects'? Those practices were make-believe. You know that. It's why we stopped engaging in them. This is entirely different. It's genetic, something to do with DNA and proteins."

"But is it right to do it?"

"We can't let this ruin our lives."

Close to Her ear, the pulsing vibrations of what Regina called the ultrasound affronted Her, followed by the baritone counsel of Dr. Geherin. "If you're planning to go ahead, this is the optimal time to do so, according to statistics. The fetus is no bigger than a lemon. If you like, we can schedule the procedure."

"Yes, please," said Regina.

Roiling rage overwhelmed Her. An image of writhing bodies in the night possessed Her. These people had created Her out of a passion She could not understand and a negligence She could not forgive, and now resolutely planned to dispose of Her. She had not asked to emerge out of oblivion nor chosen to return to it. Her existence tormented those who should love Her. The hurt became hatred, enflaming every part of Her being.

Sometime later came Regina's pronouncement. "My God, it's happening tomorrow! I'm still conflicted. I just don't know."

"Well, *I* know. It'll be all right," said Art. "You'll feel better when it's finished."

A singular intention illuminated Her sunless world.

With sound, She'd gauged the position of Her mother's organs. When Regina was still, breathing in the rhythms of sleep, She used Her nails to slash through the amniotic sac, the uterus, and the belly. The moment She encountered the air, She expanded to newborn size. Amid the rush of blood and shredded skin, She twisted and writhed, and Her claws penetrated Regina's rib cage and pierced her heart. Mother gasped but quickly died.

She had an impression of Regina's chubby face, bountiful curly hair, and oval eyes, gaping in death. She was relieved to see Her mother at last and destroy the enveloping enemy. She damned Regina silently for her pitiless choice. Now let the condemnation fall on dear Mother! She sundered the looping umbilical cord and was free.

She slithered easily through the accustomed blackness across the bed toward Art. His sonorous voice did not match his short, spindly form. She blamed him for not protecting against conception and then encouraging termination to absolve his guilt. Her anger blazed at this sniveling little man. She jabbed his throat and severed an artery, and the blood spurted on Her. He never awakened. She wished she could have made him suffer. But once he became conscious, even wounded, he could fight back, overcome her. She had to battle stealthily.

Blood soaked the bed. She slid off it until Her feet touched the carpet. A surge of energy passed through Her, permitting Her to stand. She oriented Herself from the repeated steps Regina had taken. This was the bedroom; that was the bathroom. She climbed into the shower and washed off the slime.

She found fruit and meat in the refrigerator. Eating was an interesting sensation after months of imbibing nutrients through a cord. She savored the textures, the flavors in her mouth when she bit into the flesh. Sweet, sour, salty, bitter. She easily assigned the terms. Some food needed to be cooked. She would puzzle out the method by relating Regina's gestures to the objects in the kitchen.

She had grown enough to wear Regina's clothes, though the hems of the jeans and cuffs of the shirt needed to be rolled up. She stuffed newspapers into the shoes.

She viewed Herself in the mirror in Her ill-fitting attire. She was bald, Her eyes were wide apart, Her head large for

Her body, and Her neck indiscernible. These features would change. She was evolving.

She longed to go outside but sensed that everything must remain securely hidden. The door daunted Her until she remembered jangling keys. She retrieved them from Regina's purse and locked the door behind Her. Obscured by evening, she wandered the neighborhood. It seemed as if mists were being continually dispersed before Her. She realized some things would be obvious, but some had to be learned. These were brick houses with lighted windows, surrounded by trim lawns. Here were the stark streets. Trees swayed in chilly breezes. She held out her arms, reveling in the openness—no barriers.

In the morning, She ventured out again. She passed mown fields of what she identified as standing stones and strode among them. People solemnly gathered to watch a wooden box being lowered into the earth. The pearly skies outlined their black and dark blue garb, suggesting a ceremony of regret. The box was big enough for an adult human. After the crowd dispersed, a machine pushed the dirt in.

She found a shovel in the backyard shed. With the night as a cloak, She dug a hole. She was still runty, but the harder She worked to break up the clayey ground, the stronger She became. It was a long way from the bedroom, down the stairs, through the kitchen, out the back door, and into the yard, but She steadily dragged Her rigid parents along by their legs. The corpses pressed a path in the high grass. She patted the frigid soil into place and scattered leaves and branches over the grave. From Her encounter in the cemetery, She knew She was supposed to say some words of grieving, but the welling sorrow She felt was for Herself, the loneliness She must endure. She stood a long time in the vibrating dark.

She stripped off the bedding and blankets and carried them to the basement. Figuring out the workings of the washing machine took some time, as She had no memories from Regina to guide Her. Art must have undertaken the laundry. At least he was good for something. When the sheets and covers were clean, She made the bed, mindful that everything must be tidy for unexpected "guests".

She trimmed Her claws. She no longer required them. Her intelligence was Her best weapon.

She heard the buzzing of flat, black devices on the dresser. She was aware they were phones and that Her parents conversed through them with the outside world. She ignored their summons. They could become a problem. When Regina went to what she designated as "the office", She abided the clanging chaos of traffic, the incessant conversations, the drone of machinery, and the ambient reverberations of a foreign place. A thousand stresses had infringed on Her seclusion. Now She was troubled that Art and Regina were expected at their jobs.

But time passed, and no one came to the house. She needn't agonize over the neighbors. Regina had complained that nobody on the block knew their names or cared what they did. But others would invade Her sanctuary.

In twelve days, she had consumed most of the food. She journeyed for miles in the glaring sunlight to the place where provisions were kept. A supermarket. Regina's winter coat was long on Her and uncomfortable in the heat, but She wore it with a baseball cap as a disguise. Shoppers clogged the aisles with their freighted carts in pallid light. She observed how they collected groceries and paid for them with paper money and plastic cards. She got those from Her parents' wallets. She was still so diminutive she had to strain to reach the card reader. But customers would look away when she was near. She sensed their disdain. Though Her voice was still high-pitched, She spoke little and conducted the transactions without being challenged. No one engaged Her in conversation, except that clerks asked if she'd found everything she was looking for, and she would nod. Children stared at Her, a freak.

She observed street signs and examined books and magazines; the markings became words. She went through Her parents' papers and understood that the electricity and gas must be paid for, or the services would be disconnected. The mortgage had to be attended to, or someone would take the house. She recalled how her mother sat with a computer screen on her lap and moved her fingers along the keyboard. But She didn't comprehend the procedures. In meddling with Regina's phone, She randomly found sites that explained how computers worked. She located the passwords for the accounts and took care of the bills. Everything must continue as it had, lest steps be taken that would disclose the truth. But She picked out clothing online that would suit Her size and took the chance of having it delivered. She felt exhilarated to be in clothes that conformed to Her figure, colorful pants and blouses and dresses and shoes adorning Her. She was filling out and getting taller. She had bristled red hair, and Her neck was now long and elegant. But the outfits couldn't be too tight behind; otherwise, the outline of Her tail would show. She thought about removing it but shied away from self-mutilation. She was perfect.

She watched a lot of television. The messages filled in the gaps in Her knowledge and revealed life's abundance. She desired something more than mere survival. She viewed artwork and listened to music, bathing in sights and sounds. Love relationships intrigued Her. She wondered if Her parents had loved each other. If they had, how were they able to plot to murder Her? Unless She was an abomination, a perversion of love. She couldn't bear to think that. She yearned to be in the world but was cowed by the vastness of oceans, plains, deserts, jungles, and cities. Yet it was all no more than a pebble flung into the void.

One day, three weeks after Her "birth", someone arrived. She looked out the window and saw people in uniform. She had prepared for this, having sawed a section of the floorboards in the bedroom to establish a hiding place, propped with lumber from the shed. She huddled in the constricted crawlspace. She had arranged it so a rug would slide over the telltale holes.

But the floor was uneven where She'd made the trapdoor. She hadn't tested the spot with Her weight. Would they notice something was wrong? For the first time in Her life, She was afraid and felt a tingling dizziness and the icy horripilation of Her flesh. What would they do to Her if they found Her?

She detected footsteps in the room.

"Nothing looks out of place," a man said—probably a

policeman. “No signs of any disturbance.” She worried the floorboards would creak.

“But where could they be?” A woman’s voice She recognized. “They couldn’t just vanish.”

“Well, we’ve looked everywhere. We’ve canvassed the neighborhood. No one noticed anything unusual going on here. Maybe they both went away for some reason.”

“I know my sister. She would have told me if they were going on a long trip. She was pregnant.”

A screaking sound. The officer was standing on the rug right above Her! She couldn’t breathe. All he had to do was wriggle his foot to notice the discrepancy, the “give”.

“You’ve filed a missing person’s report,” the officer said. “Without more evidence, there’s nothing to do but wait.”

“I think something terrible has happened. I can feel it.”

The officer pressed down on the loosened wood. The force of it made a squeaking noise like a questioning utterance. “I understand,” he said. “But everything seems normal. I’m sure they’ll contact you eventually.... You know, this floor seems a bit unstable. They better check for termites.” He walked away.

The people filed out. Her “aunt” continued to fret and whine. The front door opened and seemed to delay shutting, as if everyone hesitated. Was the officer looking back, feeling uneasy about the floor? She dreaded him saying, “Let me check something again.” But the door closed. A key slid, crunching, into the lock. The click resounded.

She waited a long time in case they should return. She arose from Her lair and breathed deeply. Weariness engulfed

Her. She climbed into bed, snuggling under woolen blankets to be back in the warmth of the womb.

She considered the future. Eventually, Her parents' money would run out. Sooner or later, someone would take control of the house, and the grave would be discovered.

She'd have to leave and live elsewhere, which necessitated money. She had observed homes where the elderly and vulnerable lived. Perhaps She could break into them and steal what She required. But that was risky. She was odd enough to be memorable to witnesses. Or She could find a job. She had only to observe how a thing was done to mimic it. An aberration could still be useful. She had to have a name and chose "Maya Alia". "Maya"—a word found in one of Regina's books—the illusion by which the world was manifest. "Alia" for All. "All is Maya."

Would anyone track Her down? People were too stupid to imagine how She'd been born or suspect She had survived. The authorities could classify the violent deaths and the absent fetus as the ravages of a wild animal. But what to make of the burials?

Identification was called for: a Social Security card, a driver's license, Her own credit card and bank account. The sum of a person's life. She'd get them and overwhelm all obstacles by projecting confidence, Her right to be. Nothing could hinder Her. She might live forever. Some blind force or entity—god or devil—had given Her the power to thwart death, a power that thrilled through Her.

She began to dream of others like herself, tiny malformed creatures suspended in watery prisons, conscious of Their impending execution. There were moments when She was with Them in the cloistered midnight of Their desolation, when She urged Them to strike out at Their fates. After a while, She could graze Their consciousness, and Her influence became more potent every time She touched Their minds. She emanated Her message: *Break through!* She could feel Them stirring, flailing, beginning to respond. She would show Them the way. Soon, thousands of Them would be slashing their way to freedom in blood and fury. After that, there was no limit to what They could do in the shadows. No government or society could comprehend the threat or stand against Them.

Maya's Misbegotten Army would triumph.

3:02

CARMEN DAVINLEAM

A voice whispers to me, calling for me by a name I'm unfamiliar with—mommy. It plagues me as I sleep, causing me to toss and turn. Something pushes at my shoulder and I wake with a start, but no one is there. Though the whisper calls to me again from the hall. I stay glued to my bed, too locked by fear to move.

I have no children.

I live alone.

The pitter patter of tiny feet on my wooden floors sound through the hall as the steps retreat and then finally dissipate. I take a deep breath and then reach for my phone on the table next to my bed. I move fast; fearing the person who ran away was a decoy and that perhaps someone else was waiting under my bed, ready to grab me.

After the phone is in my hand, and no one has touched me, I turn the flashlight on and shine it down the hall. It's empty, and I feel a little silly. I raise up, turn my bedroom light on and look at the clock. It's 3:02 a.m. This is the fifth time I've been awoken by this strange occurrence in two weeks.

I slide into my slippers and go into the hall, flipping the switch on as soon as I'm near it. It too is empty. I make my way toward the kitchen, turning lights on as I go from room to room. No one is in the office, bathroom, living room, or kitchen.

I head to the side door to check that it's firmly locked and the chain is in place, and know that I'll have to check the basement, just like I have for the past two weeks. The side door's chain is in place, it's not swaying at all, so no one has messed with it. I flip the basement light on, and then the sound of rain pulls my attention back to the entryway.

Water trickles so I peek out the window on the door to see if it's raining or snowing. Rain would surely turn to ice as the day dragged on.

The side light is on, but the ground is dry. I see a bunny rabbit scurry under my neighbor's bush. Other than that, all is quiet, apart from the water I still hear. I turn to head down the stairs, but I'm too shocked to move.

There's a woman, laying at the bottom of my stairs. Like she'd begun to crawl up them and stopped three stairs up. Water pools near her feet, and she's covered in moss and wet weeds.

Her white gown is drenched, soaked through so much that I can see her pale skin through it. Her hair is so wet that I can't tell if it's just wet, or if her hair is as black as night.

My body goes cold and gooseflesh rises from my arms and along the back of my neck.

Something inside me screams for me to keep my mouth shut, so I don't say a word. I slowly bring my phone up so that I can take a photo. As my screen focuses on the girl, the basement lights shut off just as I snap the picture. My flash bursts and camera clicks. I quickly turn the light back on, but she's gone.

There is no woman.

There is no water.

There is no photo on my phone.

Coldness encompasses me and every hair on my arms stands to attention. I forgo the basement check, and slowly back up the three side steps. I walk backwards all the way to my bedroom.

I gently close the door and get dressed. I'm not going to be like all those people you see in horror movies who stay in the house and die. I'm certain there's a Waffle House open somewhere close by.

I grab my purse and slip on my shoes. Slowly opening my bedroom door, I peek towards the kitchen. It's empty. I steer clear of the side entry and instead make my way to the right, and go out the front, grabbing my jacket off the back of the chair as I do. I lock it behind me, get in my car and stare at my house for a few minutes.

It was built in 1960. There were only two owners before me. The family who built it, and a man who rented it out. He'd decided to sell the house when the last family left without paying six months of rent. I've never believed in ghosts, but what else could this be? A laugh escapes my lips as I check the clock on my phone. It says 3:02 a.m. but how could that be right? Had my brain screwed up the time when

I last looked? Had my dyslexia done me a favor once again and swapped the numbers around?

It didn't matter. I wasn't going back in that house until the sun came up. I checked my local weather app for the sunrise time. 7:10 a.m. blinked at me from my screen.

It's a good thing I always carry a book in my purse. I start the car and back out of my driveway.

It might be overkill to leave the house because of something I think I heard and saw—I realize this. However, I live alone and I don't know how long it would take anyone to realize that I was missing if I died while at home because a ghost managed to kill me.

I laugh again at the absurdity of it all. I try to find some explanation for the strange things that keep happening to me. I try to apply some logic to the situation. I might need to get some sleeping pills. Starting over all on your own when your entire life has only recently crashed around you is stressful. It's probably the reason I'm not sleeping well. I've been hearing and seeing things since the day I moved in.

The yellow lights of the Waffle House sign greets me and I'm glad for it. Inside I can see a cook, a waitress, and three customers spread around, not sitting close to one another. I grab my bag, double check that my book is still in there. Darynda, it's time for you, me, and Charley to have some waffles. I mean if Charley were here, maybe she'd be able to tell me what the ghosts at my house want.

I get out of the car and head inside. A bell chimes as I open the door.

"Sit anywhere you'd like." The waitress smiles as she delivers a platter to a man on a barstool.

"Thank you." I nod and head to the left. I slide into the last booth. Put my purse down next to me and set my book on the table beside me. The waitress is filling a water pitcher now, so

I peruse the menu. Smothered, chunked, and covered is how my hash browns will be today.

Waffles, bacon, and eggs-over-easy, with a side of toast. I lick my lips suddenly ravenous. I'll also need a large cup of coffee and some orange juice.

The waitress comes over. "Hey, Hun. What can I get you?" She smiles sweetly at me but glances up toward the other patrons with a creased brow before turning her attention back to me.

I had neglected to look in a mirror before I left the house. I nervously run my fingers through my hair that most certainly looks a hot mess while I give her my order. She brings me the coffee, and then yells my selection to the cook, who starts frying it up right away. The bacon sizzles when it hits the griddle.

The warm black coffee heats me from the inside, pushing away the last bit of chill I have remaining from my house. I pick up my book to see what Charley Davidson has gotten herself into this time and I let the ghosts fall away while I dive into the story and sip my drink—knowing that out of all the disheveled people in this place, at this hour, I'm certainly the craziest of the bunch.

The waitress, whose name tag reads, 'Pamala,' sets my order on the table faster than seems possible. I put my book back in my bag to prevent any accidental splatters, and tuck into my food.

The eggs are perfect, and the bacon is crispy, but as I eat the hairs on the back of my neck stand to attention. I can't help but sweep my hand over my neck. No matter how long I leave my palm against my skin, it doesn't warm. I ask for a refill on the coffee hoping that it will cure the chill.

It doesn't.

If this room didn't have five other people in it I'd lick the plate clean. If there were no men in here, I'd order more food. I'm suddenly so hungry, though I've just eaten so much, that...

I need to go home.

I drop a twenty on the table and grab my things. Not turning back as the waitress thanks me for coming in. I get in my car and before I can blink I'm standing in my living room.

When had I started the car? Driven home? I look out the front window and my car is parked in the driveway—the windows are frosted.

Time has slipped away from me... somehow.

I walk to the kitchen to grab a glass of water, turning the heat up as I pass the thermostat.

Seventy-two degrees should rid me of this chill. I forgo the water and instead make tea as the heater kicks on. When I see that the time is 3:02 a.m. I decide Sleepy Time tea would be the best option. I pour a teaspoon of honey into my mug while the Keurig prepares my drink.

3:02 seems off though... something prickles in my head, but I can't place why.

I take my warm tea with me to the bedroom. My brow arches when I see the Darynda Jones novel open on my pillow. Had I been reading before bed?

I turn to take a sip of my tea and it's empty. I set the cup down and crawl into bed. The only explanation for any of this has got to be the horrid sleeping pattern I've had since I moved.

But being alone, is better than being abused—I suppose.

As my head hits my down pillow, the noise of that familiar flop wraps me up. I leave the bedside lamp on and allow myself to drift off.

"Mommy," whispers from beside me, but I dare not move.

Cold wafts around my feet, but I do my best to keep my breathing slow and even.

"Mommy, he's coming," comes from another small voice. The first sounded female, this other one sounded, male.

Both were the voices of children.

They both gasp as I lay there, unmoving. Their feet run pattering down the hall toward my office. The door opens and then closes gently. I gamble a peek; my room is empty. I turn over, pulling the blankets around me as I face the edge of the bed. Maybe the light isn't allowing my brain the rest it needs.

I switch the lamp off.

And that's when I see him. He is only a shadow, but he's there. Pacing next to my bed in a ball cap, is a tall man, and by the movement of his shoulders, he's angry. They rise and fall with every breath he takes.

I do not move a muscle as he paces, back and forth, up and down the length of my bed.

He takes his cap off and leans over me. He... this... shadow... takes in long slow, deliberate breaths. His hands reach out and fingers tangle into my hair. I know that he wants to kill me. How do I know... I've been in this before. I shouldn't know how angry he is, but the truth of it hangs in the air with every breath he takes.

He yanks hard and tugs me from my bed. I fall to the floor, my hands smacking it with blistering precision. I scream out as I'm dragged toward the hall by this shadow.

I take a deep breath and rise up putting a palm to my chest. My heart races. I'm safe, I'm in my bed. I don't glance at the clock, too afraid of the numbers that might blink back at me.

Instead, I look out the window above my bed.

The morning sun is rising, melting the frost from my windows. I hurriedly get up and get dressed. I throw my hair up in a clip, taking less time than I should to get ready. I just need to get out of this house. A day of working will ease my mind, and tire me out.

I'll be at work an hour early, but maybe getting a jump on the day will make my manager happy. Living on your own is more expensive than you'd think. Everything falls on your shoulders and there's no one else to help.

I don't return home until well after midnight. I'd worked until seven, and then went out with some people from work. What else is a Friday night for? It was nice meeting new people; friends would make life a little less lonely. Though, lying wasn't my forte, it was getting easier telling everyone the same backstory I'd told my boss when she hired me.

'I was an army brat, but we lived here the most times when I was a kid. My dad died recently and I've just come back to the place that felt the most like home.' When they'd ask about my mother, I'd say what I always said. The only piece of truth in my stories. 'She died when I was seven.' I never have to say how she died. Because no one asks.

Most people don't know how to handle grief, so they tend to leave you alone. They offer the shoulder rub, and the expression of sadness on their faces. They nod and allow the conversation to go to happier places. Which lets me stay off their radars.

I don't tell them that I've left an abusive relationship. I don't need their opinions on me for that. All of the regular comments. 'Why didn't you leave sooner?' the 'I'd never let someone hit me.' I don't even want to hear the, 'oh you're so strong for leaving,' comments. No matter their comments or opinions, it's always the same. Either I'm strong for leaving, or stupid for not leaving sooner. There's no understanding to be had from anyone who hasn't lived in it.

Which is why I don't tell them.

I take a hot shower, washing away the cigarette and bar smells. My strawberry shampoo takes away the bad fragrance replacing it with a pleasant one. I'll sleep like a baby tonight for sure. As soon as I'm clean I hop in bed, shut the bedside light on and drift to sleep.

"Mom!" screams out, jolting me from my bed. The screaming grows louder as I check the clock.

3:02 a.m.

"Mom! Please!" comes from down the hall.

"Dad! NO!" the little boy's voice calls out.

And then... silence.

I make my way to the office and open the door. The room is empty. The fire alarm in my kitchen rings out. I run toward it, and then I hear trilling laughter. It's the little girl again.

"Mommy, you burnt the pie," she giggles.

My kitchen window raises and I smell the scent of fresh apple pie, with only a hint of burnt. As soon as my nostrils are overcome by the smell everything around me changes. It's my house, but not my house. All my things are gone, replaced by someone else's things, and two children are running and playing. A woman with black hair is turning the oven off, before she goes to the window and waves a potholder at the pie on the sill.

Stomping comes from the basement stairs.

The kids stop immediately. The woman nods down the hall and the children race away.

Going into my office and slamming the door closed. The knob's lock clicks into place.

The angry shadow man, the one that paces by my bed every night, comes up the stairs. I can't see his face, he's not here like the mother and her children, his features are hidden from me. It's like he's in another realm—though still dangerous.

He grabs the woman by her dark hair, pulling her head back with it as he gets close to her face. He whispers something to her that I can't hear and she screams out.

He tugs her down the stairs.

I'm frozen in place, unsure what I should do. My breathing hitches as memories flash in my head. The pain I know she feels as her hair is pulled out by the roots while he drags her. The bruises on her heels from flopping down the stairs, that she'll have soon. Part of me wants to protect the children, but I know I need to protect the woman first. I throw my fear to the side and race down the basement steps.

The walls are in all the wrong places. The basement I know is gone. I turn a few corners and then hear the muffled screams and the splashing of water. I rush toward the sounds.

Opening the door I see him, the shadow man in the baseball cap, holding the woman, the mother, under the water. Her arms flail about, her screams bubble up from the water. "Please

Don! No!"

I grab the vase from the counter by the sink and throw it at his head. But nothing happens. I look over and the vase is still by the sink. I shove him, but my hands go through him.

I reach into the tub to save her, but I can't grasp anything. I can't drain the water.

It doesn't stop me though.

I try and try... everything.

But nothing works, and then I realize that ... she's no longer moving.

The shadow man paces the room and then screams into his hands. He'd done it this time... He'd killed her.

The man turned back to the tub, seeing what he'd done, then he ran out of the room.

The kids!

I ran up the stairs after him, knowing where he was headed, but on the third step something grabbed my feet, causing me to fall. My head banged against the top step, stars filled my vision. I understood this term better than most. How many times had I been blinded by light that I knew wasn't present after being knocked in the head.

Too many.

I blinked rapidly trying to regain my sight. Looking down the stairs it was her, the mother. Soaked in her gown, hair hiding her face, pulling at my legs. “It’s too late,” she whispered in a gurgled sound. A sound of lungs filled with water, but too determined to speak for it to matter.

The sound of a mother lost.

No, not lost... taken.

“I’m sorry,” I said, and then I kicked free of her grasp and raced up the remaining stairs, tripping up the three side steps, bruising my shins, and running toward my office—the children’s bedroom.

I arrived too late. The shadowy father, stood over his children. Their tiny bodies lay lifeless on the green rug of their bedroom floor. The murdering man put his head in his hands and sobbed.

He ran past me, knocking me down as he went. I scrambled to my feet in time to hear the attic ladder pull out of the ceiling.

I’d never gone into the attic. The previous owner told me all that was up there was insulation and dust. There was no storage, the stairs were for attic access by electricians or roofers. I’d never need to go up there.

And so, I hadn’t.

Until now.

The stairs were down, I took hold of the rungs and pulled myself up each step. It was dark in the attic, I felt around for anything, when something smacked my face. I gasped, taking in deep breaths. I calmed when the tinkling noise let me know it was a pull for a light. I pulled the short chain and the bulb came to life. Slowly filling the room with its dimness.

I covered my mouth, holding back a scream. There on the floor were three sheets, the outlines not what I expected, but next to the right of the sheets was a decayed body, tall, decomposed so much that if it weren't for the clothing, I'd see only bones. Atop the head was a black baseball cap.

It was him, the father. A gun lay in his left hand.

I couldn't help myself, I gathered the ends of the other three sheets in my hand, careful not to pull until I was ready to see it all at once. I took a deep breath, and then yanked the blankets upward freeing them from their place.

Dust flew about the room, released from its stillness. As it resettled in the cracks of the floor, I stared at what I'd uncovered.

The woman with the dark hair, her flesh sunken, her white nightdress still on, though covered with dirt and moss, her hair covering her face. He must have placed her that way to hide from his own shame. The children's hands were interlaced. Their heads turned so that they faced each other. They wore the same clothes I'd seen them in, when they were in the kitchen.

Matching white pajamas, with little green teddy bears all over them—decayed by time.

I backed out of the room, practically falling down the ladder. I went to my room and grabbed my phone, calling for authorities.

How would I explain my findings? I wasn't concerned with being blamed, these bodies had been here far too long for anyone to try and blame me, but... how would I explain that I'd seen the ghosts of these people?

I wouldn't.

I'd say I'd heard a sound in the attic, and brushed it off as a squirrel, and then wanted to make sure the poor creature wasn't stuck. It was a lie, but it would prevent me from being carted off to a mental institution.

The police had arrived within minutes. Not much to do on a Saturday morning I suppose.

They'd stayed for the entire day. The sun had set by the time the last vehicle left. When the bodies were removed, and everyone was gone, I stared at my house.

Though the sun was down the house seemed aglow with light. A weight lifted from my shoulders as I walked inside. I swept and mopped the floors. The coroner's office had said they sprayed some kind of treatment around in the attic. I didn't pay much attention to what, I had no plans on going up those stairs ever again.

When the house was clean, I showered. When I was clean, I made tea and settled into bed.

Delightful slumber took me quickly.

"Hey," sounded from my right. "Hey, hey," a second voice said. There was a tugging at my sleeve.

I opened my eyes, it was dark in my room, but there at the side of my bed were the two children. They smiled sweetly, standing next to my clock that read 3:02 a.m.

Movement from my doorway caught my eye. Leaning in from the hall was their mother.

Still in her gown, her hair however was pulled back, and her gown was clean. She nodded once to me. I nodded back.

"Thank you," the children said sweetly, and then their mother reached out her hands.

The children ran away from my bedside, gripping their

mother's fingers, and as their feet pattered down the hall, they vanished from my home.

I don't know why they picked me, but I was glad they had. But as I watched them disappear, I knew, if I hadn't left, I would have suffered the same fate, but no one would've ever found me. He would've made sure of that.

Made in the USA
Columbia, SC
15 September 2023

22897311R00150